BLOOM

A NOVEL

BLOOM

A NOVEL

#1 *NEW YORK TIMES* BESTSELLING AUTHOR

HELEN
HARDT

Entangled Publishing, LLC
644 Shrewsbury Commons Ave., STE 181
Shrewsbury, PA 17361
rights@entangledpublishing.com

Amara is an imprint of Entangled Publishing, LLC.

Visit our website at www.entangledpublishing.com.

Edited by Lydia Sharp and Liz Pelletier
Cover design by Elizabeth Turner Stokes
Stock art by Maya Kruchankova/Shutterstock,
Demogorgona/Shutterstock, Agave Studio/Shutterstock
Interior design by Toni Kerr

ISBN 978-1-64937-302-1
Ebook ISBN 978-1-64937-343-4

Manufactured in the United States of America

First Edition August 2023

10 9 8 7 6 5 4 3 2 1

ALSO BY HELEN HARDT

Black Rose

Blush
Bloom

Follow Me

Follow Me Darkly
Follow Me Under
Follow Me Always

Steel Brothers Saga

Craving
Obsession
Possession

Wolfes of Manhattan

Rebel
Recluse
Runaway

The Temptation

Tempting Dusty
Teasing Annie
Taking Catie

For my readers.

CHAPTER ONE

Frankie

My sister Mandy—short for Amanda—says I have two settings. High and low.

If there's any truth to her hypothesis, I've been on the low setting for the last month.

Sitting here at dinner with my parents, Mandy, and her best friend and brand-new boyfriend, Jackson Paris, isn't helping my mood. On tonight of all nights...

Did they really forget what day it is?

Mandy looks adorable, as usual. The woman can eat like a teenage boy and never gain an ounce. Plus she's the perfect height, whereas I'm the giantess of the bunch—taller than both my sister and my mother. Not that I mind my height, but that plus my wide waist and narrow hips make it difficult to find clothes that fit.

Mandy doesn't have that issue. Her cute, hourglass figure looks amazing in everything from high fashion to sweats and yoga pants. Tonight, she's wearing simple black leggings, a pink tunic, and clunky-heeled sandals, and it all works for her.

She clears her throat. "Jack and I have some news."

Mom smiles. "What is it, dear?"

Mandy raises her left hand, showing us the sparkler on her ring finger. "We're engaged!"

"That's wonderful!" Mom grabs Mandy's hand and eyes the new bauble.

"Congratulations, Jackson, Mandy," Dad says much more calmly than Mom. He's never been one to get too emotional, but his smile says it all.

This engagement isn't news to me. Mandy's been trying to hide her hand since we sat down, but I caught a glimpse of it.

I noticed it. I knew the announcement was coming. And it's been eating away at me since I saw that shimmering rock on her finger.

I force a smile. "That's great, Mand."

I should be happy for my sister, and I am on some level. Many levels, actually. She's been in love with Jackson forever, and Mandy never had a lot of dates before him. She's gorgeous, even though I was always considered the beauty between the two of us. It had more to do with Mandy's introversion than with anything else. She thought it was because she refused to wear contact lenses until recently. Something about touching her eyeball grossing her out. For Jackson, apparently she touched her eyeball, and then, about a week ago, she got laser surgery so she'd no longer have to. But the truth is that Mandy has always been attractive, glasses or not. She's the only one who didn't believe it.

So yeah, I'm happy for my sister.

But tonight? Really?

I'm trying to focus on Mandy and her happiness. Truly trying. But how did they all forget so quickly?

I don't blame Dad so much. He never remembers important dates. But I expected a lot better from my mother and my sister.

Because today…

Today is the day I was supposed to marry Pendleton Berry.

And instead?

I'm sitting at a family dinner while my sister announces her engagement to Jackson Paris, who, by anyone's standards, is a first-class stud.

I've known him forever. He's been a staple at our house since before I could talk. He and Mandy have been best friends for so long I can't remember a time when he wasn't around. I'm not exactly sure how they became an item, only that a month ago Jack was in a car accident and he woke up in love with my sister.

A few days later?

I found out the truth about my own fiancé.

So my wedding? The one that was supposed to be taking place this very day?

It was canceled, and my relationship was over.

Completely and totally over.

The fiasco with my bridesmaids' dresses, the bachelorette party… All for nothing.

One of those Long Island Playboys from my bachelorette party gave me his phone number that night and whispered in my ear for me to call him later. He was a hottie, too, with dark-brown skin and light-brown eyes. Looking back, I wish I had taken him up on his offer.

I still have his card with his number on it, but he won't even remember me at this point.

"And you'll be my maid of honor of course, Frankie."

I jerk out of my thoughts at Mandy's voice and force a smile. "Sure. Of course."

"It'll be a small wedding," Mandy says. "Just you and the best man. No other bridal party."

I don't say it, but that's because Mandy doesn't have any friends. Not close friends like I have. Isabella, Gigi, and I have been besties since college at Mellville University. Truth be told, I wish they were here with me now. I could use some support.

"This is all so amazing, honey," Mom says. "We couldn't have picked a better man for you. Jack, you're already part of the family. You have been for decades."

"I'll be honored to make it official." Jackson curves his lips up into an infectious grin.

Mandy prattles on about arrangements, and quite frankly it's getting on my nerves. I want to be happy for her. Mandy deserves everything in the world. But how could they totally not remember that *this* was the night I was supposed to become Mrs. Pendleton Berry?

Jackson asks the server to bring a bottle of champagne.

And I can't take it anymore. I stand. "Excuse me. I have to go."

"Frankie," Mandy says. "We're going to toast. I want you here."

I'm not the petulant type. I never have been. There've been times when Mandy and I didn't get along, and I know she's been envious of me, but I've never felt that way toward her.

Right now, though? I *do* envy her. I hate the feeling, but I do. Not only is she stealing my wedding thunder, but she's doing it with the proverbial perfect man, and she's doing it on the night I was supposed to get married. So yeah, I'm feeling a little cantankerous.

I scrunch my napkin in my fist and throw it on top of the table. "No, thank you."

"Frankie!" Mom admonishes.

I meet my mother's gaze, so like my own. "You really don't remember, do you?"

"Remember what, Frankie?"

Mandy gasps. "Oh my God, Frankie. I'm so sorry. We weren't thinking."

"No, you *were* thinking. Just not about—" I shake my head.

I want to cry, make them see how upset I am.

But the tears don't come.

Because I know I'm better off not being Mrs. Pendleton Berry. We were on-again, off-again so many times, and in the end, nothing would have worked between us.

But still, they could've thought about the date.

"Please, don't go," Mandy says. "We'll... We'll cancel the champagne. Right, Jack?"

"Why, Mandy Cake?" Jack asks and then darts his gaze to me. "What's going on?"

Mandy hates that pet name, but now she seems to take it in stride. "Because today is the day Frankie was supposed to marry Penn, remember?"

Jackson, my mother, and my father all drop their jaws in unison, one right after the other. It's almost comical.

Great. Here come the looks of sympathy. The looks of pity.

"Frankie," Mom says. "Oh my gosh. How could we have been so obtuse?"

"I don't know," I say, and yes, I say it petulantly.

I'm twenty-seven years old, but at the moment I feel like

I'm five and my sister stole my lunch box.

I'm being ridiculous. Childish.

Mandy deserves happiness, and she'll have it with Jackson. I have no doubt. She will be happier with Jack than I could've ever been with Penn.

But still...

It hurts. It freaking hurts. Not so much the breakup with Penn, but the fact that not one of them thought about today's date.

"Please sit down," Dad says. "We haven't ordered yet, and you must be hungry. We'll make this up to you, Frankie."

"How do you think you're going to do that? Do you think I'm not going to remember that you guys all forgot what date this was? You think you can wipe my memory clean? You think you can—"

"Please." Mom gives me a sympathetic smile. "Just sit. No one is going to try to make you forget. God knows we couldn't do that."

"What is that supposed to mean?" And yes, I'm petulant again. "I feel like I'm Samantha Baker in that old movie you used to make us watch when we were kids. *Sixteen Candles*. You know, when the whole family forgot her birthday?"

"We've never forgotten your birthday," Dad says.

True, they haven't. I sigh. "I know that, Dad."

"To be honest," Mandy says, "we thought you were okay. You didn't seem that upset after you and Penn broke up. You seemed kind of...relieved."

I won't give her the satisfaction of telling her she's right. In the back of my mind, I knew Pendleton Berry wasn't my forever. But I put so much into him. We were on-again, off-again for over five years, which should've been my first clue.

I draw in a breath, count to ten.

I don't like feeling petulant. And my sister *does* deserve a moment to shine. Even if it's on the day I was supposed to become Mrs. Pendleton Berry.

"Congratulations, both of you." I don't take my seat. "But honestly, I'm just not feeling up to this. I'm happy for you, truly. But I think I'm going to go."

"Frankie..." Mom is using her *I'm your mother* voice.

She is still my mother, but I no longer live at home. I haven't for the last five years, and I don't need to do what my mommy says just because she says it.

"I'm sorry, but I'm leaving."

"We have to talk," Mandy says. "About wedding stuff. About maid-of-honor stuff."

"We'll have plenty of time to do that. I'd rather not do it tonight, if it's all the same to you."

Mandy nods, and I can see in her gray eyes that she understands and she's very sorry.

I will forgive her. I always do. We've had knock-down drag-outs that were way worse than this, and we've always forgiven each other.

But tonight I can't be here.

"Okay," Mandy relents. "And again, Frankie, I'm so—"

I hold up a hand to stop her. I can't take any more of the pitying looks. "I know you're sorry. Please let that be the last time you say it." I grab my purse hanging over my chair, and with as much dignity as I can, I walk away from the table and out of the restaurant.

I'm not sure where I'm going. Isabella and Gigi probably already have plans. It's Saturday night. Gigi is almost always busy on Saturday, and Isabella is about seventy-five percent of the time. Neither has had a serious relationship since our college days, so they can teach me the ropes now. Show me where to meet the good-quality men.

Hell, I don't even care if he's good-quality. I kind of just want to get laid. I still have the card from the Long Island Playboy...

I haven't eaten, but I'm not particularly hungry. I went on a food bender after Penn told me he was cheating. I had been practically starving myself for the previous two months so I could be svelte on my wedding day, and I went a little overboard after the breakup. After a week of chili fries and Ben & Jerry's, I haven't been very hungry since.

Part of me wishes I'd stayed for the champagne toast, but only because alcohol sounds pretty good right now.

I duck into the first bar I see.

It's on the first floor of a residential building owned by Braden Black, the blue-collar billionaire, which means it's ultra-swanky—marble flooring, dark wood, and top-shelf liquor lining mirrored glass shelves. Lucky for me, there happen to be a couple of empty stools at the bar. I grab one and fish my credit card out of my purse.

A bartender steps forward, and boy is he hot. Blond with gorgeous blue eyes, and his name tag says Alfred.

He meets my gaze. "Hello there."

"Hello, Alfred." I try to smile at him, but it feels fake.

"You look like you could use something to take the edge off."

"My God, you have no idea. What do you recommend?"

He hands me a menu of custom cocktails. "Do you like sweet drinks? Or do you prefer them on the drier side?"

I glance at the menu but lack the mental energy to process any of the drink descriptions. "At the moment I'm thinking anything with alcohol will do."

"Been that kind of day, huh?"

"Like I said before, you have no idea."

"Tell you what." He smiles. "Let me mix you up something special. I feel like you need a dash of sweetness in your life tonight."

He probably says that to everyone. "Sure. Whatever. I'm game. But not too sweet."

Alfred turns away, and I let out a breath. I have no idea what I look like. I did my hair and makeup before I met my parents and Mandy at the restaurant, but I haven't checked it since then. And you know what? I don't care.

Someone slides into the seat next to mine.

I look up.

And I suck in a breath.

The man turns to me, his face half obscured with a white mask that covers his eyes and his right cheek. It looks glossy, as if it's made of porcelain, but it can't possibly be. That would make it heavy. It's tied behind his head with a black silk ribbon.

"I'm sorry," he says in a deep and husky voice. "Did I startle you?"

"No. It's just…your costume."

He tilts his head. "What makes you think it's a costume?"

"Well…" I look over my shoulder. "No one else seems to be dressed like you. Are you part of the entertainment for the night?" There's no stage here, so he's probably not here to entertain.

"Maybe this is what I wear all the time. Did you ever think of that?"

I can't help staring. His hair is the darkest brown—it looks black, except for the hints of gold when the light hits it just right. His eyes are the color of rich coffee, and his jawline is stubbled in black and could be sculpted out of marble. His skin is lightly tanned, and I long to see his full face. I can sort of see half of it, as the Phantom of the Opera mask only covers his eyes and the right side of it.

He's wearing a white button-down shirt with the first two buttons undone, and dark chest hair peeks out. Black jeans and black slip-on shoes, no socks.

And of course, a black velvet cape around his shoulders.

"Okay, then," I say, trying not to fidget. "So this *is* what you normally wear?"

"I didn't say that. I said what if it were?"

"Then I'd say you're trying to hide something."

He smiles. His lips are full and pink, and for a moment I wonder what they would feel like against my own.

I clasp my hands together to keep from wringing them. I'm not sure what to think of this guy yet. "Then level with me. *Is* this what you normally wear, or are you pulling my leg?"

Before he answers, Alfred approaches us. "Good evening, Phantom. The usual tonight?"

"Yes. Thank you, Alfred."

Phantom? He's actually *called* Phantom? Now that's intriguing. What is this guy's story?

"What's the usual?" I ask him.

"The usual," he says, enunciating slowly, "is a dry martini with two olives and a dash of St-Germain."

"St-Germain?" I think for a moment before it comes to me. "Isn't that elderflower liqueur?"

"It is."

"Seems out of place in a martini. A regular gin martini, I assume?"

"A martini *is* a gin martini," Phantom says, his tone almost professorial. "If you want vodka instead of gin, you specifically ask for a vodka martini."

"Yes, I know that."

"Then I commend you," he says. "Most people don't."

"I'm not 'most people.' But anyway, the St-Germain. In a martini?"

"Absolutely."

"Why?"

He smiles slightly. "Because St-Germain makes everything a little bit better."

I'm not sure what to say to his comment, so I say nothing, though his smile has me squirming.

"And what did you order?" Phantom asks.

I drop my gaze to the bar in front of me. "Honestly? I have no idea. Alfred said he'd mix up something special for me."

He leans toward me a bit more. "I see. Are you having a bad evening?"

His nearness makes me want to tremble. In a good way. "Why would you ask that?"

"I've known Alfred a long time, and he doesn't offer to whip up something special unless someone really needs it."

I sigh. "So it really is that obvious."

"What I don't understand," he says, "is how someone as beautiful as you could possibly be having a bad evening."

My cheeks warm from the compliment.

"Tell me," Phantom continues. "What's wrong?"

I sigh again. "It's a long and boring story."

"I'm not going anywhere. And I doubt anything about you could be boring."

His dark eyes mesmerize me. I wonder if that's why he wears the mask, so people will focus only on his eyes. They're deep and dark and long-lashed.

Women would kill for eyes like that.

"I just need a drink," I say.

"You have one in front of you."

Alfred's special is a light orangey brown, which of course could be anything. It's in a martini glass rimmed with white crystals. Salt? Sugar? Alfred said he'd make me something sweet, so my working guess is sugar.

I grab the glass by the stem, bring it to my mouth, and take a small sip.

As I suspected, the crystals are sugar, and they give a little sweetness to the otherwise sour lemony-orange flavor. It dances along my tongue, and I'm enjoying it until—

I set it down and push it toward Alfred. "Is this a sidecar?"

"It's a special version of a sidecar," Alfred says, "made with lemon juice and orange juice and a gorgeous brandy from France with a dash of St-Germain."

Phantom chuckles next to me. "Alfred may be a top-notch bartender, but I'm the one who introduced him to the joys of St-Germain."

Alfred and Phantom are both charming, to be sure, and they have no way of knowing, but—

"A sidecar is my sister's favorite drink. Of all the nights that I did not need to be reminded of my sister." I shove my credit card toward Alfred. "I'll take my check now, and then I'm getting out of here."

Phantom covers my hand with his own and slides my credit card back toward me. "Please. Allow me."

"Neither one of you has to pay," Alfred says. "If you don't like your drink, you're not going to get charged for it. Company policy. I'll make you something else."

"It's my own fault. I should've just ordered what I wanted.

The problem is, I don't know what I want. Not tonight."

"How about I get you a glass of water while you decide?" Alfred says.

I glance at Phantom. "You know what? It's been a long time since I've had a good martini. Make me one of his St-Germain martinis. I'd like to try it."

"You got it." Alfred turns his back and begins to mix drinks.

"It's a strong drink," Phantom says.

"Yeah? I can handle it."

I know my way around alcohol, for sure. I feel kind of bad, actually. The twisted sidecar Alfred made me was quite delicious, and it's not his fault that I'm feeling pissy at my sister—so pissy that I don't want to be reminded of her even via her favorite cocktail. It's not Mandy's fault that Penn is a jackass cheating bastard and that she finally got her heart's desire just as mine was being broken.

Of course, it *is* her fault that she forgot today was the day I was supposed to be married. It's her fault, Jackson's fault, and mostly my parents' fault. They should've remembered.

Alfred finishes our martinis and slides them toward us.

I pick mine up, and the sweet aroma of elderflower wafts toward me.

Here goes nothing.

CHAPTER TWO

Phantom

What is her name?

I don't normally concern myself with such mundane things as someone's name, but as I stare at this beauty sitting next to me, I find myself wanting to know.

Her hair is long and dark, though a few shades lighter than mine, and it falls over her shoulders in thick waves. Her oval face and high cheekbones are perfection, but the truly remarkable feature is her eyes.

They're the lightest silvery blue, and I could easily get lost in them.

I make it a requirement to never get lost in a woman. I'm not looking for companionship. I'm looking for playmates. Women whom I can take to the club and engage with in a scene.

So I don't concern myself with names.

Because if I did, I'd have to reveal my own name, and I don't do that here.

No one knows my name here, other than Alfred. I'm known only as Phantom, and I always show up in costume.

Many times, a woman has tried to get me to reveal my name.

I never have.

This is separate from my other life—the life where I make a living, do my work.

Here, I dive into the deepest and darkest parts of my desires with willing partners.

And I never tell them my name.

Nor do I ask theirs.

So why is curiosity engaging me tonight? This woman is beautiful, yes, and her outfit is stunning. Except it's only black leggings and a black tunic with a low-cut neck that shows the swells of her gorgeously shaped breasts.

Her nails and lips are painted red, and I can imagine those lips—held open with a spider gag—around my cock as I fuck her lusty little mouth.

Before she takes a drink, I lift my glass and clink it to hers. "Here's to alcohol, the rose-colored glasses of life."

She smiles. "Rose-colored glasses. I could use those about now."

"I wish I could take credit, then. But I didn't coin the phrase. F. Scott Fitzgerald did."

"The author?"

"Do you know of another?"

She smiles again. "Yeah, my butcher." Her eyes dance. "I'm kidding." She takes a sip.

"What do you think?" I ask.

She pauses a moment, cocking her head, as if she's trying to find the right words. "It's strong for sure. But it's…unique. I honestly expected the juniper of the gin to overpower the elderflower, but it doesn't. It's more like…a floral scent that comes on a light breeze. A breeze that's also scented with pine needles and wood and earth. Like the autumn. The soft breeze of an autumn day. The kind that makes the leaves rustle around your feet."

I stare at her for a moment, at those red lips, as she picks up her glass and takes another sip.

I'm not sure how she did it, but she almost took those words straight out of my head.

That's exactly what this martini is like.

It always reminds me of a line from my favorite novel, *The Great Gatsby.*

Life starts all over again when it gets crisp in the fall.

That's what this drink is like. Sure, there are other drinks that are more seasonally appropriate, like crisp apple cider, wassail, hot buttered rum.

But something about my special martini—the juniper and the elderflower—takes me to the crispness of autumn.

I need to get to know this woman better.

If she has me quoting Fitzgerald and then brings out the *Gatsby* in me, I definitely need to get to know her better.

CHAPTER THREE

Frankie

I take another drink of Phantom's special martini. It goes down way more smoothly than I expected, and I realize I need to be careful. I can hold my liquor, but this is a strong drink and I haven't eaten anything since breakfast. I skipped lunch thinking I'd have a big dinner at the restaurant, but I left before we ordered food.

I don't like myself very much tonight. I acted like an absolute baby at dinner. But on the other hand, none of them remembered what today was supposed to be.

Not that it matters. I'm way better off not being married to Penn. If he was cheating on me before we were married, he'd certainly cheat on me after. Plus, he's kind of a loser. Sure, he has a trust fund, and I would've had fun helping him spend it, but I'm better than that.

That's what Mandy told me.

"You're better than that, Frank," she said after I told her my wedding was off.

Phantom and I don't talk as we each finish our drinks, but the silence between us isn't uneasy. We don't even know each other. I'm wildly attracted to him, and just being near him has my body wound up like a bowstring.

Before I know it, I've drained the last of my martini and I'm eating the olives off the toothpick.

"Can I get you another?" Phantom asks.

"No, I'd better stop at one. I haven't eaten anything yet this evening."

"Then we should remedy that," he says. "There are a few tables available. Can I buy you dinner?"

"This is a bar," I say.

"That's true, but they still serve great food. You look like you could use a burger with all the fixings."

As if in anticipation, my stomach lets out a growl.

Phantom smiles.

"Guilty. I am hungry. I've kind of been on a diet, though."

He rakes his gaze over my body, making me warm all over. "You don't need to be on a diet."

"Well, I kind of do. I—" I stop.

No. I am *not* going to obsess about my weight. Time to turn over a new leaf.

"You know what? A big, greasy burger sounds amazing. But first you need to do something for me."

He smiles. "Other than buy you dinner?"

"I didn't mean that to sound ungrateful. I'm happy to pay for my own dinner. But I *would* like to know your name."

His lips curve slightly downward. "Why should we spoil this with names?"

"How can a name spoil it? I'm—"

He places his fingers on my lips. "Not yet. Not tonight. Tonight, I'm your Phantom, and you are my beautiful angel of music."

I suppress a shudder.

Something about his voice… The low, rich timbre of it… The slight hoarseness, just enough to be sexy.

And my God, the feel of his fingertips on my lips.

If his fingers feel this amazing against my lips, how will the rest of him feel?

And how will I ever know if he won't even tell me his name?

"Alfred," he says, "could you transfer my tab over to table seven? I see that it's available, and the lady would like a burger."

"Yeah, of course, Phantom."

"Everyone calls you Phantom?" I say.

"They do."

"Why?"

"Because, my beautiful angel of music, it's my name." Phantom slides off the stool, his cape drifting around him as if it's part of him, and then he offers me his hand.

Good thing, too, because my legs have apparently turned to jelly. His strength steadies me as he walks me toward the table, pulls out my chair for me, and then pushes it in once I'm seated.

The table is in the corner, and a small votive sits in the center, casting a glow on Phantom's face. His *masked* face. For a moment I wonder if he's scarred underneath that mask like the actual Phantom of the Opera.

And in this moment, it doesn't really matter what's under that mask.

Already I'm beguiled by this man—this nameless, faceless man.

It's silly, I know. It's the situation. My evening has been shitty, and I'm ripe for the picking.

But it's also the mystery, the enigma.

I haven't had sex in months, and frankly? Things between Penn and me were never that great. I had to teach him where some of the erogenous zones were, and once he learned, he was adequate, but don't I deserve more than adequate?

You're better than that, Frank.

The breakup was so out of the blue. Penn just announced that he had been seeing someone else and he was ending our engagement. Almost as if he'd been coerced into it, most likely by whomever he was seeing. I didn't ask. I didn't care. I still don't.

Doesn't matter anyway. It's over, and a big part of me is actually relieved.

Except…I've always dreamed of being a bride. Having a wedding. Of being a princess for a day.

It will happen for Mandy before it happens for me.

Ugh! I have to get over that silly mindset! I'll apologize to Mandy for being a brat at dinner. Then she'll apologize to me again for choosing such a rotten day to announce her engagement.

We'll be fine. We always are.

"A penny for your thoughts…" Phantom's sexy voice breaks into my mind.

"Nothing. How about *your* thoughts?"

"I think I'm sitting across from the most beautiful woman in this entire place."

The warmth again. It surges through me, and I feel like I'm a lilac flower bursting into bloom.

"You're even more beautiful when you blush," he says.

I absently touch my cheeks. They're so warm.

"So are you sure you want a burger? Or would you like something else?" He pulls the small menus off the side of the table and hands one to me.

"No, I want the burger. And I want it loaded, Phantom. With everything full of fat like cheese and mayonnaise and slices of avocado and bacon."

He laughs then.

It's a gorgeous sight and sound, indeed.

Who *is* this man across from me?

Who *is* this Phantom?

I really want to find out.

Our server, a young woman named June, according to her tag, approaches us. "Good evening, Phantom."

"Good evening, June. May I present my angel for the evening?"

Angel for the evening?

He's had other angels. Other evenings. My heart sinks. He's probably planning to let me go after tonight. What was I expecting? To meet the new love of my life behind some mask?

"Good evening," June says to me.

"Good evening," I echo.

"What can I get for you tonight? The usual for you, Phantom?"

"Yes, I believe I'll have another. Angel?"

"As delicious as it was, I think I'll switch to water. Or an iced tea if you have one."

"I absolutely do, freshly brewed." June makes a few notes. "Did you want to order any food tonight?"

"Absolutely," Phantom says. "The lady will have the third-pound burger with everything, including bacon."

"How would you like that cooked?" June asks me.

"Medium, thanks."

"Great. And for you, Phantom?"

"I was thinking I'd have the same, but I've changed my mind."

"What would you like, then?" June asks.

"What I really want isn't on the menu." Phantom sears me with his gaze. "But I'll settle for the chicken breast sandwich and a side of fries."

June must be used to his antics because she doesn't so much as flinch at the innuendo. "Got it," she says, "I'll get these right up."

My flesh is on fire. I clear my throat in an attempt to get my bearings. "So tell me, Phantom," I say. "How long have you been coming here?"

"Why do you ask?"

"Everyone here seems to know you as Phantom."

"Everyone here is paid to make sure the customer is satisfied," he says. "I prefer to be known as Phantom, so they grant me that."

"No," I say. "It's more than that. They all seem to *know* you. But you're the only one here in a mask. What gives?"

"This is just the way I prefer to dress."

"Yeah…I'm not buying it." I smile, hoping I don't have lipstick smeared all over my teeth. "I'm going to figure out all of your secrets, Mr. Phantom."

"Are you, now?"

"I am."

"Then you know what that means, don't you, Angel?"

"What?"

"That means I will find out *your* secrets as well."

CHAPTER FOUR

Phantom

Sometimes I wonder if the phantom is who I truly am and my alter ego is the one without the costume.

There are times when I feel most like myself as the phantom. I can do things as the phantom that I could never do as myself. They'd definitely be frowned upon.

When I made the comment about secrets, Angel looked down at her napkin.

So she has a secret?

Everyone has secrets. As Gaston Leroux himself said in *The Phantom of the Opera*, "Our lives are one masked ball." When I'm the phantom, others seem to feel more at ease being who they want to be in the moment as well. A lot of times, that means they let their secrets go.

My only secret is what I enjoy in the bedroom. My fantasies and tastes run deep and dark, and as I gaze at my angel of music still staring at her napkin, I'm not sure she's ready to explore that side of herself.

Still, though…I have this ridiculous need to know her name. So unlike me, and so *not* what this side of me is about.

CHAPTER FIVE

Frankie

Secrets?

I have to hold back a laugh.

I have no secrets. Everybody knows my business. Everybody knows—hell, even *I* knew—Pendleton Berry is a sleazebag. That he was running around on me.

You know what? It's kind of nice to just be by myself.

I don't know who this guy is. He's masked, after all. What are the chances that I'll ever see him again?

June slides a plate in front of me, and I inhale the robust and smoky fragrance of the beef and bacon. Once Phantom is served, I take a bite of my burger.

I don't even try to be dainty about it. When grease runs down my chin, I dab it away with my napkin, and I don't make excuses. I'm hungry, the burger is damned good, the beef is juicy, and with all the toppings, yes, it drips.

I've always been the kind of woman who tries to be ultra-feminine around men. What good did it do? I couldn't get Pendleton Berry to be faithful to me.

This man? He's wildly attractive—even though I don't

really know what he looks like—and I find myself liking him. Liking him a lot more than I should. So why do I feel like I'm more myself with this masked man than I ever was with Penn or anyone else? I wouldn't have been caught dead with grease running down my chin at dinner with Penn. No. I'd be cutting off a tiny slice of the sandwich with a fork and knife.

Nope, that's not true. I wouldn't be eating a burger at all. I'd be eating a salad with grilled chicken, dressing on the side.

"I like a woman who enjoys her food," Phantom says.

I raise my eyebrows. "Oh?"

"Yeah. You have a lovely figure, and it's great that you don't eat like a rabbit all the time to make sure you keep it."

Boy, this guy doesn't know me at all.

Normally, I love to eat, but before the food bender after Penn gave me the news, I had been eating like a rabbit.

"I exercise," I say after wiping my lips again. "I like to run, mostly."

"A runner?"

"Yeah. I'm out every weekend. Weekday mornings when the weather cooperates."

"Something we have in common, then. I also enjoy running."

Did he just divulge a piece of information to me? I can't help myself. I smile and then take another bite of my burger, again wiping the drips from my chin with my napkin and again not caring.

Sitting across from this man who's masking his identity—this man I'll probably never see again—I don't care. I don't care if I'm not ultra-perfect in my table manners. It doesn't matter.

It never really mattered.

The only thing that matters is the fact that not ever seeing Phantom again makes me feel…

Things I shouldn't be feeling.

"Tell me, angel of music," Phantom says. "Would you join me here again tomorrow evening?"

My heart flips. Perhaps I *will* see him again.

"On a Sunday evening?" I cock my head. "I work on Monday."

"So do I," he says.

"What do you do?" I ask.

He curves his lips slightly upward. "I haunt an opera house in Paris."

Can't blame me for trying.

"What do you do, angel?" he asks me.

"I'm a junior editor at—" I let a slow smile spread across my face. "I'm a soprano ingenue."

Phantom laughs then, that deep, husky laugh that I've already grown to love.

"So you are."

The game is amusing, but I believe he was truthful when he said he had to work Monday. So what does he do? Something exotic, probably. Maybe an international spy. And that's why he has to disguise himself when he goes out. Or he could be a model. Maybe I've seen him on the pages of my own magazine.

No. I'd never forget those eyes.

Maybe he works at Black Inc. with my soon-to-be brother-in-law, Jackson Paris. He could be a software engineer or a lawyer. Maybe a marketing executive like Jackson.

He could be anything.

Which is clearly the point.

For some reason, he wants to hide his true self. Why?

Perhaps there's no other reason for it than to have fun.

Because I admit… I'm having fun, too.

Wouldn't it be amazing to be an opera singer, the ingenue of the Phantom of the Opera? In my mind's eye, I'm floating with him toward his lair as he sings to me.

The music of the night…

"You haven't answered me, angel. Will you meet me here tomorrow night?"

I jerk out of my daydream. "Just here? At the bar?"

"Yes. It's masquerade night."

"Apparently every night is masquerade night for you," I say.

"True. But tomorrow is masquerade night for everyone."

"It's kind of strange that it's on a Sunday."

"What's so strange about it?"

"I told you already. We all have to work the next day."

"The party ends at eleven."

My self-imposed curfew on a work night is midnight, so what the heck? I have a strong desire to see this man again. A very strong desire—one that's directed right between my legs.

"All right."

"Where do you live? I'll pick you up."

"Oh no," I say. "You're not getting my address—or my name—if I don't get yours."

His eyes widen slightly. "I'm impressed. You have nothing to fear from me, but you're a very intelligent woman who's concerned about her own safety. As you should be. Why don't we meet here at eight?"

"All right. That sounds fine." I wipe my mouth once more.

I gobble down my burger, cleaning my plate. Good thing he likes women who like to eat.

Maybe it's time I worry less about gaining an extra pound and worry more about making myself happy. I don't need to eat a hamburger every night to be happy, but it sure is a nice treat—one I don't often allow myself.

Phantom signals June for the check. She brings it, and he hands her several bills.

No credit card. Of course not. A credit card would bear his name.

Once the check is paid, I rise. "I should go. I'll grab an Uber, and I'll see you back here tomorrow evening."

...

"I think it sounds fabulous," Gigi says at brunch the next morning.

My two besties, Isabella Phillips and Gigi Frost, always meet me for brunch on Sundays. It's one of our things.

"Yeah, but it was kind of strange. Like everyone at that bar knew him only as Phantom. Who does that kind of stuff?"

"Sounds a little psycho to me," Isabella says in her monotonic voice.

I don't like the words Isabella uses, but admittedly, I considered it myself.

"Exactly why I didn't give him my address," I tell them. "I kind of wanted to. I'm wildly attracted to the guy."

Gigi giggles. "How can you be attracted to a man you haven't even seen?"

"From what I *can* tell, he's gorgeous, but that's not even

what was so intriguing about him. It was his demeanor. He made me shiver just the way he looked at me. And he quoted F. Scott Fitzgerald."

"And you, the English major." Gigi giggles again. "He must have ESP."

"Still sounds a little creepy." Isabella takes a sip of her mimosa.

"Don't listen to Izzy," Gigi says. "You go for this. Go to that masquerade. In fact, what bar is this?"

I open my mouth but then close it. Do I want to tell them? Gigi loves a good party, and she might show up. That's not necessarily a bad thing, but she'll talk constantly and try to drag Phantom's identity out of him.

Then again, just in case, it's probably good for someone to know where I'll be.

"It's on the ground floor of that Black Inc. residential building uptown."

"I don't think I've ever been there," Gigi says.

That's something, because Gigi's kind of a barfly. She likes to party, and she's very popular with men. She's gorgeous, with blond hair, blue eyes, and a shapely booty that the guys really like.

"What kind of party is it?" Isabella asks. "I mean other than a masquerade?"

"You know as much as I know. I don't know whether it's by invitation only or not. All he said was it's masquerade night." I take a drink of my coffee.

Gigi and Isabella always have mimosas when we have our Sunday brunch, but I stopped that last year. I like to drink as much as the next person, but when I drink early, I'm not very effective for the rest of the day.

"Whose turn is it to pay this time?" I ask.

"Mine," Isabella says.

"Okay. Thanks, Izzy." I glance at my watch. "I need to go. I'm meeting Mandy at her place."

"After what she did to you?" Gigi asks.

"Yeah. She should've remembered what yesterday was, but this is my family. I can't be mad at them forever."

Neither of them replies in any meaningful way as I take off.

Sometimes I wonder if I'm outgrowing Isabella and Gigi. They're awesome people, and I love them, but they're still so much into the party scene. I enjoy a good party, but I haven't been up for much since Penn and I called it quits. The last couple of times Isabella and Gigi invited me out, I've blown them off, which isn't cool.

I grab an Uber to Mandy's place, walk to her door, and knock.

She opens the door, wearing black yoga pants and a pink cotton tank, her hair pulled up in a messy bun. Classic Mandy garb. She shoos her yapping dog, Roger, away from me. "Hey."

I walk in. "Hey." I look around. Most of her stuff is boxed up. "What's going on here?"

"I'm moving in with Jack. I wanted to wait until my lease is up, which is next week."

"You didn't mention that last night."

"I did, actually." Mandy looks down. "After you left."

Well, that didn't take long. I gulp, trying not to feel like I'm swallowing my pride. "I'm sorry I left so abruptly."

"Oh, Frank, you don't need to be sorry. *I'm* so sorry. I don't know what any of us were thinking, choosing to announce our engagement on that date."

"When you called me and invited me to dinner," I say,

"my first thought was that you wanted to get my mind off of it."

"I'm so sorry," she says again. "Mom and Dad feel awful."

Yeah, they should.

But I don't say it.

"I shouldn't have run out like a toddler," I say.

"You had every right to."

"No, I didn't. While your choice of date was not the greatest, I'm a grown-up. I should've been able to handle it."

"Will you still be my maid of honor?"

I force a smile. "Of course. I'm your sister, Mandy. Who else would be your maid of honor?"

She drops her gaze.

Honestly, I didn't mean that as a burn. Mandy has only had one best friend her entire life, and she's marrying him.

"Anyway, I just dropped by to apologize," I say.

Mandy grabs my arm. "Will you stay? I've been looking at wedding venues, dresses, everything. It's just so overwhelming."

Mandy's a virtual assistant for a romance author, so she works at home. She hardly ever goes anywhere, so this whole wedding thing is probably freaking her out.

"What does Jackson think?" I ask.

"He wants whatever I want. The problem is that I'm not exactly sure what I want."

I pull out my phone and scroll through some photos of dresses. "I was planning a fairly extravagant affair, but that's because I had Penn's sprawling estate available. Mom and Dad were going to pay for what they could, and the fact that I already had a venue really helped."

"Right." She sighs. "Would it be ridiculous if I just told Jack I want to go to city hall?"

"Mandy, he said he wants what you want."

"I know. But Mom would hate that."

I can't help laughing then. "When you're right you're right. She will hate it. But Mandy, it's not *her* wedding."

Mandy sighs again. "I know. I hate to disappoint her, though."

"You don't have to have a big wedding. If you're just going to have one attendant each, maid of honor and a best man, it can be a small affair. What about going to the Poconos? Or better yet, renting a small place upstate? It won't cost that much, and it can just be family."

"Mom might go for that," Mandy says.

"Yeah. She gets her wedding. You get your small affair. Everybody's happy."

"Maybe." Mandy crosses her arms. "I don't know how Jackson's mother will feel."

"Who cares?"

"Well, Jack will, for one."

"But Jack said to do whatever you want."

"I know. But you know Noreen. She can be a little..."

"Bitchy?"

Mandy laughs. "Okay, we'll go with your word."

"I've known the woman as long as you have, Mandy. I remember. I was never sure how she and Mom could be such good friends."

"I know, but they were. You should've seen her when Jackson was in his accident. I went over to take care of him, and she couldn't get me out of there fast enough. If it weren't for Bill, she would have moved in with Jack."

"Well, she's his mom. And she only has one kid. Mom would probably be just as protective if one of us were hurt."

"I suppose you're right." Mandy shakes her head. "I just

know she's going to want something bigger. When Bill made it big in tech and they moved out of our old neighborhood, she definitely enjoyed—*enjoys*—living the high life."

"Then I'd say if she wants a big wedding, she has to pay for it."

"Mom would never allow that. She's too proud."

"Then it's going to be your way. It's your wedding, not Noreen's."

"She'll try to put Jackson in the middle. I don't want that."

"Jack will choose you, Mandy."

"I know he will, but I don't want him to ever be in that position. I certainly wouldn't want to be."

"I'll tell you what," I say. "Why don't you, Mom, and I invite Noreen out to lunch or something? We can check with Mom and see when she's available." I scroll through my calendar. "Next week is out for me, but we'll figure it out. We can all discuss our expectations and see what she says. It's possible she'll agree with you."

"I suppose. But I know Noreen."

So do I.

But I don't say it.

Let Mandy think she has a chance for a minute, at least.

"So where did you go last night?" she asks.

"I just went home."

I don't particularly like lying to my sister, but I'm not ready to tell her about Phantom. I didn't feel quite right telling Gigi and Izzy this morning, either.

It's my own precious secret, and telling more people will make it less special.

Speaking of which…

"I should go. I've got some shopping to do."

"Okay."

No chance of Mandy wanting to come along. She hates shopping.

I take a walk around Mandy's neighborhood. It's not the best neighborhood in the world—judging by the wino hanging out by her building and staring at me like I'm a fifth of rotgut—and frankly, I'm glad she'll be moving to Jackson's. He has a great apartment near his work.

Mandy's neighborhood has a few shops, but I don't know what I'm looking for. What do you wear to a masquerade?

I laugh out loud.

A mask, of course.

But where will I find one? I don't want a basic Halloween mask. I want one of those fancy Mardi Gras masks. A party store, maybe? I honestly have no idea. If I had more time, I'd order something online.

I call for an Uber, and I have him drop me in Chinatown. Some of those shops have masks. I walk around, inhaling the umami scent of dim sum. I'm hungry again. What's with this appetite all of a sudden? I stop in front of a shop.

Golden Dragon Costumes.

Perfect.

I walk into the store, and I'm transplanted to a fantasy world.

I've always loved Chinatown. I adore Chinese culture and fashion and food. I especially love the silks in vibrant gemstone colors.

I amble through the store, taking in the beauty, until I find a display of intricately designed masks. Exactly what I'm looking for.

A light-blue satin mask draws my gaze. It covers only my eyes, unlike Phantom's mask, but the blue will be perfect with my eye color. It's trimmed with black and golden feathers.

I grab it, make my way to the counter, and pay.

What else will I wear?

I have no idea.

Until I see another store.

And in the window, a black silk dress.

I won't be able to afford it, but I can't help myself. I go in.

It's the traditional fitted cheongsam style, and the length is midthigh. But instead of the traditional high collar, it's got a square neckline that's low-cut and will show a bit of cleavage.

But what makes it even more perfect is its embroidery of yellow and blue that matches the golden feathers and blue silk of my mask.

I must have this dress.

It will be perfect for tonight, and for once, I want to buy something without looking at the price. I used to look forward to doing that once I was married to Penn. His trust fund would've supported us in a luxurious manner for all our lives.

But…it's not going to happen. I make a decent salary as a junior editor for *Lovely* magazine, but rent in New York is not cheap. Most months, I live paycheck to paycheck.

But damn, I want the dress!

"May I help you?" the clerk behind the counter asks.

"Yes, the black dress in the window, the one with the yellow and blue embroidery. Do you have it in a size eight?"

"I believe so. Let me check in the back." She returns a few minutes later with a dress covered in plastic. "Here you go—size eight. Would you like to try it on?"

"Yes, thank you."

If I'm not going to check the price, I at least need to make sure it fits.

The dressing rooms are in the back, small closets covered only by a curtain. I quickly remove my clothes and try the dress on.

And oh my God.

It was made for me.

I have a tendency to gain weight around the middle, and if I gain a single inch, the dress will no longer fit.

No more hamburgers.

At least not before tonight.

I don't want to take the dress off, but I must. Once it's back on the hanger, I carry it to the front counter. "I'll take it."

She rings me up, and I hand her my credit card.

"That will be three hundred and fifty-seven dollars and eighty-eight cents."

I gulp audibly.

But I purchase the dress.

And I hope to God this Phantom guy is worth it.

CHAPTER SIX

Phantom

She walks in beauty, like the night…

I'm not a huge Byron aficionado, but he accurately describes what I see as she walks in.

My angel of music, wearing a mask that perfectly matches her silvery blue eyes.

Her dark hair is a little wavier tonight, and it falls around her shoulders. Her chest is bare, and her plump breasts are pushed up. The dress is black silk with cap sleeves, and it hugs her luscious body, the skirt stopping halfway to her knees. Black platform stiletto pumps complete her attire.

How did she become more beautiful in twenty-four hours?

My God, I want to know her name.

For a moment, I consider escaping out the back way.

Not because I don't want to be with this woman, but because I want to be with her too much.

I want to take her down to the club. Introduce her to a scene.

But I also want to show her who I truly am.

And that never happens.

I don't do monogamy. I don't do relationships. Not anymore.

I enjoy scenes.

Sometimes with the same woman. Sometimes not.

I don't date in the traditional sense. I usually find my partners in the club, but in the rare instance that I meet someone new in the bar—as I did this angel—sometimes, if things go well, I introduce her to scenes at the club.

If things don't go well, I don't.

No harm, no foul.

I already know I won't take Angel down to the club tonight. She made a big deal about having to work in the morning. But I can at least see if she's amenable to the idea. If she's interested in exploring something unique and passionate. Something…darker.

So I move toward her, my cape floating around me—

She meets my gaze.

And she smiles.

CHAPTER SEVEN

Frankie

He seems to sail toward me, as if he's being carried by that cape around him.

His mask is the same, his tanned skin is the same; his sculpted jawline, his black stubble.

His full pink lips, his gorgeous straight teeth.

His broad shoulders, his few chest hairs peeking out… All the same.

But tonight he wears a black shirt, the sleeves rolled up to his elbows.

I suck in a breath at those forearms. So perfectly corded with muscle.

Instead of jeans, he wears black trousers, perfectly fitted over his hips. Already I know his ass is flawless, even though I can't see it because of the cape.

How can I be so attracted to someone when I haven't even seen his whole face?

How can I know, according to the thrumming of my body, that this man can take me places I've never been?

But he can…and already I know I'll let him.

He reaches toward me and trails a finger over my jawline. "Angel, you look beautiful. Where did you find that mask? It brings out the color of your eyes."

"Chinatown," I say on a breath.

"You put every other woman here to shame." He takes my hand. "Come."

I'm not sure where we're going. The bar is full, with masked faces everywhere. Some are costumed elaborately in bright colors while others wear simple masks with no adornments. Only Phantom wears the white half mask, though.

I don't see empty tables, until—

He leads me to the bar itself, to two empty seats at the very end.

"Good evening," Alfred says. "It's so nice to see you again."

"You too, Alfred."

"What can I get you tonight?"

"I think I'll have one of the Phantom specials again. That martini last night was amazing."

"Make it two, Al."

"Coming right up."

Phantom burns me with his gaze. "I have to admit, part of me wondered if you were going to come tonight."

"Why would you wonder that?"

"Some women have trouble escaping into fantasy. I wasn't quite sure which side you fell on."

"I have to admit, normally I don't do things like this."

"I'm glad you decided to do it tonight."

"Will you ever tell me your name?"

"Will you ever tell me yours?"

"You're one of those guys who likes to answer a question

with a question. And normally? That would piss me off." I boldly place my hand over his. "But for some reason with you it's simply charming."

He squeezes my hand. "I find you absolutely breathtaking, and that is definitely part of your charm."

This is so strange.

I'm never the most beautiful woman in the room, but Phantom makes me feel as though I am.

He makes me feel like I'm the *only* woman in the room.

I haven't noticed anyone else. I'm sure there are other good-looking men here. Other charming men.

But they're all a blur.

They don't exist at all.

Alfred delivers our drinks, and Phantom raises his.

"To my angel," he says.

I raise my glass and clink it to his. "And to you as well."

"To a promising beginning." He takes a sip.

A promising beginning.

Normally I'd try to dissect those words. What do they mean, exactly?

Instead, I let them slide over me, into me, with a warmth I'm not used to.

To a promising beginning…

I take a sip, and it's as woodsy and delicious as it was last night. As strong as it was last night, too. I will only be having one…just like last night.

I need to keep my wits about me because already I know I could easily lose control with Phantom.

One more perfect word from him, and I'll be hitting the sheets.

Maybe I should. After all, he'd have to take his mask off eventually.

But he won't take me to bed tonight.

Already I know this as well as I know my own name. As well as I wish I knew his name.

Tonight is not about sex.

Tonight is about the lure of the masquerade.

Tonight is about that part of myself I keep hidden.

That part of myself that only *I* see.

And somehow? I feel like Phantom sees it, too.

Which is strange because I'm not even sure what my true desires are. But I do know, now, that they were never to be Mrs. Pendleton Berry.

My whole life, I thought I knew what I wanted. Marriage, money, a big house in the best part of town.

Sitting here with Phantom, my greatest desire is none of those things.

It's simply to know this man's name.

He's going to make me jump through some hoops to get it, but already I know those hoops will open me up to a greater experience.

They will open me up to something new and exciting.

I may discover secrets about myself that even *I* don't know.

"You won't tell me your name," I say, "and I accept that. But tell me *something*. Tell me something about yourself that no one knows."

"Will you do the same for me?"

I nod and take another sip of my drink.

"Very well then, my angel of music. It may surprise you to know that *The Phantom of the Opera* is not my favorite musical."

"It isn't?"

"No. My favorite musical is *Camelot*."

"*Camelot*? About King Arthur?"

"Yes."

"No one else knows this about you?"

"No. Most people just assume my favorite musical is *The Phantom of the Opera*. Or *Gatsby*."

"*Gatsby*? I've never heard of that."

"It's a new musical based on F. Scott Fitzgerald's *The Great Gatsby*, which is my favorite novel. But because it's my favorite novel, I don't like any of the movies or the musical."

"I understand," I say. "The adaptation is never as good as the book. Except in the case of *Wicked*, in which case it's better than the book."

"I've never read it," he says.

"It's good," I say. "But the musical is better."

"Interesting. Already I found out something new about you. But you still owe me. What is something that no one knows about you?"

I don't even have to think before I reply. It's almost as if the words form in my head without any help from me at all.

"I want to find out who I truly am," I say. "Because the person everyone knows? The person *I* know? I don't think that's really me."

He doesn't reply at first, simply takes another drink of his martini and then sets his glass down.

Then he trails one finger over my jawline again, this time going down my neck to the tops of my breasts. "That's truly something no one else knows about you?"

"It's something I didn't know about myself until tonight."

"Then, my angel of music, let me help you find out who you truly are."

I gulp as fear lances through me.

Not fear of Phantom.

But fear that if he grabbed me and kissed me in this moment, I wouldn't stop him.

He seems to have some kind of hypnotic effect on me. If he took me to bed right now? I'd let him do whatever he wanted.

And already I know I'd enjoy every minute of it.

"What do you have in mind?" I ask.

"For tonight, simply being here. Enjoying the masquerade. Enjoying each other's company."

"And after tonight?"

"The sky is the limit," he says. "I'm willing to go as high as you want to go."

"What if I don't know where I want to go?"

"Then it will be my pleasure to guide you."

God, that voice. I feel it in my very bones. It vibrates through my body, culminating between my legs.

I squirm on my stool.

If he grabbed me, took me up against the wall of the bar, I'm wet enough that he could slide right in.

I grip the stem of my glass, gather my courage. "What if I asked you to take me to bed?"

"That would be very hard to turn down."

"Are you saying you would turn me down?"

"For tonight? Yes."

I suppress a shudder. "Why?"

"For the reason you just said. You don't know where you want to go."

"Wow." I take a sip of my drink, really tasting the elderflower.

"What?"

"Most men would take any chance they had to get a woman into bed."

"My beautiful angel, I am *not* most men."

Boy, is that true. Most men don't go around masquerading as the Phantom of the Opera. Normally I would think this man is a little out there, but for him it seems to work.

Everyone accepts him as Phantom.

Even though that's not who he is.

He is someone else. Someone I want to know.

But I'm going to have to get to know him as Phantom first.

"Why do you hide who you are?" I ask.

"There are a few reasons," he says. "Mostly because I prefer to keep this part of my life to myself."

"But why?"

"I think you can probably figure out the reasons why."

"Your job?"

"Partially."

"Your family?"

"Partially."

"Your…wife?"

He smiles. "I don't have a wife, angel."

I keep the sigh of relief from whooshing out of me.

I mean, come on. I had to wonder about that sooner or later. A guy who hides his identity and picks up women in bars?

That screams married.

"You must be into some kinky stuff, then," I say.

"Some would consider it kinky. To me, it's just what I like."

I turn toward him, his nearness making me woozy. Or maybe it's the drink. "Tell me. Tell me what you like."

He moves toward me, and his warm breath on my cheek makes me tremble.

He nips at my earlobe, and then he whispers, "I'd like you on your knees, in front of me, my cock between those beautiful lips of yours."

I gasp. I'm speechless for a few seconds, until—

"That doesn't sound kinky."

"Did I forget to mention your wrists are bound behind your back, and your mouth is held open with a spider gag?"

I gasp again.

Every fragment of energy in my body arrows straight to my pussy.

I squirm again on my stool.

"Does that excite you?" he whispers.

All I can do is nod.

"Good, my angel. Because that's just the beginning."

He pulls back then, and I'm sure all the color is drained from my face.

"Your cheeks are red," Phantom says.

Okay, so the color hasn't drained from my face after all. Of course it hasn't. I'm on freaking fire.

"I can't believe how beautiful you are, angel." He cups one of my flaming cheeks.

"Thank you," I manage.

"You'll be even more beautiful with your mouth held open."

I squirm once more.

"Tell me. Does the idea intrigue you as much as it intrigues me?"

Again, all I can do is nod.

He doesn't actually want me to repeat these things back to him, does he?

"Where?" I finally ask.

"Somewhere private. A place where the darkest of

desires can be satisfied. Somewhere...underground."

I clear my throat, take another sip of martini.

"When?"

"Next Saturday, angel. We will meet here again."

He moves toward me, as if in slow motion. I quake beneath his searing gaze as he comes closer, closer, closer...

And he presses his firm, full lips to mine.

CHAPTER EIGHT

Phantom

I've learned to be patient. Especially when I want a woman who's new to my lifestyle.

I can't introduce her too quickly.

When I crave a scene, I usually simply go to the club, find a willing playmate there, and indulge.

Every once in a while, I meet a woman who wants to get to know me better.

And this woman… This angel…

I have the strangest urge to let her see me as I truly am.

It makes no sense, as I barely know her.

I know she's a junior editor. She said that much before she decided to play along.

I know she has hair the color of gingerbread and eyes like a silvery lake in the moonlight. Eyes I could get lost in.

Eyes I've gotten lost in.

She didn't let me take her home last night.

Just as well. The urge to unmask myself is so great…

But I can't.

Not until I show her my darker side.

And this kiss…

This light brushing of our lips…

She affects me so profoundly. Just being near her makes sparks fly through me. Not sparks so much as firebombs. Or a fucking grenade inside my belly.

And it was just a kiss.

Mouth closed, soft lips.

Just a kiss.

And if I feel that way from a kiss…

I can't wait until next Saturday night.

We're meeting here again at the bar. Nine p.m.

And I will take her underground.

CHAPTER NINE

Frankie

My lips are still tingling the next morning as I sit in the conference room at work. Monday morning is our strategizing session. The editor-in-chief and all the junior editors sit around the conference table, drinking coffee and eating glazed doughnuts as they try to decide how to make the next issue of *Lovely* even more spectacular than the last.

"All right, people," Lisa Kingsley, our fearless leader, says, as she does every Monday morning at nine a.m. sharp, after she gobbles her first Krispy Kreme. "Let's hear those ideas."

Trixie Lamarr, a staffer who gets on my last nerve, always pipes up first with something inane.

"Flowers," she says. "The different types of roses. What they all signify, so a woman knows what her man is thinking when he sends a certain color of roses."

I resist an eye roll.

No man I know ever thought about the color of roses he was getting for a woman. They almost always get red because red are the most abundant. Probably also the cheapest.

"All right." Lisa writes *rose exposé* on the whiteboard.

Someone else at the table snickers.

Good. I'm not the only one.

Usually I'm good for at least one decent idea, but today, my mind is mush because of that kiss.

How can it be mush? He didn't even use tongue. It couldn't have been more innocent and chaste.

I value creativity. Coming up with new and innovative ideas for a women's magazine isn't easy. There are only about a zillion of those publications.

Cosmopolitan is one of the biggest, and that's kind of where we fit in. *Lovely* talks a lot about sex, about relationships, but we also publish news stories about women who make a difference in the world. I've written many of those.

But my favorite is the investigative pieces we do. We've done some good journalism on rape survivors, teen pregnancy, and internet predators.

Our investigative journalism is what sets us apart from other women's magazines. Sure, we do the confessions columns and the advice columns, but each of our issues has a hard-hitting piece of news as well.

I'm proud to say I've spearheaded a lot of those. I enjoy the fluffier pieces too, and I've contributed to those, but what I really enjoy is getting down and dirty with interviews, news, exploration.

Investigation.

"Frankie?"

My eyes pop open at Lisa's voice. "Yes?"

"You're usually a little more vocal in these meetings."

"I'm sorry. I just haven't had enough coffee yet." I smile, sort of, and take a drink from my Styrofoam cup.

"All right." Lisa nods. "But don't be shy."

I force another smile. "I won't. You know me better than that, Lisa."

"Is your broken engagement still bothering you?" Trixie asks.

I rise then, move toward Trixie's seat, pull her up by her shoulders, and punch the smug look off her face.

Just kidding.

But I sure do it in my head. I clock her good.

Another forced smile. "I'm fine."

"Trixie," Lisa admonishes, "please keep personal matters out of our meetings."

"Of course. I'm sorry, Lisa."

"You're fired," Lisa says.

Okay, that was in my head, too. Felt pretty good, though.

Jackie Swenson, another junior editor sitting next to me, leans in and whispers, "She's such a witch."

I simply nod.

Penn and I ended things months ago.

I've always felt it best to meet things head-on, so I told everybody at the office within a few days after it happened. After all, I was no longer wearing the gigantic rock—courtesy of Penn's trust fund—on my left hand.

Trixie, of course, was overwhelmingly sympathetic. Trixie-ese for, "Ha, you're not getting your rich guy."

Not that she has a rich guy. I mean, who would have her?

"I have an idea," Jackie says.

"All right," Lisa says. "Shoot, Jackie."

"How about what's going on with the singles scene in New York these days? In fact, we could include other big cities like L.A., New Orleans, Chicago."

"Singles scene?" Trixie laughs. "Everyone meets online now."

"That's my point," Jackie says. "What about people who don't *like* to meet online? I know I don't."

I back Jackie up. "I don't, either."

"Do you think there's really a story there?" Lisa asks.

"I think we have to go out and find the story," Jackie says. "I could go. Fred could go." She glances toward one of our two male editors. "I think it's important."

"All right." Lisa adds *big city singles scene, not online dating* to the whiteboard.

Singles scene.

Funny. I was at a bar when I met Phantom.

I wasn't looking to meet anyone. Certainly not a masked man who fascinates me.

And his words…

I'd like you on your knees, in front of me, my cock between those beautiful lips of yours. Your wrists are bound behind your back, and your mouth is held open with a spider gag.

Already I'm throbbing with the memory. Is it the words? His breathy whisper against my ear? The rasp in his deep voice?

Damn. I don't know. But I do know what I want to write about. What I want to investigate.

"I have an idea," I say.

"Yes, Frankie. Go ahead."

"What about"—I clear my throat—"the bondage scene? Women who are into that lifestyle?"

Lisa reddens a bit. "And you'd be willing to investigate this?"

"Well, sure. I'm not saying I want to *do* it."

I'm not *not* saying that, either.

More snickers bounce around the room.

"All right." Lisa writes *BDSM* on the board. "Any other ideas?"

Lisa writes down a few more mundane ideas from the peanut gallery.

"All right," she says. "Jackie, you start investigating your singles thing. Don't spend more than about ten hours on initial investigation, and if you don't find enough to merit the story, move on to something else."

"Sure. I understand, Lisa."

"And Frankie, take a look into the BDSM thing. Start here in Manhattan, and if you find anything worth writing about, we'll consider taking it into other cities as well."

I nod, my cheeks burning.

What the hell have I gotten myself into?

• • •

"You're seriously going to go to a sex club?" Isabella asks me at drinks Monday evening. Her cheeks are flushed pink—unusual for her.

"I didn't say that."

"You just said it was going to be an investigative piece. How do you investigate without actually going?"

"Oh my God," Gigi says. "You could go in undercover. That would be amazing."

"Maybe I should take you with me," I say.

"Would you?" Gigi's eyes go wide.

"No, because I'm not going."

Although the idea doesn't disgust me. In fact, it—

"These are from the gentleman at the bar." Our server sets down another drink for each of us.

Gigi's eyes widen. "Oh, I know him. That guy Dylan—he knows Jackson."

"Who is he?" I ask.

"Oh we met…" She blushes. "We kind of had a one-nighter. Dylan Anderson? Andrews?" She waves.

"Gigi…" I begin.

"What?"

"This is girls' night."

"Since when does girls' night mean we can't meet guys?"

"Actually…" I pull out my phone. "Do you mind if I give your number to a friend of mine from the magazine?"

"What for?" Gigi asks.

"She's doing an article about singles in big cities. You know, the people who like to meet without using apps, like most people do these days?"

"I don't do that," Gigi says.

I chuckle. "What do you think you're doing right now? You met this guy, what…two or three months ago when we were"—I sigh—"having a drink after that first fitting for those stupid bridesmaids' dresses for my stupid wedding."

"Sorry, Frank," she says.

"Don't be. It's over, and I'm better off for it. But my point is that you meet guys at bars all the time."

"So?"

"So you're doing what Jackie's reporting on. Meeting guys the old-fashioned way, without the help of dating apps."

"Do you think she'd interview me for the magazine?"

"I can't say for sure, but you're as good a place to start as any."

Gigi opens her mouth to reply, but before she can, Dylan whatever-his-last-name-is invites himself to our table.

"Hello, ladies." He gives us all the once-over, his gaze

finally landing on Gigi. "Gigi. How are you?"

"I'm just fine, Dylan. How have you been?"

"I left Black Inc.," he says. "I didn't get the transfer that I was looking for, so I began looking for another job."

"What are you doing?" Gigi asks.

"Consulting," he says.

Unemployed is what that means.

But I'm not going to tell Gigi that. She can find out on her own.

Isabella yawns.

"Are you tired?" I ask.

"No, not really."

No, she's just bored.

"Izzy," I say under my breath as I regard her still-pink cheeks. "Do you know anything about…?"

She drops her gaze to her napkin. "About that thing you're going to be investigating?"

"Yeah."

"I might."

"Oh my God."

"Here's the thing, Frank." She looks over at Gigi and Dylan, who are deep in conversation about who knows what, and then she lowers her voice. "Most clubs like that don't just let anyone in. Once you're there, you sign a nondisclosure agreement, so you can't tell anyone what goes on there. So it's going to be difficult for you to report on it."

"Oh. I didn't think of that."

"But I suppose it would be okay if you didn't name anyone or the club."

"What kind of investigative report is that? If I can't at least name the club?"

"Reporters don't have to divulge their sources. Happens

all the time."

"True… It could still be a good story."

"Here's your story," Isabella says. "Find out how many of these clubs exist in each big city. That's a start, right? Then put some feelers out online, asking people who frequent these clubs if they would be willing to speak to you—with their identities concealed, of course. You don't have to name the club, and you certainly don't have to name the people who talk to you."

"You think they'll actually talk to me?"

"If you offer them some kind of incentive."

"I don't have the authority to do that."

"Don't offer an incentive, then. Some may bite anyway. But if you don't get any bites, talk to your boss about an incentive."

"Maybe." I nibble on my lower lip. "But what about you?"

Izzy reddens again.

"Look, you brought this up to me. Will you be my first source?"

"I don't know…"

"Izzy, come on. You're the one who mentioned it, so you must've known I'd ask."

"I'll talk to you if you can't get anyone else"—she clears her throat daintily—"but I'm not really the best person. I'm new at it. I've only gone to a club a few times."

"Then you're the perfect person. We can talk about why you went. How you liked it."

"Oh, all right," she says. "But not here."

"Absolutely. I understand. How about tomorrow night? Just the two of us. Come over to my place."

"All right. It's a date."

CHAPTER TEN

Frankie

"So what do you want your alias to be?" I ask Isabella the next night.

"I don't know. You pick something."

"Okay. Jane Doe."

"You've got to be kidding me."

"You said to pick something."

"Make it Jasmine," she says.

"All right. Jasmine. Any last name?"

"Nope. Just Jasmine."

"Does that happen to be, like, a name you use there?"

"God, no. I can't give you that name. People will know."

"So that means you have a name you use there."

"Yeah. I do. Lots of people do."

Hmm. Interesting. Maybe that's why Phantom is Phantom. Except…

"You don't wear a mask, do you?"

"You mean a medical mask? To keep from catching something?"

"Not that kind of mask. I mean to shield your identity."

"Why would I do that? We all sign agreements."

Hmm… So why does Phantom disguise himself, then?

"Okay, let's start with the names people use. Tell me about that."

"Not everyone uses one," she says, "but I do. Some of the other women do. It's kind of a…submissive name."

"So you're a submissive?"

"I wouldn't say I'm a submissive exactly. This isn't really a lifestyle for me. It's just something I engage in sometimes. When the mood strikes me and when there's someone that I trust to dominate me."

"How do you decide who to trust?"

"It's a feeling, mostly. At the best clubs, people are usually vetted. Security is everywhere. There's no reason to fear."

"Security is one thing, but what about safety, though? I mean… If you're letting people tie you up, hurt you…"

"You choose a safe word. If at any time you feel unsafe, you say the safe word, and they'll stop."

"Have you ever had to use your safe word?"

"I haven't, but I know it's there in case I need it. A good Dominant will always respect your safe word. But a good Dominant will also talk to you about the scene beforehand, make sure you're comfortable with everything they're about to do, and make sure they know your hard limits."

"What's a hard limit?"

"That's something you won't ever do, no matter what."

"Do you have any hard limits?"

"Yes. Blood sports. I don't want my Dominant to ever draw blood."

My jaw drops. "Blood?"

"Yes. Some Dominants like to draw some blood, and

some submissives enjoy it as well."

I say nothing. I have no idea what to say. I had no idea this world even existed.

Scratch that. I knew it existed. I just never thought Isabella was part of it.

"Have you ever met anyone you know at these clubs?"

She looks down.

She has.

"Oh my God, who?"

She raises her head and meets my gaze. "I can't tell you. You know that."

"Yeah. I guess I do."

"So what else do you want to know?"

"How many of these places have you been to?"

"Just two. Both here in town."

I widen my eyes. "There are *two* here in town?"

"There are probably more. More people are into it than you might think."

"I know that," I say. "I read *Fifty Shades of Grey*."

"*Fifty Shades of Grey* didn't take place in a club," Isabella says.

"Right. I know that."

"Not everyone can afford to build a dungeon in their home."

"Yes, of course."

In truth, none of this ever crossed my mind. Sure, I read the book, saw the movies. But in real life?

And she's right. *Fifty Shades* didn't take place in a club. The main character had his own playroom—dungeon, apparently, according to Isabella—in his home.

"Could you take me there? To a club?"

She shakes her head. "No. I'm not a member at any of

the clubs, so I have to go as someone's guest. I can't bring guests of my own."

My mouth is dry, and I rise. "You want something to drink? Water? Wine?"

"Water. Yeah." She cocks her head. "No...wait. Wine. Red if you have it."

I walk to my small kitchen, pour a glass of Merlot for Isabella and water for me. I love red wine, but the tannins will only dry my mouth out more. It already feels like the desert.

I bring the glasses back to the living room and take my seat on the couch next to Izzy, handing her the wine glass. She takes a sip. I down my entire glass.

Then I clear my throat. Time to go in for the kill. "Why do you like being a submissive?"

To my astonishment, Isabella doesn't dodge my question.

"That's a question I've asked myself a lot," she says. "And I think the best answer I can give you is that it feels right to me at the time. I'm not a full-time submissive—"

"Wait. There are full-time submissives?"

"Sure. There are full-time Dominants, too. Meaning that's the only kind of sex they engage in."

"Okay." I try to stop the buzzing in my head. "What does that mean, exactly? That they submit to their partners all the time?"

"No," she says. "I'm talking about men and women who only engage in BDSM *sex*. I don't do that. I like it sometimes. Sometimes I like regular vanilla sex."

"Vanilla?"

"Yeah. You know. Cock in pussy. No handcuffs or other... toys."

"And that's called vanilla?"

"Yeah. Vanilla. Pure. Uninteresting."

I roll my eyes. "Have you forgotten that vanilla is my favorite flavor, Izzy?"

She laughs. "Yeah, I wasn't thinking about that. I like vanilla, too. But it's just a term, Frank. Don't read anything else into it."

"I don't actually find regular sex *un*interesting," I say.

"Neither do I. I love it. Like I said, I'm not a full-time sub."

"What is it about submission that appeals to you?"

"I think it's the surrender," she says. "I like it most when I've been through a tough time at work or a tough time emotionally. I like giving my pleasure over to someone else. Letting him or her—"

I stop typing, my jaw dropped. "Wait a minute. Or *her*?"

"Oh yeah. There are female Dominants."

"And you've been with one?"

"I have. And no, I'm not bisexual. I'm not looking for a bisexual companion. I'm looking for a man. But to be honest, the best submissive experience I've ever had was with a woman."

"Wow. I had no idea."

"Come on, Frank. We all experiment in college."

"I didn't."

"Really?

"Not with women." I narrow my eyes. "Are you saying you *did*?"

"I did. And I know Gigi did."

"Wow." I exhale slowly. "How did I not know that about my two besties? Maybe I *am* vanilla."

"Maybe you are. And that's okay, Frank. You do *you*."

"You bet I will. I'll do me."

And damn it, I don't know what Phantom has in store for me Saturday night, but I'm going to make sure I experience every bit of it.

I'll do me.

And *he'll* do me.

CHAPTER ELEVEN

Frankie

Friday night dinner at Mom and Dad's—it's a standing date, though we can get out of it with twenty-four hours' notice.

Mandy and Jackson are here, of course, and we're going to discuss wedding plans.

May I jump off the nearest cliff, please?

Apparently Mandy and Jackson don't want to wait. Mom, Mandy, and I haven't been able to nail Noreen down to a lunch date yet, but already I know she won't like the rush of all this. Why the rush anyway? The two of them have known each other forever, and neither of them are going anywhere, but of course, no one asked me.

"So how's work, Frankie?" Mandy's tone is polite, but this is obviously an attempt to talk about me before it's wedding, wedding, wedding.

"It's good. The same."

"You working on any interesting articles?" Jackson asks.

"Actually"—I draw in a breath—"I'm investigating the BDSM scene here in the city."

Everyone goes quiet.

Seriously.

I'm pretty sure we could hear a feather drop onto the carpeting.

I can understand why my mom and dad might be a little freaked out about that. Who wants to hear that their younger daughter is investigating an alternate sexual lifestyle?

"It's not like I said I was doing it or anything."

"That sounds…interesting." Mom's face has gone as white as her china.

"Yeah, I think it would be, but it's difficult to get information. Apparently people who engage in this lifestyle are very quiet. They can't talk about it because everything is confidential."

"Well"—Dad clears his throat—"as long as you enjoy your work, Frankie."

"My work doesn't entail me actually doing the stuff, Dad. I'm *investigating* it. It's of interest to our readers."

"Honey, whatever makes you happy."

My God. My parents really think—

Then I look at my sister. I look at her fiancé.

Neither of them says a word. They're just chewing their food ferociously.

No. Way.

Seems my big sister and I need to have a little chat.

Alone.

I swallow my bite of peas. "So, Mandy, what kind of wedding do you envision?"

Mandy looks visibly relieved. "Nothing huge. We decided to have it at Jackson's parents' house because it's so big."

"And Noreen's okay with that, Jack?" I ask.

"It's what Mandy and I want," he says, "so she'll be okay."

Mandy doesn't look so sure.

"Don't you want to get married in a church?" Mom asks.

"We could if it means that much to you. But Jack and I don't think we need a church. Our vows will take no matter where we are. And this way we don't have to wait. Bill and Noreen's place is always available."

"Then whatever you want," Mom says.

"My parents' backyard will make a great place for a ceremony and a small reception," Jackson says.

Mom nods. "Yes, I can see how that would be beautiful."

"How many guests do you plan to invite?" I ask.

"Probably only about fifty or sixty," Mandy says. "Just family, close friends, a few work associates."

"You really just want one attendant each?" I ask.

"Yeah." Jackson nods.

"Okay. What kind of wedding dress?" Mom takes a bite of her roll.

"Something simple. Mom, can you take me shopping this weekend?"

"Of course, dear." Mom glances at me.

Please, please, please don't suggest that I come along.

"Are you busy, Frankie?"

I put on my happy face. "No. I'm happy to go."

"It's okay." Mandy comes to my rescue. "Mom and I can handle it."

"If you're sure."

"Absolutely. What kind of dress would *you* like to wear as maid of honor?"

"Whatever you choose will be fine," I say.

"I want you to have a dress you like," Mandy says. "One you can wear again."

"Please. You just pick it."

"Francesca," Mom says. "You should come with us. Help choose your own dress. If you don't want to help Mandy pick out hers—"

"That's not what I said. I'm happy to help Mandy pick out a dress. And if it means that much to all of you, I'll choose my own dress."

"Well, the decision ultimately rests with Mandy," Mom says.

Dear Lord, get me out of here without pulling all the strands of my hair out one by one. "I know that. That's why I said whatever she picks will be fine."

Mandy shakes her head. "I seem to be doing everything wrong. I haven't been thinking about anyone but myself, and I apologize. There's no excuse for it."

And now I feel like shit again.

This is my sister. My older sister, Amanda, who's been in my shadow her whole life.

And now, I'm in her shadow.

You know what? It fucking sucks.

Is this how she's felt her whole life? And she being the older sister and all.

I've got to get over myself. I draw in a deep breath.

"Mandy," I say. "I am so, so happy for you. You too, Jack. The two of you belong together. You always have. I'm not sure why I never saw it before. You just shine when you're together. I want you to have the wedding of your dreams. If that means you want me to help choose your dress, I will be there for you. After all, you were there for me."

"Thanks, Frankie." Mandy smiles. "We'll find the perfect dress for both of us."

• • •

The next morning, Saturday, after doing some online research for my article, I go shopping.

Alone.

I'm not supposed to meet Mom and Mandy at Macy's until two o'clock, and I want to find an outfit for tonight.

I'm meeting Phantom again.

He really liked the blue mask and silk dress that I wore to the masquerade.

But I want to look sexy tonight.

Little-black-dress sexy.

The only problem? All the little black dresses I own, I wore for Penn. They feel…not *tainted* so much as…

I just want something special for Phantom. Something I've never worn for anyone else.

I head into Treasure's Chest, a lingerie store that also sells sexy garments and…other things. Things that may aid in the research for my article.

"Hello there," a young woman with auburn hair says. "Can I help you find anything?"

"Yes, actually. I want a sexy black dress. I have a date tonight."

She smiles. "You've certainly come to the right place. We have some gorgeous evening wear. Let me show you."

Mary—her name tag reads—leads me toward the right side of the store. I wouldn't exactly call these dresses evening wear. None of them are long or cocktail length. All the dresses are short, and many are quite revealing.

I zero in on a simple black sheath with black sequins around the low neckline.

"See anything you like?" Mary asks.

"This one." I finger the stretchy fabric.

"Yes, that one is gorgeous. What size are you?"

"I'm an eight."

"Then I'd recommend medium."

"Medium?"

"Yes. All of our dresses come in small, medium, large, and extra-large. Some come in extra small as well. Because all of the fabric is stretchy, these sizes can accommodate most figures." She glances over me. "I have a really good eye. I'd say you're definitely a medium." She pulls a dress off the rack. "Would you like to try it on?"

"Yes. Thank you."

She leads me to the back of the store—and through aisles devoted to corsets, bustiers, stockings, and then leather attire. And…

Toys. Handcuffs. Ropes. Chains. Whips.

My skin tightens.

Then I notice a sign. It's small with black lettering, but it flashes at me as if it's neon.

Classes available.

"What kind of classes do you offer here?" I ask.

"Just some introductory classes to alternative sexual lifestyles."

"Really? You mean like BDSM?"

"Yes. We have classes in domination, submission, and bondage."

I inhale, gathering courage. "I might be interested in one of those."

"If you spend more than four hundred dollars, you get our introductory class free."

I haven't even looked at the price tag on the dress. This isn't a good habit I've gotten into. "How much will I spend if I purchase the dress?"

"Three fifty."

Three hundred and fifty dollars? Do I have some kind of magnetic pull to dresses that cost that exact amount?

"Okay. Well…I'll think about the classes." I take the dress and head into the dressing room.

I disrobe quickly and pull the dress on. Mary was right about the elasticity. It forms itself to my body and accentuates every curve.

Damn.

I was hoping it would look terrible. Seven hundred bucks in a week on dresses? I'd better do a top-notch job on this article. I'm going to need a promotion if I keep spending money like this.

I peel the sheath off, get dressed, and return to Mary. "I'll take it."

"Perfect, and I have excellent news for you. I just checked with my boss, and she said you can take the class for free with this purchase."

"Oh?" I should be happy about this, but I'm a little freaked. "When does the class meet?"

"We're starting a new one next week. Thursday evening at eight."

Shivers rack my body. But why? It's only a class. Just a class.

It's for work. It's just for work.

"I'll see if I can make it."

Better not to commit. Not just yet.

CHAPTER TWELVE

Frankie

"I think you should wear white," I say.

Mandy blushes. "Really?"

"Mandy, I'm not trying to ask about your sexual history."

I'm pretty sure my sister was a virgin before Jackson, but I honestly don't know.

"White just seems so…"

"It's what brides wear. It's what I was going to wear. And God knows I was no virgin."

Mandy reddens further. "I do like this one." She pulls a white sheath off the rack.

A sheath isn't the right design for Mandy. She has a sweet little hourglass figure, but a sheath is more appropriate for someone long and lean, like Isabella, who needs to add the appearance of curves. Mandy already has curves.

But I keep my lips shut.

Mom, however, doesn't. She pulls another dress from the rack. "How about this one, Mandy? I feel it would flatter you more."

Mandy widens her eyes. "Wow, Mom. It's beautiful."

Indeed it is. It's satin with a white lace inlay and some subtle beading, fitted around the bodice but flaring out at the hips. It will be perfect on Mandy.

Mom smiles. "This is your size. Why don't you try it on?"

Mandy takes the dress from her and heads into the fitting room.

Mom turns to me. "You holding up okay, Frankie?"

"Yes, Mom. I'm fine."

"Dad and I still feel awful about last Saturday night."

"Don't. Please. I'm over it."

Or I'm trying, anyway. I do *want* to be over it. I'm definitely over *talking* about it.

"I hope you're happy for Mandy," Mom says.

"Of course I am. Why wouldn't I be?"

"It hasn't escaped Dad's and my notice that you were ahead of her in everything, even though you're two years younger."

"I never tried to be."

"Oh, we know that, Frankie. But in a way, this is amazing for Mandy. She gets to be a bride first."

I open my mouth, but Mom holds a hand up.

"I don't mean that in a bad way. Seriously. Dad and I were never thrilled with the match between you and Penn, and you knew that. But we would be just as happy if this were happening for you."

My mom is a good person—even though she just mentioned Penn. Again. So is my dad. They were great parents, and I imagine they had to soothe Mandy many times when I was getting ahead of her. It couldn't have been easy for them.

So I make myself a vow here and now.

I'm going to be happy for my sister. She deserves love,

and she's found it with her best friend. With Jackson.

Besides…

I've met someone new.

Granted, I've never seen his face, and I don't know his name. But for some reason, I'm more excited about this prospect than I have been for a long time.

I was with Penn for over five years, since I was twenty-two.

I'm not in a huge hurry. I'm twenty-seven, and sure, my biological clock is ticking, but I've got time. Women are having children well into their thirties these days, some in their early forties. And who says I have to have children? Sure, I always thought I would, but if I don't? That will be okay, too. There's no law that says a woman must have kids to be fulfilled.

Mandy steps out of the dressing room, and I can't help but smile.

The dress fits my sister beautifully, and she looks radiant. Truly radiant. And happy.

I never looked that way when I was talking about Penn. I never even felt that look on my face.

"You look absolutely beautiful, sis," I say. "Absolutely beautiful."

"Really, Frank?"

"Really. You know I've always been the first to tell you when something is not flattering." I walk around her, checking out the fit from every angle. "This is your dress. It was made for you."

Mandy smiles ear to ear. "Thank you for saying that. I do like how I look in it. It looked great in the mirror, but I wondered if I was just seeing something I wanted to see."

"Absolutely not," Mom says. "That dress is lovely."

"Now we have to find something for you, Frank," Mandy says. "The perfect dress for my maid of honor."

"What color are you thinking?" I ask.

"Well, I was going to ask you. As I told you, it's going to be a smaller wedding. I haven't decided on a color scheme yet, so I figured why not let you pick the color of your dress? Then we can work around that."

"Mandy, this is your decision."

"Actually, Frankie," Mom says, "I think that's a marvelous idea. And Mandy, that's very nice of you."

I sigh. "Well, all right. If you'd like for me to choose, I think I'd like something silvery blue. Kind of like our eyes."

Mandy's eyes are a little grayer than mine. Mine are lighter silvery blue. I always thought mine were prettier, but now, as I look at my sister glowing in the essence of her love, I'm not sure how I ever thought I outshone her. She's beautiful.

I'm going to make sure she has the most perfect day.

"Silvery blue sounds great," Mandy says. "We can probably get any of these dresses in that color."

"Let me have a look around," I say.

It seems strange shopping for wedding garments at Macy's when I went to a bridal shop for mine, but I was planning a more elaborate celebration. Mandy is no doubt trying to keep expenses down for Mom and Dad. They're doing fine, even though they live in the same house on Long Island that we grew up in. I know they have a wedding fund, because we talked about it when Penn and I were engaged.

Still, Mandy doesn't want to overdo it.

Which is classic Mandy.

She always thinks about others before she thinks of herself.

I need to be more like her.

I zero in on a cocktail-length dress in a gorgeous color called *livid*. I let out a chuckle.

"What's funny?" Mom asks.

"The color of this dress. It's perfect, but look at the name of it."

Mandy fingers the tag. "Livid? Frank, you're not—"

"No, Mandy. I'm not still angry about the other night. How many times do I have to say it? It's just pretty funny, the name of the color. Livid."

"Livid can mean a grayish blue," Mom says.

"Really?" Mandy raises her eyebrows. "I've never heard of it as a color."

"Neither have I," I say. "But I love the style of this dress. The halter style on top and the draping at the waistline will work perfectly on my figure."

"It is gorgeous," Mandy says. "You should definitely try it on."

I check the size. "This one's a six. I'm an eight."

"Are you sure?" Mom asks. "You've lost weight, Frankie."

"Well… I suppose I could try the six. We can always have them order an eight."

I already know it will flatter me. I'm taller than Mandy, with narrower hips and a slightly wider waist. Not everything looks great on me, but this dress will—in an eight. But to appease them, I go back to the dressing rooms. I want to see how the color looks against my whole body anyway.

As I suspected, the six is a tad small. I return to Mom and Mandy.

"I'm going to need an eight."

"That's no problem," says a salesperson who seems to have appeared from nowhere. "I'll get that ordered for you.

In the meantime we can ring up your dress, ma'am."

"Thank you so much." Mandy hands her the bridal dress.

I take my chance to duck out. "If you don't need me for anything else, I have some research I need to do for work."

"Are you working on a new story?" Mandy asks.

"The same one." I clear my throat. "About alternative sexual lifestyles in Manhattan."

Mandy stares at me a moment, going slightly rigid. Same as she did at dinner. Strange.

"Goodness." Mom shakes her head. "Well, as long as your readers are interested."

"Lisa seems to think they will be," I say. "I've already started doing some research. It's actually very interesting."

Again, nothing from Mandy.

Maybe I'll ask her later. Certainly not in front of our mother.

"Anyway," I say, "I have to be going. Mandy, your dress is beautiful."

And again…Mandy says nothing.

CHAPTER THIRTEEN

Frankie

I fidget as I sit at the bar.

Alfred brings me a glass of water.

I'm tempted to order one of Phantom's special martinis, but I need to stay focused.

I have no idea what awaits me.

Until—

"Hello, my angel." Hot breath fans the back of my neck. "You look lovely."

I turn as he takes the stool next to me.

He's wearing his black cape, of course, and the white mask that covers nearly all of the right side of his face and the eye on the left. His stubble is thicker and darker today, and God, it's sexy. His full pink lips are curved into a smile, and he's wearing all black. Black leather shoes, black pants, and a black button-down shirt.

"Thank you." My cheeks are blazing. "You look nice too."

"Nice?" He grins.

"Very nice?"

"I'll take it."

I pick up my glass of water.

"I'd like to take you somewhere," he says.

His previous words emerge in my mind.

Somewhere private. A place where the darkest of desires can be satisfied. Somewhere…underground.

I swallow another sip. "Where?"

"Somewhere you will be completely safe," he says. "You have my word."

His word?

Odd how I want to believe him. I don't even know him.

"I don't know you well enough to accept your word," I say.

"That's true. You don't. But I hope you come with me, anyway, for after tonight, you'll know for sure that I'm a man of my word."

How I want to. I want nothing more than to go with him, see what he has to offer me.

He hasn't tried anything with me so far, other than to brush his lips over mine. Then again, we've always been here, at the bar. In a very public place.

"Perhaps…we should stay here," I say. "Maybe get to know each other better."

"I think we've done all we can here."

"Try to understand. I'm a woman. I'm vulnerable. I don't even know your name."

"I don't know yours either, Angel."

"It's Francesca," I say. "Frankie for short. Frankie Thomas."

Phantom says nothing, but his smile fades. Have I upset him?

"Are you looking for a date, Francesca?"

"I don't know what I'm looking for." I stand. "Scratch

that. I know exactly what I'm looking for, and this isn't it."

He touches my arm gently. "Please. Don't go."

"I told you my name. Now you tell me yours."

"I can't tell you my name," he says.

Is that a touch of remorse in his voice? I'm not sure.

"But," he goes on, "I *can* tell you something else about myself."

"All right. I'll take it."

"We have something in common."

I lift my eyebrows. "Oh?"

"Yes, I'm a writer."

"What makes you think we have that in common?"

He smiles. "The first night we met, you told me you're a junior editor."

My cheeks warm. He's right. I did, before I decided to play along with his fantasy.

"Is there a lot of time for writing while you're busy haunting the opera house?" I ask.

"You'd be surprised how much free time I have," he says, chuckling. "I'll make a deal with you. Come with me. Let me show you what I want to show you. If you like it and you choose to stay, I will tell you my name."

"Where do you want to take me?"

"A place where all your dreams can come true." He pulls a piece of silk out of the pocket of his pants. "But first, I need to put this over your eyes."

Oh hell no.

I take the last sip of my water and set the glass down on the bar. "I'm so out of here."

"I understand." He pulls a card out of his front pocket and hands it to me. "Call me if you change your mind."

The card is black with a white mask on it. It says simply

Phantom with a phone number.

I hold the card. It burns against my fingers.

I want to go with him.

But I'm a smart woman. What kind of woman lets herself be blindfolded and led…who knows where?

Except–

"Phantom?"

"Yes?"

"Is the place you're taking me some kind of club?"

"Perhaps."

"And you promise my safety?"

"Not only do *I* promise it." He glances at Alfred. "Tell her, Al."

"Phantom here's a good man," Alfred says. "He can guarantee your safety, and so can I."

"All right. But why the blindfold?"

"The club requires it. If you're not a member, you can't know where we're going."

"How will I get there, then?"

"Very simple," Phantom says. "I will lead you."

What I'll do for a story.

My intuition doesn't often fail me, and I feel very safe with Phantom. It makes no sense, of course, and the place he's taking me may not be a BDSM club after all.

But I think it probably is. He already told me he'd like to bind me and gag me, so he's into that kind of kink. Why else would it be so secretive?

Phantom leans close to me, brushes a kiss over my cheek, and I swear sparks shoot all the way through me.

Then he ties the blindfold across my eyes. "We'll be there soon. I'll tell you where to go. Tell you if you need to step up or down."

"Okay." My heart flutters.

But not out of fear.

No.

As much as I *should* be feeling afraid, I'm not.

My heart is fluttering out of anticipation. Out of… *arousal.*

The silk is cool and soft against my eyes, and Phantom takes my hand.

"Come with me," he whispers.

I go willingly, not knowing who I'm with, not knowing where I'm going.

But I'm exhilarated. Excited. Electrified.

I'm seeking a thrill.

And I know I'll find it.

He guides me through what feels like a hallway, with carpeting under my feet, and then down some stairs.

Then another flight of stairs.

And another hallway, this one also carpeted.

Until we finally stop.

"We're here, my angel. You may take off your blindfold."

CHAPTER FOURTEEN

Phantom

Francesca. Frankie.

I prefer Francesca.

I thought I'd prefer not to know her name at all, but this woman is different. I've wanted to know her name since I first set eyes on her.

A frightening thought, no doubt.

She's not the first woman who questioned whether she'd be safe with me.

Women always find that they are safer with me than with most men.

Francesca *is* safe with me, and she will find that out soon enough.

Black Rose Underground is the safest club of its kind in Manhattan.

I've been a member here for several years, and I've never shown my face. Not that it would matter. Everyone who comes here is sworn to confidence. But for me, it adds to the dazzle. To the excitement. And it keeps me extra safe with regard to my real life.

I've brought women here in the past, but only rarely. I usually come here and find another member who's willing to participate in a scene. If I do find someone outside the club who intrigues me, I like to meet them at the bar first a couple times. Get to know them—as well as I can get to know anyone when I don't divulge much about myself.

Francesca—my angel of music—is something special. I knew the moment I saw her.

And I know it even more so now.

She's a smart woman.

She was apprehensive about putting on a blindfold, about trusting me.

That is normal, and I respect that.

But now she's here.

And we stop in front of the door that will lead us on a new voyage.

As the Bard himself said, "To unpathed waters, undreamed shores."

CHAPTER FIFTEEN

Frankie

I'm surprised Phantom doesn't take the blindfold from me, but the fact that he gives me permission to take it off empowers me.

Then I understand why he wanted me to take it off myself. He's allowing me a bit of control, a bit of freedom, in a place where he ultimately wants me to submit.

He's showing me that I'm safe here. That I'm safe with him.

I remove the black silk, and we stand in front of a plain white door. Phantom slides a card through the scanner on the door, and we walk into a foyer where a large man sits behind a desk.

"Good evening, Claude."

"Good evening, Phantom. I see you brought a guest this evening."

"Yes, please meet Francesca. Francesca, Claude."

"Hello, Claude."

"Hello, Francesca. I'll need you to sign some papers before you can go into the club."

"Oh?"

"Yes," Phantom says. "Everyone who enters must sign a nondisclosure agreement. You cannot mention that you've ever been here, who you see here, or what you see here. It's pretty straightforward."

Claude shoves some papers toward me. Yes, the confidentiality agreement that Isabella told me about. Has she been here? To this club? Has she signed this very document?

"I'm surprised you don't have these on an iPad to sign electronically," I say.

"Our owner likes to do things the old-fashioned way. He prefers a paper trail."

I read through the document quickly. It's pretty standard—not that I've seen a lot of nondisclosure agreements in my life, but I've been in the magazine industry long enough to know how to read a contract.

"Wait," I say after reading. "You're going to take my phone?"

"No photography is allowed in the club." Phantom hands his phone to Claude. "But I think we can make an exception for your first time. Right, Claude? If she promises no photos?"

Claude nods. "To help you feel more secure. But no photos. Understand?"

I nod, gulping, and I hastily scribble my signature at the bottom and hand the papers back to Claude.

"Understand," Claude says, "that your safety here is guaranteed at all times. I can give you a pager if you'd like. It will bring a security guard to you if you ever feel unsafe."

"I..."

"I promise you'll be safe with me, Angel," Phantom says.

"But to be sure..." He removes a pearl necklace from his pocket and clasps it around my neck.

"What's that?"

"A signal. It shows that you're mine for the evening. That way no one else will approach you."

"What if I *want* someone else to approach me?"

"Then we may as well leave now," Phantom says. "Because that's not what *I* want."

But I *want* to talk to people here. To get information for my story. The nondisclosure agreement is a problem, but Isabella warned me about such things.

What if Izzy *does* come here? What if I see her tonight?

If I see her here, I can't tell anyone, and neither can she. We both agreed to that.

Besides, what does it matter? This is just a club.

"I'm sorry." I touch the necklace, finger each separate pearl. "I guess I'm not understanding. Why would anyone approach me? Or why would that even be a problem?"

"We're about to enter a leather club, Angel," Phantom says. "If you're not wearing a collar, any man can approach you—or any woman, for that matter—and they can ask you to...play."

Is that a bad thing?

I don't ask, because I can tell by the look on Phantom's face that yes, he considers that a bad thing.

"You're here under my protection," Phantom says, "but I can't guarantee that protection unless everyone else here knows you're mine."

"Excuse me? *Yours?*"

"Only for the evening, and only while we're here."

"Ms."—Claude looks down at the paper—"Thomas, if you have any reservations at all—"

I hold up my hand. “No, I’m absolutely fine. Just… You know. First-time jitters.”

Claude seems to buy my lie.

The fact of the matter is, I *want* to talk to people here.

I want information.

“Everything’s in order,” Claude says. “You may take your guest in.”

We meander through the entryway, into—

Another world.

I have to keep my jaw from dropping to the ground.

At first glance, this could be any dance club, right up to the disco ball above. Dark red decor, dim lighting. Soft jazz plays, and a large bar sits at the far end of the room.

People dance. People sit at the bar. People talk huddled in corners.

Except some of them are naked. Completely naked. Others are dressed normally, like Phantom and I are—if you can call Phantom’s mask and cape normal.

And others are dressed still differently. In leather or lingerie.

One person is even dressed in rope.

“What do you think?” Phantom asks.

“I think…I want to know more.”

“This is a place, Angel, where your wildest fantasies can come true. But first, I need to know what those are.”

“What are *your* fantasies?”

“I disclosed one the other night. How I’d love to see you on your knees, bound, your mouth held open.”

I squirm, my pussy aching.

“Does that sound good to you?”

I squirm again. “It sounds…intriguing.”

“Tell me something, Angel. Have you ever been tied up?”

I shake my head.

"Would you like to be?"

Would I? "I've honestly never given it any thought."

I look around. Per the contract, I can't take any pictures, so I want to memorize this place.

"Think about it," he says.

"I will."

"What would you like to do? We can get a drink at the bar. We could dance. I could show you the other areas of the club."

"What other areas?"

"The public exhibition rooms. And then there are private rooms for partners who don't want to play out in the open."

"Do you play out in the open?"

"I have in the past, but I don't prefer it. Sometimes, though, with a new partner, she prefers to be out in the open for her own safety."

"But you've guaranteed my safety. So have Alfred and Claude."

"Absolutely. Look around you. There's security everywhere."

"Cameras?" I ask.

"No. Cameras aren't allowed here. But there are security guards posted everywhere."

I cast my gaze around the room. Sure enough, burly security men stand at nearly every entrance.

Every corner.

"What would *you* like to do?" I ask.

"What I would like to do has no bearing, because you're not ready for that."

"What if I am?" I say boldly.

"Then you're lying to yourself. You don't know me yet,

Angel. But I'd like to change that."

"How am I expected to know you when you won't tell me your name?"

"Because this is fantasy, Angel. Pure fantasy. I would like nothing more than to make your fantasies come true."

His deep and raspy voice makes my skin heat.

I don't even know what my fantasies are.

To be swept off my feet? To be fucked into oblivion?

Sure, that works. But isn't that every woman's fantasy?

What do *I* want?

What does Francesca Maria Thomas want?

"So you want to know my fantasies." I smile.

"More than I want my next breath," Phantom says.

"I want to see your face," I say. "I want to look into your eyes when I kiss you."

"The mask doesn't keep you from looking into my eyes, Angel."

He's right about that. His eyes are beautiful, and maybe the mask makes them even more so, because they stand out so darkly against the white. His long lashes, his deep brown irises. In the dim light, his pupils are large and black, his irises a thin rim around them.

"I don't show my face here," he says. "I have my reasons for that. Reasons I may tell you sometime. But not yet, Angel. We don't know each other that well."

"That's my point. Shouldn't we know each other before we… You know."

"We're engaging in the physical," he says. "I know all I need to know about you to do that."

"You *don't* know me, though. For all you know, I could go running and screaming out of here. I could tell everyone what goes on here."

"But you won't."

"How are you so sure?"

"Call it intuition. Call it clairvoyance if you want to. Most people are trustworthy, and you're not one of the ones who isn't."

He's right, of course.

But I *am* going to write an article. I just won't write about the name of this place. Or him. Or Claude. Or anyone else I might see here.

Already I hear my lead in my mind…

At first glance, it's a club like any other. The wooden bar in the back that stocks top-shelf liquor. A large dance floor with strobe lights and a disco ball. Tables line the dancing area, and couples talk intimately. Jazz plays across the sound system, and a few people take to the dance floor.

Only then do you notice their garments.

This is going to be an amazing story.

But to write the story, I have to *see* the place.

"What else is here?" I ask.

"As I told you. Exhibition rooms. Public playrooms. Private playrooms."

I draw in a deep breath to gather my courage. "Show me."

"Come with me, my angel."

CHAPTER SIXTEEN

Frankie

Phantom takes my hand, and together we walk through a door into another hallway.

"These large rooms on this side of the hallway are exhibition rooms. There, you're allowed to look. The people playing are exhibitionists who want to be seen. The people watching are voyeurs."

"Are you a voyeur?"

"Not usually. But when I bring someone new to the club, I want to satisfy her curiosity."

"What kind of things do they do in these rooms?"

"There's a bondage room, a role-playing room—"

"What do you mean, a role-playing room?"

"Would you like to see?"

"Yes, I would."

We walk to the third door, and Phantom opens it.

A security guard stands by the door. "Good evening, Phantom," he says.

"I'm just showing my guest around."

"Absolutely. Enjoy yourselves."

I have to stop my jaw from dropping.

The first thing I notice is a man dressed in leather—leather from head to toe—and a naked woman walking him on a leash.

"See anything that interests you?"

I gulp. "No, not really."

"Animal play is big with some people," he says. "But it's not my cup of tea."

"What *is* your cup of tea?" I ask, my skin tightening.

"I could show you. If you're ready to go to a private playroom with me."

"I…don't think I'm quite ready for that yet."

"That's okay. If we don't get there tonight, we don't have to. This is all in your own time."

In the corner, a woman dressed as Wonder Woman is getting pounded by Superman.

Still not a huge turn-on, but it makes a lot more sense to me than playing like a dog.

In another scene, a man and a woman are biting each other…with fangs.

"They don't really…"

"Drink each other's blood? Perhaps. But not in here. Blood sports can only be done in private. It's a sanitary thing."

I gulp. And then I nod.

Right. A sanitary thing.

This is all too much. I'm about ready to go into work Monday and tell Lisa I can't do the story.

"It's important not to be judgmental," Phantom says.

"I'm not," I say. "It's just…new."

"Clubs like this are places where people can meet like-minded people. After all, most people won't walk up to someone on the street and ask if they'd like to be led around on a leash."

"Or if they'd mind if you drink their blood?"

"Exactly."

"Who *are* these people?"

"Pretty much normal people, just like you and me," he says. "They just have some different tastes, and this club allows them to indulge."

"I see."

"Perhaps I shouldn't have brought you in here. This is not a room for beginners. Maybe the bondage room would be better."

"Or maybe bondage light?" I suggest.

"Actually, that's a good idea. We'll just go into the basic exhibition room. There you'll see scenes, but they won't include a lot of toys. It's a place where people can have sex and be watched. That's the turn-on."

I nod. "That sounds like something I can handle."

He guides me to a different door. Another security guard stands inside. Phantom murmurs a few things to the guard, and we enter.

Beds. Beds and stools and armchairs. And people naked, having sex.

Some are kissing, some are having oral sex, and others... Others are fucking.

Normally my jaw would be on the ground, but after what I just witnessed? This is completely normal.

Simple vanilla sex, in myriad positions, and I find myself...

Wondering...

Wondering how I'd feel having sex here, others watching me...

Phantom has already said he's not an exhibitionist, so if we do anything together, it will be in private.

"What are you feeling?" he whispers to me.

I shudder as his warm breath caresses my neck. "I don't know what I'm supposed to think."

"You're not *supposed* to think anything, Angel. Just tell me what you're *feeling*."

"I feel..."

Somehow I have to commit all of this to memory. I have to...

"I feel like I want to kiss you," I say.

Never in my life have I asked to kiss a man.

Either he asks me, or it just happens. I've never initiated it.

But I've known Phantom now for just over a week, and even though I know nothing about him, I desperately want to kiss him.

I expect him to turn me around and bring his lips to mine, and when he doesn't, disappointment surges through me.

I've done something wrong.

"Come with me," he says.

We leave the large room, and he leads me to another door, where he slides a card through the lock. "We can be alone in here."

"Is this yours?"

"No, but I was hoping you and I might need some privacy tonight, so I reserved it." He opens the door and allows me to walk in ahead of him.

"Wow."

It's a beautiful bedroom. I'm not sure why I was expecting anything else.

The king-size bed sits on one side of the room, covered in a glorious royal blue quilt. Where are the toys? The tables, the ropes?

Phantom closes the door. “Come here, Angel.”

His presence is imposing, yet I feel no fear at all. Only anticipation as I walk toward him and he pulls me into his arms.

His lips touch mine.

It’s a soft kiss, but it has my heart thrumming.

He slides his lips over mine, and then his tongue probes the seam of my mouth.

I part my lips, and his tongue delves in…

And no longer is the kiss gentle.

He devours my mouth, sliding his lips, his tongue, his teeth, and then he growls into me, vibrating through me.

This kiss.

How could it start so gentle and then…

But my God, I love it. I melt into it and into him.

My nipples are hard against the stretchy fabric of my black dress.

I don’t care about the article anymore, and I don’t care about the black dress or the three hundred and fifty dollars that it cost. He can rip it into shreds.

All I care about is Phantom and this kiss.

Even if I never learn his name, it’s all worth it for this kiss.

This kiss that’s better than the hottest sex I ever had with Penn or anyone else.

All of it… Love. Peace. Goodness. The whole world.

All of it is in this kiss.

CHAPTER SEVENTEEN

Phantom

At his lips' touch she blossomed for him like a flower and the incarnation was complete.

I've never really been into kissing.

I like it, but it's not the crux of what I'm after during a scene.

Scenes, for me, while they're definitely about the sex, aren't about emotion. Kissing is about emotion. Consequently, I'm not that into it.

I give my partners pleasure, for sure. Pain if they want it.

But I don't get attached, and I rarely kiss them unless they ask me to.

With Francesca, though?

I've never enjoyed a kiss so much.

I couldn't wait to get my lips on hers, my tongue inside her mouth.

I couldn't wait to touch her soft cheeks, to thread my fingers through her silky hair.

I truly get what Jay Gatsby was feeling. She's blossoming

like a flower under my kiss.

Perhaps I shouldn't have brought her here. I want her more than anything. My cock is hard as a rock, and I long to thrust it into her lush body. I come here for one purpose—to satisfy my hunger, my desires.

She came here with me. She's seen the place. She knows what happens here.

And she hasn't asked to leave.

That's all I can think as she melts farther into me, farther into the kiss.

My God… The feelings swirling through me. I wasn't sure I could ever have them again.

I still don't know much about this woman. I know her name, now, and a bit about what she does.

I certainly know more about her than she does about me.

And what's truly frightening?

I *want* her to know me. I want to show her who I truly am.

But if I do, will she be as enamored by me?

Women like the mystery of my costume, the darkness, the desires shrouded in a conundrum.

I've never had trouble attracting women without this getup, but I like the mystery, too. I like how excited it gets them.

And I like how I can be someone other than who I am, if only for a moment.

But no matter what I look like on the outside, I'm the same person on the inside.

I never forget that, though my partners probably do. They probably never think about who I am on the inside.

Francesca seems to be the exception.

She's asked me many times to level with her. To tell her something personal about myself.

I've done that, and I want to tell her more.

I want to very much.

Which means I cannot. I unequivocally cannot.

CHAPTER EIGHTEEN

Frankie

The decision turns out to be an easy one.

I'm going to let Phantom take me. Right here in this private suite.

I may let him tie me up. I may let him do whatever he wants. If he wants me on my knees in front of him, my mouth held open… Well, I may even consider that.

Yes, it will be good information for the article, but that's not the ultimate reason why I'm considering it.

I'm considering it because this whole atmosphere—this whole fantasy—intrigues me.

I want *him*.

In all my life, I never imagined wanting to be with a man whose identity I don't even know. So why do I feel closer to Phantom than I ever did to Penn or anyone else?

On some level, he seems to get me. He's admitted that we have things in common. Running. Writing.

He understands me.

That's why he brought me here.

That's why I, twice now, have dressed in a way that I

knew he would like.

I pull back hesitantly, break the kiss.

"Please," I say softly. "Take me. Take me right here in this private room. Please."

He stares into my eyes, his own so deep and dark. "Are you certain?"

"I wouldn't say it if I weren't."

"Then I have your express consent?"

"Of course you do."

"I will guarantee your safety, Angel. That, I promise you."

"I know that."

I do. From the bottom of my heart, I know this man will never harm me.

"We don't know each other very well yet," he says, "so we'll start with the basics. Undress for me, my angel."

Undressing won't take long. I'm only wearing my stretchy little black dress and a pair of black panties. No stockings or pantyhose, only my platform pumps. No jewelry other than stud earrings and the pearl necklace Phantom placed around my neck, designating me as his for the evening.

Such a freaking turn-on.

I begin with my shoes, but—

"No, Angel. Keep the shoes on."

I nod, and then I pull the dress up around my hips and over my head.

My breasts fall gently against my chest once free of the stretchy fabric.

I am naked but for my panties and my shoes.

Phantom sucks in a breath. A deep, gasping breath.

He likes what he sees.

I like that he likes it.

"Will you undress for me now?" I ask boldly.

"When I'm good and ready," he says. "I make the rules in here, Angel, but you do have a chance to say no each time."

I smile. "Then I say no. I want *you* to undress now."

He chuckles huskily. "That's not exactly the way it works, and I have a feeling you know that."

"Can't blame a girl for trying."

"Indeed I can't. But what I could do is tell you that you're not going to speak for the rest of the evening."

I drop my mouth into an *O*.

"But I won't. Frankly, I like it when you speak. Your voice is sexy, and I love to hear it."

"That's good, because I don't have a very good record of keeping my mouth shut."

"I want to hear what you have to say tonight. If we choose to continue this…"

"This what?"

He's silent for a moment.

And I wonder… What *is* this? It's certainly not a relationship. Is that the word he was trying not to say?

"Playtime," he finally says. "If we choose to continue this playtime, we'll make the rules as we go."

"*We* will?"

"I'm a Dominant by nature, Angel. I'm used to making the rules during a scene, though you always have the chance to say no. But because you're new at this, I'm bending things a little."

"Does that mean *I* get to make the rules?"

"No. If that were true, I'd be undressed by now."

I can't help the smile that spreads across my face. "Touché."

"I knew you were beautiful, Angel. But even I couldn't

imagine the true splendor of your soft flesh, your perfectly formed breasts, those brownish red nipples." He walks toward me and tweaks one.

I suck in a breath as the tingles travel straight to my pussy.

"Take off the panties, Angel."

I slowly slide them over my hips, down my legs, and I step out of them, still wearing my platform pumps, and kick the satin panties to the side.

Phantom groans. "My God..."

My pussy is freshly shaved, and it's also very wet right now.

"Sit down on the bed, Angel. Spread your legs for me. Let me see the jewels you're hiding."

I walk to the bed covered in blue silk, and I sit down on the edge. Then I spread my legs.

No one's ever asked me to do this before. Correction–no one's asked me to spread my legs just so he could *look*.

I'm already wet and glistening, so swollen, because I can feel it pulsing with that hungry need, that need to be filled.

But does he fill me?

No. He simply walks toward me, staring. Then he kneels before me, spreads my legs farther, and pushes my thighs upward.

"Very beautiful," he says. "Pink and plump and perfect."

"I..."

"What?"

"Thank you. I guess."

"No, thank *you*."

He moves forward then, and just when I think–hope, pray–he may slide his tongue across my folds...he stops, his face mere inches from my slit.

"So beautiful." He inhales. "So fragrant. You're wet for me, aren't you, Angel?"

"Yes," I breathe out.

"Would you like me to suck on that pussy, Angel? Perhaps slide a finger into your cunt?"

His use of the C-word shocks me, but the shock wears off in a millisecond, and I find myself liking it. Liking the taboo of it. The dirtiness and the darkness.

Phantom is so suave. So debonair. Such a forbidden word from his full lips seems out of place.

Yet not so out of place.

"God, yes."

"Tell me. Tell me in explicit detail what you'd like me to do to your pussy right now."

I close my eyes, as if that will somehow bring the words to my lips. Because I want to answer him.

"I want your tongue on me," I say. "Inside my pussy, on my clit."

"And?"

"Fingers. Your fingers inside me. And your… Your cock. Your cock inside me, too, Phantom. Please. God, please."

My nipples are so hard and straining. They feel like they're on fire. The only thing that will ease the ache is Phantom's lips or his fingers.

But he's focused solely on my pussy, and that's a great place to be focused on.

"Is that all?" he asks.

Is that all? I basically just told him I want him to fuck me. What else is there?

"I'm glad to do what you ask," he says. "But I wonder… Isn't there more?"

"Kisses. My nipples. Suck my nipples."

"There you go. But think outside the box a little, Angel. I can suck on your sweet nipples. I would enjoy that very much. I could suck that treasure between your legs, and I *know* I'll enjoy that. And I can fuck you. I can fuck you hard and fast with my big cock, and yes, I will really enjoy it. You'll enjoy everything too. I promise. But tell me, Angel. Tell me what has *never* been done to you. Tell me what you dream about in your deepest, darkest, forbidden fantasies."

I gulp audibly.

"I… I don't know, Phantom."

"Surely you've desired more than just a quick fuck."

"A slow fuck?"

"That would be nice. But you know what I'm talking about."

For the first time, he reaches toward me and touches me, brushing one finger over my clit.

I gasp. Tingles shoot through me, and I swear to God, I almost feel like I could orgasm from that light caress alone.

"We'll have it your way tonight. I'm going to suck on those beautiful little nipples of yours. I will suck this paradise between your legs. And I'll fuck you. Slowly at first, and then hard and fast. And if you enjoy that, Angel, I will take you home and let you dream about better things."

He comes forward, his mask still on his face, and he tweaks one of my nipples while lowering his head to the other one. He draws it between his lips and sucks.

Torpedoes shoot through me, and again, for a blissful moment, I'm sure I'm going to climax from this alone.

He pulls on the other nipple as he sucks on the first, moving in tandem. I'm getting wetter by the second, and I want so much to pull him toward me, run my fingers through his silky hair, but that may jar his mask.

Though I desperately want to see his face, make him show me who he truly is, it would spoil this moment, and we both know it.

I will *not* spoil this moment.

Because like the kiss before this, I'm getting more out of having my nipples played with than I've ever gotten out of the most intimate lovemaking with any other man.

Phantom licks my nipple, running his tongue all over the areola and then sucking it deeply between his lips.

He cups my other breast, pinching the nipple, and then, after torturing my nipple with his tongue, he moves toward my mouth, kisses my lips, swirls his tongue with mine.

The next moment, he's back to my nipple, licking, biting, sucking. And then my mouth again, kissing me, cupping my breasts, squeezing my nipples.

He pulls his lips away, then, so that only our tongues are touching. God, so powerful. Just the loving movement of tongues as he pinches my nipples.

I could kiss this man for hours and never tire of the spicy taste of his tongue on mine, the rough feel of his fingers pulling at my nipples.

But my pussy… My aching pussy…

And then I wonder if he's truly clairvoyant, because he leaves my mouth, my breasts, and he kisses down my abdomen, trailing his tongue over my flesh, and finally, finally, his head is between my legs.

The side of his mask rubs against my thigh as he licks my clit.

"Oh!" I gasp.

He chuckles, growls, and nips at the hard nub again.

My hips rise, fall, undulate, reach for that precipice that is so close. When he slides that velvet tongue between my legs, against my hot core…

My God. This isn't going to last long.

When have I… When–

"Oh my God!" I cry out.

Already I'm coming, coming so hard beneath his mouth.

Normally I like a finger in my pussy when I come, but Phantom's tongue is all I need. His tongue working me, sliding through my slit, landing on my clit.

The man is magic, and as I move my hips, he holds me down by my thighs, continues to assault my pussy, and oh my God, I'm coming again.

I'm coming again and again and again.

Is this a long orgasm, or is it multiple orgasms? Whatever it is, it's something I've never experienced before. It's blinding me. Burying me. Taking me under…under…under…

"That's it," he says. "Keep coming, Angel. Come for me. Come for your Phantom."

And then, like Christine Daaé herself, I scream out at a high pitch, almost in song.

"Yes, sing for me, my angel of music."

"Yes!"

My eyes are closed, and I'm not sure how it happens, but within another second, his large cock is inside me.

Thrusting, thrusting, thrusting…

Burning, burning, burning…

I haven't seen his dick, but my God he must be huge. Huge and perfect and everything good. And still I'm coming, coming, coming…

My God, this can't be happening.

But it is.

It is, and–

"Yes, Angel! Yes!" He sinks inside me deeply, releasing.

I'm completely spent, and he stays inside me for a wonderful moment, keeps me full of his huge cock, and I relish the feeling.

I whimper when he finally withdraws and disposes of the condom.

When did he put on a condom? Thank God he was responsible. I certainly wasn't, and that's not like me at all.

All I know is that I just had the most amazing fuck of my life…from a man whose face I've never seen.

"Well, my angel of music?"

"Amazing," I breathe out. "Absolutely amazing."

"And, Angel, this is only the beginning."

CHAPTER NINETEEN

Frankie

After the rest of the weekend dreaming about Phantom—and recalling that he promised to tell me his name but he didn't—I arrive at work Monday morning, only for my boss to ask me how the story's going.

The BDSM-in-Manhattan story.

If she only knew.

The problem is my nondisclosure agreement. That's also the problem with talking to Isabella about the story. Has Isabella ever been to the club I went to? I'll never know because she can't tell me. And I can't tell her I was there.

Because of the NDA, I resort to an ad on social media asking for people to contact me—people who frequent leather lifestyle clubs in the city and are willing to speak to me confidentially.

I don't expect to get a lot of responses because these things are confidential, so I'm more than surprised when I check my inbox during the afternoon and I find over thirty.

About two-thirds of the respondents are women, and the remaining third are men. That doesn't surprise me. Women are more likely to talk than men are, but I want information from both.

I reply to each of them, asking if any of them would be willing to come into a private chat room with me and answer questions. Within five minutes, one man and four women respond affirmatively, so I set up the chat for the next day.

Then I think about Phantom.

I have a date with him at the bar next Saturday night. I still have the card he gave me, and I've been tempted to call him, but…I can't. I can't ruin the fantasy.

I have another hour to kill before I leave for the day, so I reach out via direct message to one of the female respondents who didn't agree to a private chat.

Frankie: *Do you have a few minutes to talk now?*

Candy: *Yes.*

Frankie: *Can you tell me your age?*

Candy: *I'm forty-seven.*

Hmm. Surprising. I expected her to be in her twenties.

Frankie: *Are there a lot of people in your age group at your club?*

Candy: *We have all ages. But most people are in their forties. Some in the late thirties, early fifties.*

That's a surprise.

Frankie: *I know you can't tell me the name of the club, but can you tell me a little bit about it?*

Candy: *I can try. I've been to a few here in the city.*

Frankie: *Which one is your favorite?*

Candy: *I don't know that I can say I have a favorite. They all offer different things. For example, one of the clubs I like gives you a lot of privacy for your scenes. I'm not an exhibitionist by nature, so that's what I prefer.*

Frankie: *Do you know a lot of exhibitionists?*

Candy: *I know a few. But I never see them in my favorite club, because there isn't a lot of exhibition there.*

Frankie: *I understand. What kind of activities do you engage in at the club?*

Candy: *I'm a submissive by nature, so I play with Dominants.*

Frankie: *Men or women?*

Candy: *Mostly men, but I've played with a few women Doms. I prefer men, but once in a while, it's fun to shake things up a bit.*

Frankie: *Is there anything specific that women do differently from men?*

Candy: *Honestly, it depends on the Dom. They're all different, male or female.*

Frankie: *What about sex? Men and women have sex differently.*

Candy: *The female Doms I've played with used strap-ons, so it's pretty similar.*

Huh?

Frankie: *You mean…*

Candy: *Yes. Exactly what it sounds like. A strap-on dildo. They come in all shapes and sizes.*

Frankie: *All shapes?*

Candy: *Yes. Most are normal shaped, but some of them are differently shaped, which allows for fantasies of aliens and such.*

That comment would freak me out had I not been in the role-playing room just last night. I know what some people like to do.

Frankie: *So you prefer men. Any particular reason for that?*

Candy: *Probably because I'm straight.*

Frankie: *Okay, that makes sense. So you prefer to play in private. With just one partner or multiple partners?*

Candy: *Usually with just one partner.*

Frankie: *Have you ever played in a public setting?*

Candy: *Once or twice. It's not really my jam.*

Frankie: *I understand. When did you first find out you like this kind of play?*

Candy: *I'm a late bloomer. I've only been doing this for a few years. I got a divorce five years ago, and I just wanted something different. I wanted to try something I'd never tried before, so I got online and looked around. When I found a BDSM chat room, I was intrigued.*

Frankie: *How long after that did you actually get into the lifestyle?*

Candy: *I kind of dived right in. That's not really the norm for me, but like I said I had just gotten out of a marriage, and I'm not getting any younger, so I wanted to try things.*

Frankie: *Do you have a specific partner you play with?*

Candy: *No, I'm not interested in a relationship. But there are people out there who play only with each other.*

Frankie: *I see.*

Candy: *I'm happy to talk again, but I'm running late for a meeting.*

Frankie: *That's okay. Thank you so much for your candor, and I'll definitely be in touch with you again. Is there a certain way you'd like to be credited in my article?*

Candy: *Yes, call me Candy.*

Frankie: *You got it, Candy. Thank you again.*

Next, I reach out to one of the men who didn't want to take part in the group chat. He agrees to message with me.

Frankie: *I understand that all the clubs here in the area* *require confidentiality agreements, so you can't tell me the names of the clubs or where they are, and you probably won't want to use your real name, either. Is there a name you'd like to use in my article?*

Erik: *Yes. Erik.*

Frankie: *Very well, Erik. How long have you been involved in the lifestyle?*

Erik: *About ten years at this point.*

Frankie: *May I ask how old you are?*

Erik: *Of course. I'm thirty-five.*

So that means he started when he was twenty-five. Interesting.

Frankie: *How long have you known that you're interested in this kind of thing?*

My heart beats rapidly as I watch the three dots move.

Erik: *I think subconsciously I've always known. I like regular sex as much as the next person. It's great. And I enjoy it. But I always felt like something was missing. I crave danger. I crave the forbidden. I crave taboo.*

Frankie: *Why do you think that is?*

Erik: *I don't know. Maybe because my life is a little bit mundane without it.*

Frankie: *It is? What do you do for a living?*

Erik: *I'm a medical doctor.*

Frankie: *What kind of doctor?*

Erik: *I prefer not to say.*

Frankie: *Why? Because you think it would make you more recognizable?*

Erik: *Maybe. Maybe I just don't want to say.*

Frankie: *Does anyone in your life know that you participate in this lifestyle?*

Erik: *No. It's very private to me.*

Frankie: *I understand. So does that mean you have a specific partner that you play with? Or do you play with multiple partners?*

Erik: *Multiple partners, but not multiple people at the same time. I play with only one person at a time, but I'm not in any kind of relationship.*

Frankie: *Why?*

Erik: *Because I choose not to be.*

Frankie: *Are you a Dominant or a submissive?*

Erik: *I'm a Dominant.*

Frankie: *What do you like about being a Dominant?*

Erik: *You're probably looking for some kind of answer that makes sense. Like I love having control over my partner. But that's not really it, at least not in my case. My sub is my equal in every way, more so than in a conventional relationship in some ways.*

Frankie: *I'm not sure I understand.*

Erik: *My submissive consents to everything I do. We talk beforehand about what her limits are and what my limits are. About what I expect out of the scene, about what she expects out of the scene.*

Frankie: *So in that respect, you're both getting what you want.*

Erik: *Exactly.*

Frankie: *What kind of activities do you engage in with your partners?*

Erik: *Bondage, flogging, sometimes nipple torture, labia torture.*

Labia torture? Good thing he can't see my face about now.

Frankie: *Can you elaborate?*

Erik: *Bondage is pretty self-explanatory, I think. I like to* *use leather bindings, sometimes silk. I don't use ropes very often because I never took the time to learn the intricacies of it.*

Frankie: *And flogging?*

Erik: *What about it?*

Frankie: *What instruments do you use?*

Erik: *It depends on my partner, but most of them like what I do with a riding crop.*

I gulp audibly.

Frankie: *And the rest?*

Erik: *What do you mean?*

Oh, God. He's going to make me say it.

Frankie: *Nipple torture.*

I can't bring myself to type "labia torture."

Erik: *Right. Nipple torture. Most submissives love that. Especially if they have sensitive nipples. I use clamps for the most part.*

Frankie: *And the rest?*

Erik: *Labia torture? Again, clamping mostly.*

Frankie: *And women enjoy this?*

Erik: *You'd be surprised.*

God, yes, I'd be surprised.

Frankie: *Anything else that you engage in?*

Erik: *I've tried a lot of things. These are the things I enjoy the most. But if there's something that a submissive wants that I don't normally do, I will entertain the idea if I feel I can do it without putting either one of us in any danger.*

Frankie: *Danger? What could be dangerous?*

Erik: *There have been times when my partner has asked me to draw blood.*

Blood sports. Isabella mentioned that. So did Phantom. Still…acid crawls up my throat.

Frankie: *Drawing blood? Is that safe?*

Erik: *Absolutely, when done correctly. And I will not engage in it unless I feel that I can do it with absolutely no danger to my partner or myself.*

Frankie: *How do you do it?*

Erik: *There are many different ways. Needles probably are the most common.*

I'm afraid to ask him to elaborate. But this is research for work. I have to ask. Before I can, though, another message pops up.

Erik: *All the instruments are sterilized beforehand, and an antibiotic ointment is applied when we're done. I also make sure that she checks in with me both twenty-four and forty-eight hours later.*

Frankie: *And clubs let you do this?*

Erik: *Actually, not all clubs do. But some will. Then of course you can do anything you want if you have the privacy of your own dungeon.*

Frankie: *Do you have your own dungeon?*

Erik: *Not at the moment.*

Frankie: *I see. Thank you so much for your candor. May I contact you again if I need more information?*

Erik: *Absolutely. And remember it's Erik. Erik with a K.*

CHAPTER TWENTY

Frankie

At my apartment that evening, I begin to compile the notes into a rough draft. I need lots more information, but I certainly have a good start.

The problem is…what do I do about clubs? No one was willing to go into detail, and I understand that. I know of one, but I can't mention it.

My phone buzzes.

It's Isabella. Perfect. She's a source.

"Hey, Izzy," I say.

"Hey, do you feel like getting a drink? I'm restless."

I check my watch. "I'm actually working on a story, but I could use a break."

"Great, meet me over at Rossi's? We can have a glass of wine or something."

"I'll be there."

Half an hour later, I'm sitting with Izzy, pouring out what I learned from the people I chatted with online.

"I never thought of that," she says. "That's the best way to get information. Nobody has to worry about the confidentiality agreement, because they're not identifiable."

"Right? I'll be very good about not mentioning any clubs or anything."

"How could you? You don't know any of them."

I look down at the table. "Right. Of course."

I hate lying, but Isabella is lying to me as well. By omission. Of course, she's bound by a confidentiality agreement.

"Thanks for being one of my sources." I smile.

Izzy crosses her legs. "I've been thinking about that, Frank, and I've already told you too much."

"Why do you say that? I don't think anything of it."

"I know you don't, but it's just such a private thing, you know?" She takes a sip of wine. "I don't want to say anything more."

"Yeah, I do know. I get it."

More than she knows. Good thing I have other sources online.

"May I still use what you've told me?"

"Yeah. That's fine." She takes another sip of wine. "So… how are your sister's wedding plans going?"

I roll my eyes. "I had to go wedding dress shopping Saturday. And get my maid of honor dress as well. We went to Macy's, which is so totally Mandy. Saving pennies anywhere she can."

"How come you didn't get the frugal gene?"

"I was marrying the son of a multimillionaire. The guy has a trust fund. I didn't have to be frugal."

"True. But his trust fund wasn't big enough to overlook cheating." Izzy sighs. "Did you ever find out who he was fucking behind your back?"

"Nope."

"Don't you want to know?"

I pick up my wine, swirl it in the glass. "Not really. I mean sure, I'm curious. But it's probably some skank."

Isabella laughs, which is interesting. Isabella doesn't laugh that often.

"Anyway, I'm over it."

"Are you really?"

"Over Penn? Absolutely. Over the humiliation of it all? Not so much."

"No one thinks any less of you, Frank."

"I know that. In fact, I'm finding out that no one wanted me to marry Penn in the first place."

"Yeah."

"My mom and dad made it very clear. So did Mandy. They all thought he was no good. And I'm like, why didn't you tell me you felt like this before we set a date?"

"For the same reason Gigi and I didn't tell you," Isabella says. "Because we love you. We wanted you to be happy."

"But apparently none of you thought Penn was going to make me happy."

"Yeah, I know. Doesn't make a lot of sense now that I look at it in hindsight."

"Well, I won't hold it against you. I'm the one who was going to marry the dickhead. I'm not sure what I was thinking."

"You were thinking that you had been on and off for so long, that he was good-looking and rich, and you thought you loved him."

"I did think that. But now that I look back? I'm not sure I ever did. I'm not sure I've ever been in love."

"Then you haven't. Because if you've been in love, you know it."

"I thought I was. But my bruised ego hurts a lot more than losing Penn."

"And then there's Mandy..."

"Right. Mandy." I slosh my wine in my glass again and take a drink, letting it drizzle over my tongue. "Mandy, who radiates happiness when she and Jackson are together. And God, he does, too. It took them twenty-nine years to find each other when they were right in front of each other the whole time. And I'm not jealous. I mean, Jackson's a hottie. He always has been. But I've never felt that way about him. Not for more than about five minutes, anyway."

"I have," Isabella says. "He never gave me a second look."

"He danced with you that night, after we went for that first bridesmaid fitting."

"He was just being polite. In fact, I think maybe I asked him to dance. I can't remember."

"Doesn't matter anyway. He's head over heels for my sister. And I *am* happy for them. Truly."

Our waitress comes by and asks if we want a refill on our Chardonnay.

"No, I'm good," I say. "Work tomorrow and all that."

Isabella nods. "Me too."

"All right," the server says. "I'll be right back with your check."

A good-looking man approaches our table. "Would you like to dance?" He nods to Isabella.

"Sure." Isabella rises, and she looks good in her skinny jeans and tight T-shirt. She's so long and lean. No boobs, though, which Mandy and I both have in abundance. Well, maybe not abundance, but more than a handful for sure.

I run over my notes in my head as I watch Isabella and the man—who's slightly shorter than she is but really good-looking and built—dance.

I've only talked to two people so far. Candy and Erik. Erik with a K.

So strange that he made it clear it was a K. Sure, most of us would automatically go to Eric with a C. But what does it really matter? It was over DMs, so I could see it was spelled with a K. Plus, it's just a pseudonym for an article.

Erik with a K.

Well, if he wants to be Erik with a K, he'll be Erik with a K.

"Would you care to dance?"

I look up.

A gentleman stands in front of me. His hair is sandy blond, and his eyes are blue. So different from Phantom.

In fact, this is the anti-Phantom. Light hair, light eyes, and no mask and cape.

Since I don't even know Phantom's name, I'm free to dance with whomever I please.

I'm free to dance with whomever I please anyway, so why do I feel like I'm cheating by dancing with this man?

I rise and smile. "Absolutely. I'm Frankie."

"Nice to meet you, Frankie. I'm Tom."

I follow Tom to the dance floor, and we end up next to Izzy and the guy who asked her. It's a fast song, so we don't have to touch each other, which is fine with me. It also means we don't have to talk, since we're not close enough to hear each other very well.

Once the song is over, I make my getaway. "Thanks so much. It was great meeting you, but I have an early day at work tomorrow."

He follows me back to the table where the check is lying. He grabs it. "Please, let me get this."

"Oh, that's not necessary."

"I insist." He lays a credit card on top of it.

Tom Carson. Thomas J. Carson, actually. That's the name on his credit card.

"So what do you do for a living, that you have to be there so early tomorrow?" he asks me.

"I'm a junior editor at *Lovely* magazine. My day starts early, sometimes by seven a.m."

"I suppose it's a lot of work to get a magazine out every month."

"It is. But I like the work."

"That's good. I'm an attorney."

"Oh? What kind of an attorney?"

"Corporate attorney. I work for Black Inc."

"Really? My sister's fiancé works there. Maybe you know him. Jackson Paris?"

"Sure. I know Jack. Good guy." Then: "Wait, you're Mandy's sister?"

"Guilty."

"Francesca. I guess I didn't put two and two together, though now that I look closer, your eyes are similar. Frankie is a nickname for Francesca."

"No one calls me Francesca, but how did you know Mandy had a sister named Francesca?"

"She mentioned you once when she was in the office bringing Jack lunch. I happened to be talking to him at the time."

"She brings Jack lunch at the office?"

"Yeah. And I love them both, truly, but I have to say, they're a little nauseating sometimes."

"Oh my God, you have no idea."

"As I understand it, they've been friends forever?"

"Longer than forever. Mandy crushed on him for years, but he never thought of her as anything more than a friend. But somehow, he finally saw her."

"He's pretty damned whipped, from what I can see," Tom says.

I sigh.

"Everything okay?" he asks.

The waitress comes by and takes Tom's credit card.

"Yeah, I'm fine. But my God, it seems like everywhere I go, I find some tie to Mandy and Jack."

"Black Inc. is a big company."

"I know. But New York's a bigger city. And to be honest, you're the first person I've met in a while who actually *knows* my sister and future brother-in-law. I guess I'm just feeling…"

"What?"

"Nothing. It's a long, boring story, and I come off bad in it."

"I can't imagine you coming off bad in any story."

"Maybe we all come off bad in it. Which is just as bad."

"Feel like talking?"

I glance to the dance floor, where Isabella is still clinging to the dark-haired man.

"Not particularly."

"I'm a really good listener."

I definitely don't feel like conversing, but this man is very attractive and clearly interested. So why am I feeling nothing? Why am I not thinking about how to jump his bones?

What the heck is wrong with me?

Granted, I was on-again, off-again with Penn for so long, but during our off-again times, I never had any problem going to bed with another man.

Now we're off-again permanently, and all I can think about is the masked man with the mesmerizing dark eyes.

Tom Carson seems like a good guy. He's an attorney, and he works for Black Inc., which means he does well. He's tall, though maybe not quite as tall as Phantom, with broad shoulders and a corded neck, at least from what I can see above his collar.

"I just got out of a relationship," I say. "Broken engagement."

"Oh. I'm sorry."

"Don't be. I should've gotten out of that relationship a long time ago. Apparently I'm the only one who couldn't see that he wasn't right for me. But I sure see it now."

"That's not a bad story."

"Isn't it? I stayed in a relationship for over five years with a man who never appreciated me. We were on-again, off-again for so long that sometimes I didn't know which end was up."

Tom nods. "I think I'm beginning to see the issue."

"You think?"

"Now your sister and Jackson are engaged and planning their wedding. Just as you're going through a breakup."

"Yeah. I told you I come off bad in it."

"Do you wish your sister ill?"

"Of course not."

"Then I don't see how you're coming off bad in the story, Frankie. It's okay to feel a little sad. To feel like this is supposed to be your time to shine, and it turns out it's not."

"You don't think that makes me childish?"

"Maybe slightly, but we're all childish sometimes."

"I'm actually happy for Mandy and Jack. I love my sister,

and I love Jack. I've known him forever. My sister… Let's just say she deserves this. She's been pining away for Jack for so long that she never really had another satisfying relationship. So I'm thrilled for her. For both of them. So why can't I…"

He slides his hand over my arm. "Because none of this exists in a vacuum, Frankie. It's okay to be happy for them and still feel a little sad for yourself. One doesn't negate the other."

"I just feel like I should be a bigger person than that."

He laughs then. "And all this time I thought I had found the perfect woman. I mean, look at you. You're beautiful. Stunning, actually, and clearly very intelligent. And available, from what I can see." He shakes his head and then laughs. "But you're just not perfect, damn it. I'm afraid there's no future for us."

I join him in his laughter. "Okay, you've made your point. No one is perfect. It's okay to have these feelings."

"It's not only okay. It's normal. I'd probably be feeling the same way if I were in your shoes."

What a nice guy.

If it weren't for that damned Phantom, I'd be all over Tom.

"Would you like to go out sometime?" he asks.

"Sure."

Although I'm not excited about it.

"How about Saturday?

Saturday. I'm supposed to meet Phantom again on Saturday.

"Maybe Friday instead?" I have a family dinner at Mom and Dad's every Friday, but I can cancel.

"Are you busy Saturday?"

"Yeah. Family plans." Again, I don't like lying, but I don't even know this guy.

"I'm going out of town later this week, and I get home Friday afternoon. But I suppose I could make that work. Maybe a late dinner date?"

"How late?"

"About nine, at The Glass House?"

I force a smile. "Sure. That sounds great."

He pulls out his phone. "Perfect. Let me make a reservation."

"All set." He hands me his business card. "If anything comes up, just give me a call."

"Sure." I grab my purse and pull out one of my own cards. "Here's my information for if anything comes up with you."

"Frankie." He meets my gaze. "Trust me. I will be keeping this date."

CHAPTER TWENTY-ONE

Frankie

I arrive slightly late to The Glass House on Friday. I don't want to appear overeager, and oddly, I'm not overeager at all. I kept the date because Phantom and I have nothing going on.

I do have a number for him, but I don't even know his real name.

So why not date Tom as well?

"Good evening," the host says. "Do you have a reservation this evening, ma'am?"

I hate when people call me ma'am. But to this woman, who looks all of eighteen, I guess I'm a ma'am. "I'm meeting someone. Mr. Carson?"

"Tom Carson? Yes, he's already here. Let me show you to your table."

I follow the hostess to the back, to a very private table.

The restaurant is dimly lit, but already I can see that Tom looks amazing. I expected him to be in a suit and tie, but he wears black pants and a white button-down unbuttoned at the neck.

Then I see his suit coat and his tie over his chair. I can't blame him for discarding the tie. He said he'd be traveling today, and he's probably tired.

He rises when he sees me. "Frankie, I was beginning to think you were going to stand me up."

"I apologize. I got delayed."

A glass of amber liquid sits in front of him. "The server already came by and asked for drinks." He waves to a woman who comes over quickly.

"I see your companion has arrived. What can I get you to drink?"

"A martini," I say automatically. "But could you put a splash of St-Germain in it?"

"Absolutely." She makes a quick note and then cocks her head. "You're actually the second person to order that tonight."

My eyes widen, and my heart nearly skips a beat. "Is the person who ordered it still here?"

"No, it was a few hours ago. I'm pretty sure he's gone."

"But it *was* a he."

"Yes, it was."

"Did he have brown hair and brown eyes?"

She wrinkles her forehead. "I think so. But honestly, I see so many diners each night, I can't be sure."

Oh my God. Phantom was here.

"Please tell me he wasn't wearing a mask."

She laughs. "No, of course not. Why would he be?"

"Do you remember what time he was in here? Did he have a reservation?"

"He most likely had a reservation. We're usually fully booked on Fridays and Saturdays. No one can get in without a reservation unless they want to wait for two or three hours."

I don't know much about Phantom, but I don't think he would tolerate a two- or three-hour wait. Besides, he's gone already. If he didn't have a reservation, he'd still be here waiting.

"I'll get your drink ordered." The server walks away quickly.

"You certainly gave her the third degree," Tom says.

"Yeah. I only know one other person who drinks martinis that way."

"The brown-haired and brown-eyed man, I guess."

"Yes."

"Why didn't you just ask his name?"

"I… I don't know his name."

Tom tightens his lips. "Is this mystery man my competition?"

"Oh, no. It's nothing." I pick up my menu and pretend to look at it. "I met him at a masquerade ball, and he wouldn't tell me his name, but he introduced me to this martini with a splash of St-Germain. It's amazing. You should taste it when it gets here."

"I'm not much of a martini man. I prefer good bourbon or scotch."

"You may change your mind when you taste it."

He laughs. "Okay. For you, I will taste the amazing St-Germain martini."

I can't help squirming in my chair. My skin is on fire.

Phantom was here!

Unless there's someone else who drinks a martini like that, but I don't think there is, or the waitress wouldn't have been so surprised that I ordered the same thing.

Brown hair and brown eyes… Of course, she wasn't sure, but she probably would've remembered if he had searing blue eyes or something.

You're on a date, Frankie. You can't spend the whole evening fantasizing about another man.

I heed my own advice and look up from my menu. "So where were you? You said you were traveling for business this week?"

"Yes. I was in L.A. Then Boston, and I just flew back this afternoon."

"Right. Black Inc. is headquartered in Boston."

He nods and takes a sip of his bourbon. "It is. Though we do a lot of work here."

"Have you ever met Braden Black?"

"Yeah, a few times. Him and his father and brother. They work mostly from Boston, but they're here several times a month."

"Interesting."

"Is it? They're good guys, all three of them. But I have to tell you that Braden is most definitely taken."

"Oh, I know that. I read all about his engagement to some photographer or influencer."

He clears his throat. "Yeah, her name is Skye."

"I find their story fascinating. The blue-collar billionaire. I mean, the three of them worked in construction, and now look at them."

"Yep, pretty amazing. It's a great place to work, too. Wonderful benefits. They take care of their people."

Such a nice guy, this Tom Carson.

And I'm bored out of my mind.

It's my own fault. I'm the one who asked about Braden Black. I am interested. I mean, he's an amazing success story, but now we're talking about all the benefits he offers to his employees.

Bo-ring.

The waitress—her name tag says Summer—returns with my drink. "Here you go. I hope you enjoy it."

"I'm sure I will."

I pick it up and take a sip.

And I'm transported back, back to the bar, sitting with Phantom. The marble tile floor, the dark-wood bar, the mirrored shelves with top-shelf liquor...and those dark eyes blazing into my own...

"Uh...Frankie?"

I widen my eyes as I take another sip. "Sorry, what?"

"You seemed a million miles away for a moment."

That's because I was. Though only about six miles away, to be exact, sitting at the bar with Phantom.

"So you promised me a taste."

"And as I recall, you said you'd rather not."

"But then you pressed, and you talked me into it."

He's right. I did. But for some reason, I feel very possessive of this drink right now. Like it's my only link to Phantom, who I'm pretty sure was in this restaurant earlier. Unmasked and everything.

I reluctantly hand the martini glass to Tom.

He takes a tentative sip and then makes a face. "Ugh. I guess I'm still not a martini fan."

"This isn't just any martini," I tell him. "Can't you taste the floral from the elderflower liqueur? It mingles with the juniper, and it's like a crisp autumn day."

"All I taste is rubbing alcohol." He hands it back to me.

"To each his own, I guess." I take another sip.

And I wonder how I can cut this date short.

Summer returns to the table. Though I hid behind my menu, I didn't actually read it. I'm nursing my martini, trying to make it last, because I can't have another one. I don't want to lose my faculties and end up falling into bed with Tom Carson.

Not that I have any desire to, but if I keep drinking, I may see things differently.

"I'm so sorry," I say. "I haven't even looked at the menu."

"You need a few more minutes?"

"No." I open my menu, my gaze landing first on the rack of lamb. That won't do. I don't like lamb. I don't like eating baby animals, and I hate the taste anyway.

I glance up above the rack of lamb. "I'll have the Muscovy duck."

I've never had Muscovy duck. I've had regular duck, and I like it.

"How would you like that cooked?"

"Medium, please."

"Any soup or salad with that?"

"No, thank you."

I don't want this date to last any longer than it has to.

One sip of the martini and all I can think about is tomorrow night, when I'll see Phantom again.

"And for you, sir?"

"I'd like to start with the calamari, and then a house salad with ranch dressing, please, followed by the prime rib, medium rare."

What? No chocolate soufflé for dessert? This date is going to go on forever.

"Perfect," Summer says, "and would you like to add any sides to that?"

Tom glances at the menu. "Asparagus spears sound good."

"And ma'am, I forgot to ask if you wanted any sides?"

"It says the duck comes with wild rice pilaf and green beans."

"Yes, it does. But did you want anything else?"

I close the menu and hand it to her. "No, thank you."

"Perfect. I'll get these in. And sir, your calamari should be out soon."

Great. Tom ordered an appetizer *and* a salad. Which means I get to watch him eat while I wait for my food. Here I thought I could get out of here quickly if I only ordered an entrée. I didn't consider the fact that he might want something more than an entrée. He'll probably want dessert, too. And coffee.

My martini is about halfway gone. I desperately want it to last, because with each sip I take, the floral and woodsy flavor slides over my tongue and I remember more and more about Phantom.

Then I have an idea. "Would you excuse me?"

"Of course."

"I'll be right back."

I grab my purse on the pretense of going to the bathroom, but I edge past the restrooms and back to the host's podium.

"Excuse me," I say to the host who seated me. "Would it be possible for me to find out who had a reservation here earlier?"

"I'm sorry. We don't normally give out that information."

"I know, and I understand. It's just that I think a friend of mine was in here earlier."

"What's your friend's name?"

I don't actually know his name, but I can describe his dark eyes in detail, and he ordered a martini with a splash of St-Germain.

Yeah. That won't fly.

I move my head, trying to see the computer screen where I assume the reservations are kept.

The hostess frowns. "Uh…ma'am? The name?"

So much for my bright idea.

"Never mind. Thank you anyway." This time I head to the bathroom. I don't actually have to go, but I look at myself in the mirror.

My makeup still looks good, and my lipstick—lip stain from Susanne cosmetics—is still perfect. That stuff doesn't ever move. I run a comb through my hair quickly and add a bit of gloss to my lips. Then I wash my hands and head back to the table.

Tom's calamari has been delivered, and he's munching on it. "This is delicious," he says. "Can I tempt you with a piece?"

"Sure, maybe just one." I grab my fork, spear a piece of calamari, and dip it in the marinara sauce. It is good—nice and crunchy and not too rubbery.

"So tell me what you do at the magazine," he says.

I like talking about my work. I love fashion, I love women's interests, and I especially love it when I get to do some of the investigative reporting.

"I do a lot of things," I say. "I write stories, I edit, and sometimes I even do some photography."

"You're certainly a Jacqueline of all trades." He chuckles. "Photographer, too?"

"Very amateur, but with the photography equipment available today, even an amateur can make something look good. We do have photographers on staff, though. I only take my own photos if one of them isn't available to go with me."

"What are you working on right now?"

"An investigative piece. I'm not at liberty to say what it's about."

Actually, I can tell anyone what I'm working on. I'm not under any nondisclosure agreement with the magazine. But this seems very private to me. I don't want to tell Tom Carson about it.

In fact…I really want this date to end.

He's a perfectly pleasant gentleman. Very nice-looking, professional—everything I should be wanting in a man. But I can't get Phantom off my mind.

Especially when I take another sip of my martini.

So crisp, like a blustery fall day. With the warmth of Phantom's cape around me.

"You seem to be really enjoying that," Tom says after swallowing another bite of calamari.

"I am."

"You seemed so surprised when they said someone else ordered it."

"Did I?"

"Frankie, what's going on here? Are you involved with someone?"

"If I were, I wouldn't have accepted a date with you, Tom."

It's not a lie. I wish Phantom and I were involved, but we're not. Sure, we had amazing sex. But how can I be involved with someone when I've never seen his face? When I don't know his real identity? When he promised he'd tell me his name last Saturday, and I was too flustered by my afterglow to press him on it?

And to think… He was in this restaurant tonight.

If Tom and I had come earlier…

But I wouldn't know him if I saw him.

I've never seen his face. Only his eyes.

Would I recognize him?

I know his general build. His jawline. His hair and eye color. His deep and melodic voice.

"You're a million miles away again," Tom says.

I take the last swallow of my martini, feeling a strange loss that it's gone. "I apologize. It was just a long day at work."

God, I hate lying! Makes me feel like a heel.

"Why did you accept this date with me?" Tom asks.

"Because you're a nice guy. Why wouldn't I accept?"

"Your mind is definitely somewhere else, Frankie. I realize this is only our first date, but I don't normally have this hard of a time capturing a woman's attention."

"I'm so sorry." I shove the martini glass to the side of the table for the busboy to pick up. "You have my undivided attention now."

"Good." He smiles. "Tell me what you like to do in your spare time. What are your hobbies?"

"I love to read. I like to cook. And I exercise a lot. I like running, yoga, Pilates."

"I love running. I'm training for a marathon. Maybe we should run together sometime."

"If you're training for a marathon, I'm sure I'd hold you back," I say. "Five Ks are my limit."

"Then let's do a Five K run sometime. You up for one tomorrow morning?"

Am I? I do usually run on Saturday mornings.

"Sure," I say. "You want to meet in Central Park?"

"Sure. Or I could come pick you up."

"It's no problem to just meet."

"I see." He looks down.

"I'm just being cautious," I say. "You and I hardly know each other. I'm not ready to give out my address yet."

"I understand, but you're going to find out, Frankie, that I'm a stand-up guy."

"I'm sure you are, but a woman in New York can never be too cautious."

"I suppose you're right." He smiles.

And then he takes another bite of calamari.

Dear Lord, this is going to be a long night.

And I'm going running with him tomorrow.

The great thing about running is you don't have to talk while you're doing it. In fact, if you're talking, you're not working hard enough. Since he's training for a marathon, Tom will understand that.

Summer comes by to check on us. "Can I get you anything else?"

I nod to my martini glass, breaking the earlier rule I set for myself. "Another one of these, please."

CHAPTER TWENTY-TWO

Frankie

I get a quick brush on my lips from Tom, and I keep my lips sealed. I like him, but I can't get Phantom out of my mind.

He puts me in a cab, and when I open my mouth to tell the cabbie my address, the address of the bar where I'm going to meet Phantom tomorrow comes out instead.

Fifteen minutes later, the cabbie stops, and I pay him and then head toward the bar, hoping Phantom will be there.

I'm wearing the same shoes I wore last Saturday night—my black platform pumps. But other than that, I'm dressed much more casually. Tonight, I wear black skinny jeans, a white camisole, and a black leather blazer.

I walk tentatively into the bar.

I've been to this bar many times. But now? It has a whole new meaning for me.

This is where I met Phantom.

The Phantom of the Opera is one of my favorite musicals, but I'm not sure I could say it's my favorite. I was taken aback when Phantom himself told me that *Camelot* was his favorite and that his favorite book is *The Great Gatsby.*

I read *The Phantom of the Opera* once, back in college. Even then I was mesmerized by the Phantom, whose real name was—

I drop my jaw.

The Phantom of the Opera's name isn't given in the musical, but it *is* in the book.

It's Erik. Erik with a K.

Oh my God.

Was I actually talking to Phantom in my chat earlier this week? And then I just missed him at the restaurant, too? Hmm. Phantom said he's a writer, and Erik said he's a doctor. But doctors can also be writers... Phantom clearly likes literature.

This is all circumstantial evidence to be sure, but...

I walk to the bar. Alfred is tending, as usual. Does he ever take a night off?

"Hey, great to see you again. Frankie, isn't it?"

"Yes. Hi, Alfred."

"Don't tell me you're meeting Phantom tonight."

"I wasn't planning on it. Why? Has he been in?"

"I haven't seen him. Can I get you a drink?"

"Yeah, but I've already had two martinis tonight, so make it a Diet Coke."

"Absolutely." He turns, squirts Diet Coke into a glass from the fountain, and slides it across to me. "Anything else?"

"This is fine for now."

"Are you hungry? I can order you some food."

"No, I just had dinner."

Indeed, my dinner tasted kind of like cardboard. I usually enjoy duck, but this was a little overdone. The skin was soggy more than crispy. Very odd for The Glass House. They usually serve a great meal, not that I go there very often.

"Well, look who came in tonight." Alfred glances toward the entryway.

I turn and—

My whole body goes numb.

It's him. Phantom.

We weren't supposed to meet here, which means…he might be meeting someone else.

If only a giant hole would appear beneath me and swallow me. Whoever Phantom is meeting, I don't want to see her. I don't even want to think about the fact that she exists.

He approaches. "Good evening, Angel."

I swallow. "Hello."

"Did we have an engagement this evening?"

"No. I just decided to come have a drink."

"That doesn't look like a drink to me."

I hold up my Diet Coke and take a sip. "It's a liquid, and I drink it."

"Have you eaten?"

"I have. Have you?"

"I have."

"Then what are you doing here?" I ask. My voice reeks of annoyance. He's clearly here to meet someone—someone who isn't me.

"I like it here," he says.

"Who are you meeting?" I blurt out.

"No one but you at the moment."

"You were at The Glass House tonight, weren't you?"

His eyes widen slightly. Only slightly, but I notice. It's

that much more obvious behind the mask.

"No."

"Well, I was."

"Were you? When?"

"At nine o'clock."

"I was not there this evening."

"You're lying."

"Excuse me?" His voice goes dark.

"My waitress said someone else ordered a dry martini with a splash of St-Germain. Who else would've ordered that drink?"

He shakes his head. "Any number of people."

"Why don't you start telling me the truth, Erik with a K?"

This time his eyes don't widen. They look more... confused. "I'm afraid that's not my name."

"Oh, isn't it? Erik with a K? As in *The Phantom of the Opera*? Or haven't you read the book?"

"I've read the book. I'm very familiar with most world literature."

"Oh?" Another hint. Perhaps he's not a doctor after all.

"Yes. And my name is not Erik, with a K or without a K."

"It would be much easier to believe you if you would tell me your name."

"That's not how this works, Angel."

"Isn't it? You promised me you'd tell me your name if I went to the club with you last week."

"Yes, I did."

"So tell me."

"I don't recall putting a time limit on it," he says, this time with a sly smile. "I simply said I'd tell you, and I will. Just not yet."

Anger curls up my spine. "You know my name. Francesca,

Frankie for short. You know I'm a junior editor at *Lovely* magazine. You know where I had dinner tonight."

"All information that you voluntarily gave me."

"And why won't you volunteer any information to me?"

"Why destroy the fantasy?"

"Maybe this isn't my fantasy," I say. "Maybe my fantasy is to meet a man who's truthful with me, who's open with me, and who lets me see his fucking face."

"I'm afraid that's not me, Angel."

"Frankie. The name is Frankie, not Angel."

He frowns. "Perhaps you're not the woman I thought you were."

"How *can* I be? I don't know anything about you. I have no idea what kind of woman you're looking for."

"Perhaps I'm not looking for a woman at all."

"Seriously?" I take another gulp of my soda. "What is it with you?"

"This is why you came here this evening? To find me and pick a fight?"

I sigh and drain the rest of my Diet Coke. Then I turn to him. "No. I didn't come here to find you, and I don't want to fight with you, Phantom." I shake my head. "You know how ridiculous that sounds? Me calling a grown man Phantom?"

"So you don't enjoy the fantasy?"

"We were in the role-playing room, Phantom."

"I told you I don't role-play."

"And that's a big fucking lie. You're hiding behind a mask. You're pretending to be some opera ghost. Erik with a K. You won't tell me anything. For example, I know you were at The Glass House tonight. And I know you messaged with me."

"Why would I be in a chat room with you?"

"For the ar—" I close my mouth quickly. I can't tell him I'm writing the article. Then he'll know about my research. "Curiosity. I'm curious about your lifestyle. Who wouldn't be?"

"You're wrong," he says. "That is not my name. I was not chatting with you earlier."

"Right. And you weren't at The Glass House, either."

He does not reply.

"Tell you what, Phantom," I say. "I'll make you a deal. You can take me back down to the club tonight. Now. And I'll let you do whatever you want to me. In exchange? You take off the mask when we're done."

"I'm afraid that's not how the game is played, Angel."

"It's Frankie, and you admit it's a game?"

"I admit it's a fantasy," he says.

"Why can't you engage in your fantasy unmasked?"

"Because I like doing it this way."

"What if I chose to wear a mask?"

"No one is stopping you from doing that, Angel."

"Damn it. It's Frankie."

"You're not making this easy for me, Frankie." He leans in and whispers, "Do you have any idea how much I want you right now?"

I suppress a shudder.

Yes, I know. Because I want him just as much.

Why? How can I be so physically attracted to someone I've never seen? Who's making me so damned angry? When he fucked me last time, I was naked, but he wasn't. I haven't seen his face, and I haven't seen his body.

So strange.

"Why are you here?" I ask. "Were you hoping to find someone else tonight?"

"What if I were?"

I scrunch my napkin in my hand. "Then I'm not sure I want to keep our date for tomorrow evening."

"Why?"

"Because I don't want to be…intimate with you if you're seeing someone else."

"I see."

That's it? He sees? "Why are you *here*?" I demand.

"Because I like to come here."

"You like to come to find people to play with."

"If that were the case, I would go straight to the club. Why stop in the bar?"

"You're not really answering my question."

"Aren't I?"

"So this is your MO. You answer my questions with questions. It's getting old, *Phantom*." I cross my arms.

"Perhaps I just came in here for a drink."

"You already had a drink tonight at The Glass House."

He doesn't reply.

"Let me make my position clear," I say. "I don't want to keep our date tomorrow evening if you're sleeping with anyone else."

"Oh?" He grins. "You think *you* make the rules now?"

"I absolutely think I make the rules about who I sleep with. It's something I feel strongly about. I don't have multiple sexual partners."

"Ever? I assure you I always practice safe sex, and I'm tested regularly."

"I'm always safe as well," I say. "That's not really the point."

"Then what is the point?"

"The point is that I feel strongly about it. I suppose you

think that makes me some kind of square."

"No."

"Call it a hard limit, then. I don't want to have sex with you if you're having sex with anyone else."

He stays quiet for a moment, but then he trails his finger over my cheekbone, leaving sparks in its wake.

"You drive a hard bargain. So I'll promise you this. As long as we're playing together, I won't play with anyone else."

"And by play you mean..."

"Kiss. Touch. Have sex. Fuck. You will be my only playmate, Francesca. Until you say otherwise."

CHAPTER TWENTY-THREE

Phantom

I can't believe those words just came from my mouth. My cock is so hard, so straining, to the point that I don't think I can make it to the club. I want to find a secluded area in the hallway and take Francesca up against the wall.

This woman—Francesca—who has no interest in being my angel of music, just made me promise something I've never promised another woman, at least not recently.

Emotion is roiling through me. Emotion I'm not used to. I like to concentrate on the physical for both of us.

I draw the line at emotion.

But my God…

I'm feeling something for this woman.

She says she doesn't even know me, but do I know her any better? I know her name. I know what she does for a living. But that's all. I don't know anything else about her. Where she went to school. What she likes to do in her spare time. Her family.

I want to know these things.

I want to take my mask off with her. Let her see who

I truly am.

I want to give up the fantasy for reality.

We could still have fun. We could still go to the club. We could still have any kind of physical intimacy that we both agreed to.

But we could also have more.

For the first time in a long time…I consider what having more could mean.

And I like the idea.

CHAPTER TWENTY-FOUR

Frankie

I have no reason to trust that he's telling me the truth. I know next to nothing about him.

But the sincerity in his voice is unmistakable.

He's willing to play only with me for as long as we play together.

It's far from a relationship, but do I want a relationship with someone I don't even know?

Whose face I've never seen?

All I do know is that I've felt more in the short time we had together at the club than I ever felt with Penn or anyone else.

I want to feel it again.

And again.

I want him to show me what he desires, and I want to be the person who can fulfill those desires.

"All right," I say. "Let's go."

"Now?"

"Why not? You're here. I'm here. The club is here… somewhere."

"What about our date tomorrow night?"

"I suppose if you want to wait, I can wait," I say.

"Sometimes," he says, "anticipation makes things better."

"I've been anticipating for a week."

"Have you?"

"But I suppose I should be honest with you about something."

"By all means."

"Although…why should I be? You're hardly honest with me."

"You need to do what you feel is right," he says. "As do I."

"All right," I say. "I'll tell you this because I would want to know it if I were you. I went on a date tonight with another man."

His jaw goes rigid. "Oh?"

"But I'm not with him now, as you can see. Somehow I ended up here."

"So you didn't sleep with him."

"If I had, I'd probably still be there."

"Indeed. Why didn't you?"

"Isn't it obvious? I can't get you off my mind. You, who won't tell me your name, who won't let me see your face." I caress the stubble on the unmasked side of his face. "Why do you have this enigmatic hold over me? I can't figure it out."

"Perhaps it's *because* I won't tell you who I am. Perhaps it's *because* you can't see my face."

He raises a good point. I smile. "There's one way to find out. Tell me who you are. Show me your face. Then I'll know if I'm still as intrigued by you as I am now."

He pauses a moment. Then, "Would it surprise you to know that I actually *do* want to show you who I am?"

I lift my eyebrows. “As a matter of fact, yes, that surprises me. Clearly you’ve been Phantom for a long time around here.”

“I have, because it works for me. At least it has up to this point.”

I gasp with hope. “So you’ll show me your face? You’ll tell me your name?”

He chuckles, and that sexy and raspy voice of his makes me shiver.

“Not quite so fast, Francesca.”

I smile. “I noticed you stopped calling me Angel. But I still prefer Frankie.”

“I’m doing what you asked me to do. I’m calling you by your name.”

“And I’d like to do the same for you.”

“Perhaps in time.”

“I saw a few other people in the club who wore masks,” I say. “But very few, actually. Most people go in there showing the world who they are. Why don’t you?”

“I’ve told you. I like the fantasy.”

“Is this fantasy for you? Or for your partners?”

“For both. My partners find it as exciting as I do.”

“You mean you’ve never had a partner who’s asked you to take off the mask?”

“Occasionally I have. But for the most part, no. We play together for a scene. Maybe two or three if we like each other and have good chemistry. We’re only playmates, Francesca. I’m Phantom, and they are who they are. Our day-to-day lives have nothing to do with what happens at the club.”

“So that’s really what it is,” I say. “This is something you consider much different from your day-to-day life.”

"Don't you?"

"I've been to the club once. I never gave it an inkling of thought before that."

"Perhaps you should."

"I'll never get back in the club without you being with me."

"You could become a member yourself."

I lick my lower lip. "How do you do that? I would have no idea. I don't even know where the place is, and I'm sure I couldn't afford it."

"Membership is by invitation only."

"Then how could I become a member?"

"I've been a member in good standing for years. I could see that you get an invitation."

"So that's what you want, then? You want me to become a member?"

"That's not what I said."

I clench my hands into fists, ready to pull my own hair out. "You're driving me to the brink here, Phantom. What is it that *you* want?"

He pauses a moment, and just when I think he's not going to answer at all—

"At this moment, I want nothing more than to kiss those ruby red lips of yours."

I look around. "I don't see anyone stopping you."

"I'm stopping myself. Because while I could say all I would do is softly brush my lips over yours, I know I can't stop with that."

"So?"

"Look around," he says. "This is a classy place. Do you see anyone else making out in here?"

"Fine. Then take me to the club."

"I didn't bring my blindfold with me," he says. "Which should prove to you that I didn't come here looking to pick up another woman to take there."

"Then I'll close my eyes."

"I believe you would. But the owner makes the rules. I don't."

"You don't think he would trust me to keep my eyes closed?"

"Whether he trusts you is irrelevant. The rule is the rule. No guests go to the club without a blindfold. Only members."

"So you're saying you can't take me there tonight."

"That's correct. I can't. I didn't bring my blindfold or my collar."

"I'd bet Alfred has one."

"He may."

"Why don't you ask him?"

"Because I think we should wait until tomorrow evening."

"And why, exactly?"

"Because..."

"You can't even think of a good reason."

He clears his throat. "Alfred?"

Alfred comes toward us. "Yes, Phantom? Did you need a drink?"

"This young lady and I would like to enter the club, but I find myself without a blindfold and collar."

"Not a problem. I can hook you up." He leaves the bar and then returns with a black silk blindfold and a velvet ribbon, which he hands to Phantom. "Here you go."

"Thank you, Alfred." Phantom turns back to me. "May I?"

"Absolutely."

CHAPTER TWENTY-FIVE

Frankie

Tonight is different.

Claude, looking just as burly as before, lets us breeze right through.

"Don't I need to sign something tonight?" I ask Phantom.

"No. The NDA covers you for a year."

"I see."

"We'll be limited as to what we can do tonight," Phantom says. "Because I didn't expect to meet you or anyone, I didn't reserve a private suite."

Disappointment courses through me. My nipples are hard and my pussy is already wet, and I was hoping…

"What do we do, then?"

"I suppose we could play in one of the open rooms, but as I told you, I'm not an exhibitionist, and I'm pretty sure you're not, either."

"You're right about that."

At least I think he's right. I honestly never gave it much thought, but the idea of having sex in front of a bunch of other people? And knowing that they're getting turned on by watching me?

Actually…doesn't sound all that bad.

In fact… It's a little freaky… Kinky… And exciting.

"What if I wanted to try that?" I ask.

"Exhibitionism isn't a hard limit for me," he says, "but it's not how I would prefer to be with you. What we do together is our business and no one else's."

"When you put it that way…"

"Are you thinking you might like to try?"

"I don't know. Part of me would like to. The other part of me agrees with you. It's not anyone's business."

"You can be assured of your privacy here—I mean as far as confidentiality goes. Everyone here takes it very seriously, and all the years I've been a member, there's never been a breach."

"What would happen if there were?" I ask.

"Obviously the person would be expelled from the club. As for any other damages, I don't know."

"Everyone takes a big chance being here," I say.

"Yes, you have to have a certain amount of trust in your fellow club members. But people who are serious about the art of BDSM also take their privacy and the privacy of their fellow human beings very seriously."

"How do you know that?"

"Because most people are like me. This is a side of themselves that some people on the outside wouldn't appreciate, and we all understand that."

"That makes sense."

"So…as I said, exhibitionism is not a hard limit for me, but are you sure it's something you want to try on your second time here?"

He makes a good point. No, I don't want to have sex in

front of other people here. At least not yet.

"Can we go to the room again? The room where people are playing without…toys?"

"Of course."

"I'm not saying I want to do anything, but I'd like to see what *they're* doing."

"Absolutely."

We walk through the club, and I glance here and there at the people out in the open. One couple is dancing completely naked, gazing into each other's eyes. Another couple wears club clothing—the blond woman dressed in a tight blue miniskirt and a tube top, and the dark-haired man in jeans and a white button-down. Then, of course, many are dressed in leather attire. We pass through the dance floor and into the hallway where the exhibition and private rooms are.

"Here you go." Phantom opens the door to the room I chose, waving to the security guard as we walk in.

Scenes take place before my eyes in all parts of the room. There are beds, armchairs, and tables, most of them occupied. One young man is masturbating as he watches.

Instinctively, I look away.

"He wants you to watch him," Phantom says.

"But it's very private."

"This is an exhibition room."

"Oh my God, so he's an exhibitionist? I thought he was here to watch. A voyeur."

"He's clearly both. If he were simply a voyeur, he wouldn't be masturbating here, where anyone can see him."

I move my gaze toward the couple the man is watching.

The man's back is to me as he thrusts his dick into a woman who's bent over an armchair.

My gaze falls on the strawberry birthmark near his waistline. My God, it's just like—

I gasp.

"Francesca?" Phantom says. "You can't do that in here. It's considered—"

"You don't understand. That's—" I walk toward the back of the man.

Yes, I was right.

It's—

Phantom tugs on my arm, leads me out of the room, and back into the hallway.

"I'm sorry, but this was a mistake. You can*not* act like that in here."

I gulp, trying to swallow down the nausea. "You don't understand."

"Believe me, I do. Sometimes I see things here that make me want to gasp. But you must not be judgmental."

"Judgmental? About what was going on in there? It was just sex." I swallow down the puke that's ready to erupt out of my throat. "But I recognize that guy. It's Pendleton Berry, my ex-fiancé."

CHAPTER TWENTY-SIX

Phantom

Francesca's eyes glisten.

Pendleton Berry.

I know the name. Everyone knows the Berrys. They're old Manhattan money. Penn Berry is a newer member, but if he and Francesca only broke up a month or two ago…

He's been coming here for over a year.

I don't need to tell her that.

"I'm sorry," I say.

"Just get me out of here, please."

We whisk out of the club then, and after I blindfold her, I lead her back up to the bar, where I remove the silk from her eyes.

They're still glistening, as if tears are going to emerge at any moment.

My heart sinks. I can't bear to see her hurt, and I really can't bear to see her hurt over another guy.

"I can't believe it," she says, sniffling. "He told me he was seeing someone, but I never imagined that…"

"That he was into the same things I'm into?" I can't help

the anger that laces my tone.

"I didn't mean it that way."

"Do you still have feelings for this man?"

"No." She shakes her head adamantly. "That doesn't mean I want to see him fucking someone else in a sex club."

"Did you not consider the fact that you might see someone you know there?"

"Of course I considered it. I just didn't think it would be him."

"I once saw someone I knew," I say. "In fact, that's what led me to begin masking myself."

"Who did you see?"

"Just someone from my work. Luckily, she didn't see me."

"What kind of work do you do?"

I stroke her cheek gently. "You know, I *will* tell you, Francesca."

"I'm listening."

"I can't. Not yet. But the fact that I want to is strange indeed."

"Why is it strange?"

"Because," I tell her, "it's the first time I've ever wanted to."

CHAPTER TWENTY-SEVEN

Frankie

My jaw drops.

"That surprises you."

"Yes, it does." I grab a tissue out of the box Alfred pushes toward me. "I'm also just… I never imagined Penn…"

"Perhaps you and I should wait," Phantom says. "Postpone tomorrow evening's date until you're sure that your feelings for Penn are in the past."

"Phantom, they *are* in the past." I dab the tissue at my eyes. "They've been in the past for a long time. Even while I was planning the wedding. I just can't believe what I saw. And if he was coming here while— I mean, who knows who he was fucking?" I squirm on the stool.

"Part of being a member of the club is submitting to monthly STD testing," Phantom says, his voice irritated. "You have nothing to concern yourself with."

"My God, I didn't even *think* of that!" I shake my head. "The entire world is imploding."

"Which is why I think we should wait," he says.

"So you won't be here tomorrow night, then? Looking

for someone else to play with?"

"Didn't I just promise you earlier that while you and I are playing together, I won't play with anyone else?"

He did, of course. Just… Seeing Penn… I'm not thinking straight.

"I don't know. I need to go home."

"All right."

I pull my credit card out of my purse. "I have to pay for that Diet Coke I ordered."

"Don't worry about that. I had Alfred put it on my tab."

I sniffle. "That's kind of you. Thank you."

"Let me take you home," he says.

"I… I'm usually more careful than that. I don't let anyone know where I live when I don't know his name."

"If I tell you my name, will you let me see you home?"

"Will you take off your mask?"

"No. But I will give you my name. That is, my first name."

I sigh. "All right. But I don't know why you need to take me home. I can easily catch a cab or an Uber."

"Because I want to know that you got there safely. I want to see you to your door and make sure you get in. You're distraught right now, Frankie, and I want to know you're safe."

His words could so easily be a silver-tongued lie, but I believe him. Against my better judgment, I believe him.

"All right. Thank you for your concern…Phantom."

He kisses my cheek, and tingles float through me. "It's Hunter," he says. "My name is Hunter."

Hunter.

Such a sexy and masculine name. "Hunter," I echo.

"Francesca," he says.

"I detest the name Francesca. You seem to like to call

me by my given name, but please just make it Frankie."

"Okay. Frankie it is. But Francesca is so beautiful. It fits you."

"It's not beautiful. It's ugly. It means Frenchman."

"Where did you get that idea?"

"I looked it up once."

"Probably on some search engine and you just believed the first thing you read."

"Well…maybe."

"You should know, then, that Francesca simply means free. And free is a beautiful thing. Free to be who you are. I think Pendleton Berry was most likely holding you back."

"That's a given."

"You're free of him now. Free to be who you're meant to be. Would the Frankie who was with Penn ever think about entering such a club?"

"No. And I guess he knew that, too, because he certainly never invited me there."

"You came willingly with me."

"That's different. I was looking for something. For excitement."

"I believe you were, but I also believe you're not the type of woman who normally would go to a private club with someone you just met."

"And who wears a mask," I add.

"Precisely."

I laugh. Sort of. Then I meet his gaze. "How do you know what my name means?"

"I'm a student of language."

I smile. "You just revealed something about yourself."

He returns my smile. "So I did."

"So what do you do, then?"

"Does it matter? Anyone can be a student of language. Perhaps I'm a mechanic who fixes cars all day but who also loves the study of language and beauty."

"Anyone can appreciate that sort of thing, but somehow I don't see you as a mechanic."

"Why?"

I grab one of his hands. "There's not a speck of dirt under these fingernails."

He smiles. "Observant."

I lightly caress his hand. "Your hands, while they're very clean, are clearly not professionally manicured."

"True."

"Which means…you probably don't come from wealth."

"I know several men who come from wealth," he says, "and none of them get professional manicures."

"Penn used to."

"I'm glad I don't, then. I don't want to ever remind you of him."

"God, you don't. You're everything that Penn isn't."

"Although we both appear to be members of the same club." He looks around.

"I suppose we shouldn't be talking about this."

"Not at the bar, anyway." He rises from his stool. "Let me take you home, Frankie."

CHAPTER TWENTY-EIGHT

Hunter

Hunter *is* my name.

I considered giving her a fake name, but I did promise to reveal it, and lying didn't feel right. I wanted her to know my real name, just as I know hers.

Francesca.

I love that name, but she doesn't, so I'll call her Frankie.

Because I want to please her.

I want to please this woman more than I've ever wanted to please another. And that's saying a lot for me because as a Dominant, it's imperative that I please my submissive.

Frankie will be a good submissive.

But I'm not thinking of her in that way. At least not *solely* in that way. I'm already considering her to be more than a playmate.

It's frightening but also invigorating.

So invigorating that I actually gave her my own first name. She now knows more about me than any woman I've been with in the last several years.

I get into a cab with her, and she gives the cabbie her

address. She lives in a decent area, in a building with a doorman and security. I breathe a sigh of relief.

I live in a converted brownstone in an area that's safe but not quite as nice as her building. I could afford better, but my flat suits me.

When we arrive, I help her out of the cab, still wearing my mask and cape.

"Please let me see you up," I say.

"I'm perfectly safe, Phantom." She laughs lightly. "I mean Hunter."

I warm at the sound of my name from her lips.

Warmth with goosebumps. An odd sensation.

"Hunter is a beautiful name. I'm not a student of language, but I'm pretty sure I know what it means."

"In this case, it means exactly what you think it means."

"Does your family hunt?"

"No. Hunter is actually my grandmother's maiden name."

"Well, it is a beautiful name."

"So is Francesca."

She makes a face. "If you say so."

"I do. And I also insist that you let me walk you up."

She sighs. "I suppose it's okay. You already know where I live now."

We walk past the doorman.

"Good evening, Ms. Thomas," he says.

"Good evening, Clancy."

Once in the building, we take the elevator to the fourth floor. She leads me down the hallway to apartment 471.

I etch it into my memory.

Not that I'll forget anything about Francesca Thomas anytime soon.

She pulls out her key, and I take it from her, unlocking

her door. Then I kiss her on her lips.

"Good night, Frankie."

"Good night, Hunter."

She doesn't invite me in, and that's okay. This was a rough night for her, seeing her ex at the club. I wait until she's inside and the lock clicks.

Then I leave.

CHAPTER TWENTY-NINE

Frankie

Hunter.

It's late. After one a.m.

Hunter.

It's not much, but it's something. It's a first name.

I also know he's well-versed in world literature, and that he's a student of language. His favorite musical is *Camelot*. His favorite novel is *The Great Gatsby*. He kisses like a dream.

And his first name is Hunter.

Not Erik with a K, although I suppose he could still be the person I spoke to in the chat room, since I asked for pseudonyms.

But already I know he's not.

I know because when I ask a question he doesn't want to answer, he doesn't lie to me. He just doesn't reply.

Interesting.

I'm exhausted, so I wash my face quickly and head to bed. And I hope to dream about a masked man named Hunter.

• • •

Morning comes quickly, and I get up for my jog—

And I remember.

Crap.

I'm supposed to meet Tom Carson for a jog in Central Park.

I could easily break the date. I have his number, and I could text him. But I'm not a rude person. And Hunter and I… Well, he's agreed not to have sex with anyone else as long as we're having sex, but he didn't agree not to go jogging with anyone else.

So why should I agree to that?

I take a quick shower, dress in my running shoes with some leggings and a sports bra, and I head to Central Park.

Tom is already there, stretching. "You're not known for your punctuality, are you?"

"Nope, just running a little bit late." I give my hamstrings a stretch. "Sorry about that."

"No problem. Let's go."

"What route do you like to take?"

"The full loop is about six miles. So a quarter? A mile and a half and then back? We can keep track with our apps."

"Sounds great to me," I say. "Let's go. Last one there's a rotten egg."

I have no idea why I said that. I never race when I jog. We end up keeping pretty much apace with each other, and it gives us a good chance to not talk.

I'm used to doing Five K runs, so this is easy. The run takes only twenty minutes, and soon we're back where we started, wiping off with towels and taking deep drinks from our water bottles.

"How about a cup of coffee?" Tom says.

What the heck? I could use some caffeine, and coffee is just coffee. "Sure. Sounds good."

We walk a few blocks to a Bean There Done That and enter. I grab my credit card out of my phone case, but Tom shakes his head at me.

"Please. My treat."

"No, let me. You paid for dinner last night."

He smiles. "Okay. But just this once."

It may only be this once, but I don't say that. "Black coffee for me," I tell the cashier. "Whatever he wants."

"I'll have a cinnamon mocha," he says.

Ugh. He likes froufrou coffee drinks.

Not that I don't like a cinnamon mocha on occasion, but it's mostly just empty calories. Of course, Tom is training for a marathon, so he doesn't have to worry about calories.

I slide my credit card through the reader and add a tip while the barista pours my black coffee. "The cinnamon mocha will be up in a few minutes."

"Sounds good."

I turn and find Tom at a table by the window. I join him. "Your cinnamon mocha will be up soon."

"Great," he says, "and thank you again."

I pull the lid off my coffee and inhale the aroma from the steam that rises. "I love the smell of coffee."

"Do you? I can only drink the stuff when it's loaded with cream and sugar."

"And cinnamon and chocolate," I say.

"Yeah, that helps."

"I like it just black like this. Been drinking it since I was a kid. This new coffee shop is even better than Starbucks, in my opinion."

"I wouldn't know," he says. "They all taste the same to me."

"Definitely not a coffee connoisseur."

He laughs. "No, I'm not. But I can give you good bourbon any day. Or a single malt scotch."

I wrinkle my nose. "Yuck."

"What can I expect from a woman who likes martinis and black coffee?" He smiles.

I take a sip of the coffee, let its robust goodness slide across my tongue and down my throat.

"What are your plans for the rest of the day?" I ask. Then I want to kick myself. He's going to think I want to get together.

"Unfortunately, I have to go into work for a few hours."

Saved by work. "Yeah, I should work as well."

My group chat with the five sources is scheduled for tomorrow, but I need to get my materials and questions together.

I take another sip of my coffee. It's the perfect temperature now. It's always too hot when I first order, so I always take the plastic lid off of it and let the steam escape. A few minutes later, it's the perfect temperature—still hot but not scalding.

"Black coffee, please. Leave room for just a touch of cream."

I jerk at the voice coming from the counter.

I know that voice.

Deep and husky and—

I see only his back. He's tall, and he's dressed in running shorts and an Under Armour T-shirt.

His legs are long, covered in the perfect amount of dark

hair, and oh my God, his calves… Did he swallow a couple volleyballs?

Broad shoulders, the sleeves of his T-shirt are tight around his biceps, and—

The barista hands him a cup of coffee, and he turns—

Those eyes.

I'd know those dark eyes anywhere.

Phantom.

Hunter.

That jawline, those full lips.

And oh my God… Seeing him without the mask? He's everything I imagined he would be and so much more.

High cheekbones, perfect black stubble, a few creases on his forehead, and a straight Grecian nose. His dark hair is slightly wavy—not slicked back like he wears it with his costume—and sticks to the sides of his face.

I gape.

I can't help it.

His eyes widen when he recognizes me, and he heads straight for the door of the coffee shop.

I rise abruptly, nudging the table and nearly spilling my coffee. "Excuse me for a moment," I say to Tom.

I race toward Hunter just as he's exiting.

"Hunter!"

He doesn't stop, but his shoulders tense.

Only subtly, but I notice.

I close the distance between us with rapid steps and touch his arm. "Don't run away from me, Hunter."

"I think you've mistaken me for someone else."

"You really want to pull that?"

He says nothing for a few moments, and we simply stand there, staring at each other—he holding his coffee—about ten feet from the entrance to the coffee shop. Through the window, Tom watches us.

"I can't lie to you," Hunter finally says. "I don't lie."

"Good. I don't want you to."

"You were never meant to see my face."

"Well, now I have. Does that mean we don't have a date tonight?"

"Seems you already have a date." He cocks his head toward Tom through the window.

"He's just a friend. We went on a jog together this morning."

"And I'm supposed to believe that? He's the guy from last night, isn't he?"

None of his business. "Believe what you want. But look at how I'm dressed. How he's dressed. How *you're* dressed, for that matter."

"I run every day," he says. "I already told you I enjoy running. I'm training for a marathon."

"Are you? So is Tom. I'm not, though. I only run Five Ks at a time."

He doesn't reply for a moment, but then, "Don't let me keep you from your companion."

"Why are you doing this?" I blurt out.

Again, no response. At least not at first.

Until—

"I'm uncomfortable, as you can well see. This isn't how I..." He rubs at his forehead, "Damn it!" He sets his coffee on a window ledge, grabs me, and presses his lips to mine.

I open for him instantly. Our tongues tangle. Yes, we're making out, right here in public in front of Tom and everyone else in the coffee shop.

And I don't care.

I absolutely don't care.

Until Hunter breaks the kiss abruptly. "Forgive me," he mumbles.

"Forgive what? Did you see me resisting?"

"I'm not good at this," he says.

"And that's why you hide behind a mask?"

"I've already told you why I wear a mask," he says. "It's part of the fantasy for me."

"Fantasy," I repeat. "What's your *reality*, Hunter?"

"I don't discuss my reality with sexual partners."

"What if I were more than a sexual partner? What if I were a friend?"

"That's not the way I do things," he says simply.

"Why is that?"

"Does there have to be a reason?"

"I think there's usually a reason for most things you do in life, whether you realize it or not."

Two young women walk by us. "Hi, Professor Stone," one of them says.

Professor Stone? He knows literature. He's a student of language.

Of course. A professor.

"Good morning," he says, waving to them.

"Professor Stone..." I say.

"Frankie..."

"Professor Hunter Stone. Someone who knows literature. Someone who's a student of language. I'd say you're an English professor somewhere."

He doesn't say anything.

"So I'm right, then. Where do you teach?"

"Frankie..."

"Hunter, I can easily search for you on the Internet.

Professor Hunter Stone. I *will* find you."

He gazes at the coffee shop window. "Don't you have someone in there you need to attend to?"

I glance over to the table where Tom was sitting. He's gone.

"Apparently not. I guess he saw us kissing."

"I'm sorry."

"Why? I'm not. I told you he's just a friend."

"If he were a friend, he'd still be there. Apparently he wanted a little more from you than friendship."

"He's not going to get it. I'm only interested in one man, and it's not him."

"You don't even know the man you're interested in," Hunter says.

"I'd like to."

He sighs. "Come on." He takes a seat at one of the outside tables and motions for me to join him.

I sit across from him, give him a good once-over. He's clearly been exercising, as his hair is messy and slicked down with sweat at his hairline.

"I'm a professor of English literature at Mellville," he says.

My alma mater, no less. "I see. Where did you study?"

"Mellville."

"So you didn't stray far from home, then."

"No. I'm comfortable there. It's a good school."

"I know." I smile. "I went there too."

"Oh? What did you study?"

"English and journalism. But I only got my bachelor's. I went straight into the workforce after I graduated."

"When did you graduate?"

"Are you asking me my age? I graduated five years ago.

I'm twenty-seven."

"And you're already a junior editor at a major magazine? That's pretty amazing, Frankie."

"Believe me, I've paid my dues. I did nothing more than get coffee for the first two years. But I'm happy with how things are going."

"Good."

"What about you? When did you graduate?"

"I finished my PhD five years ago. In English and comparative literature."

"*The Great Gatsby*."

His brown eyes brighten. "You remembered. My favorite book."

"So that doesn't really tell me how old you are, Hunter. People finish graduate work at all different ages."

"I'm thirty-five."

"How did you end up as a professor back at Mellville?"

He doesn't respond at first.

"The cat is already out of the bag, Hunter."

"This is difficult for me," he says. "No one at the club—other than the owner, who had to approve my application, and Claude—knows who I really am. I keep that part of my life separate."

"I understand. Your secret is safe with me."

"I'm not worried about that."

"That's good, because I signed that nondisclosure agreement. So even if I wanted to, I couldn't say anything."

He doesn't reply.

"And I don't want to, Hunter. I would never do that to you. I'd never do that to anyone."

"What about your ex-fiancé?"

"I can't tell anyone else I saw him there, but I can

definitely mention it to him."

"Will you?"

"No. I don't want to talk to him—especially not at the club."

"Does this mean our date is off? Are you uncomfortable at the club?"

"No. I don't want it to be off, Hunter. I'd like to go."

"What if he's there again?"

"It doesn't matter. Not if we're in our own private room."

"You don't care if he sees you there?"

"I assume he signed the same NDA that I did."

"He would've had to."

"Then what does it matter?"

"I don't want to be a pawn in some kind of game," Hunter says. "Maybe you *want* him to see you there."

I shake my head. "Did you really just say that?"

"It's a valid concern."

"Penn and I are over, Hunter. He admitted to me that he had been cheating on me, and now I know where it went down."

"Did you and he…?"

"Do anything kinky? No, we didn't. Totally vanilla sex, usually in missionary. In fact, he was pretty boring."

"Does it bother you that he never wanted to do more with you?"

"You want me to be honest?"

"Of course."

"It irks me a little. But honestly, I'm over him. It was a lot easier getting over the loss of him than it was getting over the humiliation of the whole thing."

"So you've said."

"Yes, so I've said. And I'm not a liar, Hunter, and I resent the implication that I am."

"I wasn't implying any such thing."

"Weren't you?"

Anger nips at my neck. I like this guy. I really like this guy. What's going on with him? He clearly had a good time with me, or he wouldn't have asked me out again.

"Why were you convinced that my name was Erik with a K?"

Okay... That's a little out of left field. But why not level with him?

"I'm doing an article on the BDSM lifestyle in Manhattan for the magazine, and I—"

"You're *what*?"

"Researching an article, and—"

"Frankie, you can't do that."

"Why not? Everything will be anonymous."

"I don't want to be the subject of any article."

"I didn't say you would be, Hunter."

"How can I *not* be?" He takes a sip of his coffee and then sets the paper cup down so harshly that some of the hot liquid spills onto the table.

"You won't be. I won't—"

"This part of my life is personal," he says. "I've already shared too much with you. I should've known better." He rises and tosses his nearly full coffee cup into a nearby trashcan. "It was nice knowing you, Frankie. Don't bother going to the bar tonight."

CHAPTER THIRTY

Hunter

Now I know why Frankie was hanging around that bar. Why she was so eager to go to the club with me.

It was the plan all along.

A plan to get information for a magazine story.

I won't be a part of it.

I keep my private life private for a reason.

I'm not ashamed of what I do at the club. I'm not ashamed of my proclivities. I never have been.

But professors have to be careful. The university would frown upon one of its tenured professors frequenting a leather club.

And yes, the confidentiality agreements provide safety, but only to a certain point—as evidenced by Frankie's admission that she's researching an article.

I'm angry, yes.

But more so I'm…sad.

I was feeling something for this woman. For this woman I barely know.

Something drew me to her.

I know her address, but I don't know how to reach her.

Maybe she'll show up at the bar.

God, I hope so, but why would she? I treated her like shit.

Maybe…

She works for *Lovely* magazine…which means she may have a work email that's public.

I get to my brownstone as quickly as I can. It's small, only one bedroom and an office, and it takes up half of the second floor of the brownstone.

I fire up my computer to find Francesca.

Doesn't take long. Francesca Thomas, junior editor. Frankie@lovelymag.com. Getting in touch with her is a different matter. I can email her at the magazine, but she may not get that until Monday morning.

But it's my only shot. I'm not a stalker. I could look her up on social media, but I can't stand social media. I have accounts on each of the big ones, but I never use them. It's better not to, because it's difficult when you get friend requests from your students.

I compose an email.

Frankie,

I'm sorry about today. I was so out of line, and I hope you can forgive me. You probably won't get this until Monday, but on the off chance that you do, I'm going to be there tonight at the bar at eight o'clock. I hope you'll be there, too. I do want to know you better.

Hunter

I considered signing it Phantom, but she knows who I am now. There's no need to hide behind a mask.

Besides…we can still have the fantasy.

Will she show up?

I have no idea.

But I will be there. In the meantime? I'll be reading term papers.

Fun afternoon. A day in the life of Professor Hunter Stone.

I love my job, but I also love my sex life.

Maybe this can work. Maybe I can get to know someone both in and out of the club.

Maybe…

CHAPTER THIRTY-ONE

Frankie

I shower, trying to wash the memory of Hunter Stone from me, but to no avail. I exit the shower, squeaky clean, still wanting him as much as ever.

Nothing that a few hours of work can't erase from my head. Right? I fire up the laptop to get some research done.

And–

On my work email…

Frankie,

I'm sorry about today. I was so out of line, and I hope you can forgive me. You probably won't get this until Monday, but on the off chance that you do, I'm going to be there tonight at the bar at eight o'clock. I hope you'll be there, too. I do want to know you better.

Hunter

I can't help the ridiculous squishy feeling that consumes me. He's right. He was an ass this morning, but this email is good news. I smile as I continue to work. What shall I wear this evening? I don't have any sex clothes, and frankly, those aren't really me anyway.

So what if I run into Penn?

Except…I'd rather not.

I could wear the blue mask again—the one that I wore to the masquerade.

If Hunter can use a mask for fantasy, so can I. Even if I am using it so Penn won't see me if he's there. But I'm being ridiculous. He and I were together for five years. Of course he'd recognize me. Fuck.

I'm ready by seven o'clock in the black dress and mask from Chinatown and my platform pumps. I need to go shoe shopping. I've already called an Uber to take me to the bar. The ride should be here in five minutes.

But then a knock on the door. I peer through my peephole—

It's Hunter. Masked and caped and luscious.

I open the door. "What are you doing here?"

"I sent you an email."

"I know. I got it." I smile.

"You did?" He widens his eyes. "I wasn't sure you'd get it until Monday, and…"

"And what?"

"I didn't want to wait until Monday to apologize to you. I'm sorry, Frankie."

I warm all over. "Thank you for that."

"If you got my email, why didn't you respond?"

"Is it such a bad thing to keep you guessing a little bit?"

"It's not a bad thing," he says in his deep voice. "But I feared you wouldn't come, which is why I came here."

"Right, because you know where I live."

"Yes."

I hold the door open. "Won't you come in?"

"Thank you." He enters.

My phone dings. “My Uber is here.”

“So you *were* going to go to the club.”

I gesture to my outfit. “Uh…yeah. Do you think I dress this way for my health?”

He smiles then, and I desperately want him to remove his mask. I already know who he is. But I can’t ask him to do it. I feel like he needs to do it of his own accord.

And I’m surprised when he does just that, removing it along with his cape and hanging them on my coat rack by the door.

“Should I cancel the ride?” I ask.

“Yes,” he says. “For now, anyway.”

I cancel the Uber and then turn to Hunter. “Can I get you anything? I’m afraid I don’t have the ingredients to make one of your famous martinis, but I have white wine. And some red.”

“Red would be nice,” he says.

“I’ll get it for you. I don’t have much to eat in the house. I usually do my shopping on Sunday afternoons, but I can probably scare something up.”

“No, I’m fine. I had dinner.”

I nod and head to my small kitchen, pull a bottle of Pinot Noir off my rack, and uncork it. I pour two glasses and bring them to the couch where he’s sitting. I hand one glass to him. “It’s Pinot Noir from Washington state. I hope you like it.”

“I usually like anything red, as long as it’s not sweet.”

I smile. “So do I.” I take a sip.

He does the same, and then he takes another.

“So why did you come here?” I ask.

“I wanted to see you.”

“I was planning to meet you at the bar, as you know.”

"I had no reason to believe you would, especially after my behavior today."

I say nothing. What is there to say? He did behave badly.

"Would it be so bad to get to know each other?" I finally ask.

"No," he says. "It's just that…I haven't had a relationship with a woman in over five years."

I'm not overly surprised, considering he's already told me he only plays at the club. "Why?"

"It seems easier to just keep things…*professional*, you know?"

"No, I don't know. Having sex with someone isn't professional."

"I didn't mean it that way. Not like I'm having sex for money or anything. I guess a more apt term would be *impersonal*."

"But how can anything that intimate be impersonal?"

"It's a transaction. Scenes at the club for me are a way to live out my needs and help another live out hers, with nothing else between us."

"And your partners are always okay with that?"

"Yes. We lay out our expectations beforehand."

"What about the people like me, who you meet at the bar and then take to the club?"

"Actually…"

"Don't tell me I'm the first. You said—"

He covers my lips with his fingers. "I know what I said. You're not the first person I met at the bar as Phantom. And you're not the first person I took downstairs. But you're the first person I've wanted to reveal myself to."

"I see. What made you change your mind for me?"

"I don't know, Frankie. I wish I did. Something about you…"

"You're attracted to me." I give him the words.

"I think that's pretty obvious."

"But I assume you're attracted to the other people you play with."

"Of course I am. Physically."

"So it's more than physical for you with me?" I warm inside.

"It is, and what I can't understand is *why*."

"Here's a thought, Hunter." I playfully elbow him in his ribs. "Maybe you *like* me."

"I do like you. I like everyone I play with. But with you, it's…"

"It's more. You want to get to know me."

"Yes."

"And what exactly is wrong with that?"

"It's not something I do."

"All right." I take a drink of my wine. "Let's lay it on the line, Hunter. Who burned you in the past?"

He goes quiet, then.

Yep. I nailed it.

"You heard *my* story," I say.

"Yes, left at the altar."

"Not quite. We didn't make it to the altar. I can at least thank him for saving me *that* humiliation."

Hunter shakes his head and swallows another sip of wine. "That's looking at the glass half full."

I chuckle. "That's what Mandy, my sister, would say. She's a glass-half-empty kind of person. I'm the opposite." I sigh. "At least I was."

"You still are. One bad experience doesn't change who you are."

I lift my eyebrows. "Oh? It doesn't?"

Hunter doesn't take my bait—not that I'm surprised.

"Do you think Penn would have left you at the altar if it had gone that far?" he asks.

Great. We're still talking about Penn. "I don't know. He said he'd been cheating on me for a year, so why did he stay with me? Why did he continue the charade of being with me? Why did he finally set a wedding date? He was obviously already cheating on me at that point."

"I don't know. Maybe he got cold feet."

"No. Penn only does things if there's something in it for him. I would have made the right kind of wife for him. Young, professional, you know."

"And, of course, gorgeous."

My cheeks warm. "If you say so."

"I say so." He takes another sip. "There must be some reason why he decided to level with you before the wedding."

I shrug. "Maybe he fell in love with somebody else? One of his partners at the club?"

"Or maybe… Maybe someone saw him… Told him he'd better tell you."

"Who could've seen him? It would have to be someone who knew him and who knew me."

"And you don't know anyone who goes to the club."

"Besides you? I sure don't."

"Why do you think you don't?"

"What are you saying?"

"I'm saying someone must have seen him there. Someone who knows you. Given what you've told me, it's the only explanation that makes sense."

My curiosity is piqued. Who do I know who goes to the club? Only Isabella, and I don't know if she was at that particular club. Besides, if she were the one, she'd have leveled with me when she admitted to being in the lifestyle.

Doesn't really matter.

I already know what Hunter's doing. He's deflected the conversation to me when we were supposed to be talking about him. How *he* got burned, not how I got burned.

"Nice try," I say.

"What do you mean?"

"Getting me to talk about Penn instead of you talking about who burned *you*."

Another sip of wine. "I don't talk about that."

"You just said you wanted to get to know me."

"I do. And damn, that bugs the hell out of me."

I can't help chuckling. "You know what? I think you got burned badly. Really badly."

He says nothing.

"You know what else? I bet it happened more than once."

"What makes you say that?"

"I did an article a year or so ago for the magazine, all about the psychology of people who get burned by someone they care about. I recognize the signs. You could be the poster child."

He raises his eyebrows. "So now you're a psychologist."

"No. I'm a magazine writer and editor who did a lot of research on this particular subject. That's what I am, Hunter."

"I see."

"And you're a professor. A learned man. A teacher. A scholar. A student of language. A student of love."

He sets his glass down on my coffee table. "A student of love?"

"You teach literature, Hunter. What is the greatest theme in all of literature?"

He smiles, then—a big, beautiful smile.

My God, he's handsome.

"I suppose you're right," he says.

I smirk. "You *suppose*?"

"You're absolutely right, Frankie."

"So you understand love, and you've been burned."

"As have you."

"We have that in common. And I still say you've been burned more than once."

"All right. I'll bite. You're correct. I have been burned more than once. But the first one wasn't her fault."

"What happened?"

He clears his throat. "She died, Frankie. She died."

CHAPTER THIRTY-TWO

Hunter

I don't talk about Allison. Not ever. It was ten years ago now, and at the time I thought she was the love of my life. I didn't think I'd ever feel anything again.

Until I met Teresa.

She turned out to be...

Well, I don't like to use those words.

"Tell me," Frankie prods.

And I want to.

I want to tell her the whole damned story. Want to pour out my soul to this woman I hardly know. This woman who somehow managed to crawl under my skin and start to chip away at the cement around my heart.

And I don't even know her. I don't get it. This is so not me.

"Her name was Allison," I say. "We met our first year at Mellville. Our first week, actually. We lived in the same dorm, and our eyes met during orientation."

"Love at first sight?" she asks.

"No. More like lust at first sight. Kind of like..."

"Like you felt with me," she says.

"Yes."

She places her hand on my forearm. "That explains why you're fighting it so hard. Go on."

I close my eyes, but the images flash before me. Allison, with her reddish blond hair and light brown eyes, the spray of freckles across her nose. She wasn't classically beautiful like Frankie is, but she had a girl-next-door quality that men found irresistible. She was pursued by several upperclassmen, but for some reason, she chose me.

"She was smart, and we shared a lot of interests," I say.

"And…?"

"We were friends first. For about two months, but I was falling hard, and one day I took a chance. I kissed her."

"And she kissed you back."

"Yeah. It turned out she felt the same way. She had been dating this upperclassman, and I was so jealous."

"So she dumped him for you?"

"She did, and we were together for the next six years."

"What happened?"

"Car accident," I say matter-of-factly. "She died instantly, which I was thankful for. I mean, later. At first, I wasn't thankful for anything."

Frankie pauses. "I'm so sorry. Did you have any plans to get married?"

"We had just set a date. I hadn't bought the ring yet, though."

"And did she…share your proclivities?"

I nod. "She did."

"Did you ever take her to the club?"

"The club didn't exist at that time. It's only about six years old. And I didn't belong to any club back then."

"So how did you…"

"At home. In our bedroom."

"So you lived together."

"We did, since our junior year of college."

"I'm so sorry, Hunter."

"I've made my peace with it," I say.

The words are true. If Allison had lived, we'd probably still be together. But she didn't live. I mourned for nearly a year, until I decided it was time to move on. With the help of a therapist, I did.

"So who's the next one who burned you?" Frankie asks. "Or I should say, *the* one who burned you. Because with Allison, it wasn't her fault."

"No, it wasn't Allison's fault, but that didn't make it hurt any less. Didn't make it any easier to go forward and try to find a new relationship."

"But you did," she says, "because you said you were burned more than once."

"I did. I figured, what were the chances of me losing another woman I love to a freak accident?"

"Pretty low."

"Exactly, and call me naive, but because what Allison and I had was so special, I never imagined…"

"You never imagined that a person you loved could turn out to be something different."

I nod.

I don't feel any words are necessary.

Frankie and I both know what we're talking about.

My relationship with Teresa nearly cost me my sanity.

After that, I began masking myself and going to a club. Playing only with submissives who wanted what I want, without a relationship of any kind.

"It's still difficult to talk about," I say.

"I'm curious," she admits, "but if you can't talk about it, Hunter, I understand."

"Maybe if you told me a little about you and Penn."

"Penn and I were together for nearly six years. We were on-again, off-again so often. We actually met at Mellville as well. We didn't get together until our senior year. He's a trust-fund baby. He never cared about his studies. He was kind of a bad boy, and, well…I was a good girl, so that attracted me." She looks down at her lap. "Plus his trust fund didn't hurt."

I suppose at some point I need to tell her I have a trust fund of my own. Not yet, though. "College professors aren't exactly overpaid."

She grins. "You don't think I'm after your money, do you?"

"I know you're not."

She laughs then, and it's a joyful sound. A sound that makes me feel happy inside. Like I want to hear that laugh every day.

"But that's the thing about Penn," she continues. "He was nothing like what I thought he'd be. He had this bad-boy reputation, but he wasn't a bad boy. He was a dick but not a bad boy. I can't believe I actually saw him at the club, because, like I said, all he was into was the purest vanilla sex."

"And that wasn't enough for you?"

"I pretended like it was. I pretended a lot of things with Penn. I kind of fell into a routine, and part of it was great. It was great being able to go to the most expensive places in town, to have him buy me lavish gifts. But we fought a lot. He'd say something stupid, and I'd walk out on him. A few weeks later he'd come back, and I'd forgive him. It was horribly codependent. Not healthy at all."

"Then maybe it's good that he came to you and confessed that he was cheating, so you could break the engagement."

"Oh, absolutely. I should've ended things with him years ago. But you just get used to the bad parts, you know?"

I know more than she knows.

That was part of the problem with Teresa. We had an intense physical chemistry, and I mistook that for something deeper.

Something deeper that she apparently never felt.

I thought I could replicate what I had with Allison. That it would be the same, just with a different person.

I learned it's never the same.

"Anyway," Frankie continues, "I learned a lot. Wasted five years of my life along the way."

"Time is never wasted if you learn something," I tell her.

It took me a long time to realize that myself.

But what I *did* learn was that I could never reproduce what Allison and I had, so I was no longer going to try. I'd find a place where I could satisfy my sexual desires without commitment, without a relationship of any kind. Where I didn't have to reveal anything more about myself than what I wanted in a scene.

And I found it.

I found Black Rose Underground.

CHAPTER THIRTY-THREE

Frankie

"Sounds like we're in kind of the same boat," I say. "You had Allison and then your next relationship, and that's it. I've pretty much only had Penn. I dated a little bit in high school and in college, but I never had anything serious. Penn was the first guy I said 'I love you' to. And the last."

"I've only said it twice," Hunter says.

"To Allison…and the other one."

"Teresa."

I resist widening my eyes. This is a big step for him already—I can tell. He said her name to me. For a man who wanted to keep himself masked, he's revealed more than I ever thought he would.

"She's the one I never talk about," he says.

Curiosity is of course gnawing at me, but he's already disclosed so much. This is a man who normally disguises himself to hide who he is from his sexual partners.

"Tell me something, Hunter," I say. "If I hadn't recognized you in the coffee shop, would you be telling me all of this now?"

He pauses...clearly thinking. Then, "No."

"Why? You've already said you're developing feelings for me."

"I am. And I've been fighting them, Frankie."

"Then why? Why did you come here? Why did you send me that email? You could've walked away."

"True. And I probably should have."

"How can you say that? After all you just shared with me. After all I've shared with you."

"Maybe I'm having second thoughts."

"Are you really?" My heart drops.

He sighs and finishes his glass of wine. "Actually, Frankie, I'm not. I'm not having second thoughts at all. I want to tell you everything. I want to tell you the hell Teresa put me through and the reason I stopped seeing women with the goal of having a relationship. Hell, I want to tell you what my favorite flavor of ice cream is. And it's driving me to the brink of madness."

I want to smile. A great big smile. But I don't. Because even though he wants these things, he's not happy about wanting them. I'm trying to understand, but I just don't.

"My favorite ice cream is vanilla," I offer. "Would you like some more wine?"

He shakes his head.

"A glass of water, maybe?"

He nods, so I rise, pad over to my tiny kitchen, and get a glass of water from the faucet. I return and hand it to him.

He downs almost all of it in one gulp.

"You okay?"

He sets the glass down on the table as if he's just taken a shot. "I'm so far from okay. I mean... Hell, I don't know what I mean."

My God. That woman—Teresa—must've done a real number on him. Is it possible she was worse than Penn?

"We don't have to talk, you know," I say. "There are… other things we could do."

He widens his eyes a bit, and then he scans my small apartment. "I don't see any toys here."

"Do we need toys, Hunter?"

"My God," he says. "I want to say no, we don't."

"Then say it."

"But that would mean…"

"That would mean regular old sex, Hunter. And you've trained yourself to think that's not what you want anymore."

"It's usually not."

"And…"

"I want it now, Frankie." His eyes narrow, darken. "I desperately want to fuck you, and I don't care if you're tied up. I don't care if you're gagged. I don't care if I don't get to spank that sweet little ass of yours. All I care about is getting my dick inside you. That's all I care about in this single moment."

This time I don't hold my smile back. I stand, and I begin to peel my dress from my shoulders. "Then what are you waiting for?"

CHAPTER THIRTY-FOUR

Hunter

God, she's so beautiful.

I suppose there's no rhyme or reason to love, is there?

God knows I've read enough books.

In *Pride and Prejudice*, Mr. Darcy fought his love for Elizabeth Bennet, but in the end it consumed him.

In *Jane Eyre*, Mr. Rochester was willing to commit bigamy to have the woman he loved.

In *The Scarlet Letter*, Hester paid dearly for falling in love with Arthur Dimmesdale.

In *The Great Gatsby*—my favorite novel of all time—Daisy Buchanan was married, but Jay Gatsby still loved her, still pursued her.

Why is it my favorite novel? Love and marriage are hardly portrayed in a positive way.

Yet it speaks to me on a visceral level.

That's probably why I've become so hard-hearted about the idea of relationships.

I decided, after Teresa, that I would only engage in transactional sex with submissives who were in it for the same reason I was—pure physical pleasure devoid of emotion.

I never thought I would want anything other than that.

But I do.

I want it with this woman.

This woman I barely know but who has somehow softened me.

Of course there's still the matter of the article she's writing. I don't want to be part of that.

But that thought disappears from my mind as she undresses in front of me.

She has a beautiful body. Long yet buxom, with slim hips and legs.

She's tall, and even after she kicks off her platform pumps, she's still tall.

She stands naked before me, her cheeks pink, her lips scarlet with lipstick, her fingernails and toenails both painted the same color—a blackish red.

Very vampy.

I suck in a breath at her beauty.

"Time for you to take off your clothes," she says.

"Maybe you're not understanding how this Dominant-and-submissive thing works," I say. "You don't tell me what to do. I tell *you* what to do."

"You didn't tell me to get undressed."

I rake my gaze over her—my God, she's beautiful—and she's also right. I didn't tell her to get undressed. Perhaps she should pay the price.

"True. And I'm going to have to punish you for that."

A subtle shudder racks her body. "Oh?" She tries to remain calm, but her voice cracks a bit.

"Yes. You may as well learn that lesson now."

"Look around," she says. "I don't have any rope here. No handcuffs. Not even a blindfold. No toys of any kind."

"Any good Dominant knows how to improvise." My voice is dark. "Believe me. I'll figure it out."

The tops of her breasts turn pink. Her nipples are protruding, so hard and ripe for my lips. I will suck on them, but not now. Right now, I promised her punishment, and if I renege, I won't be her Dominant. And I desperately want to be her Dominant. That has never been a question.

I want to be her Dominant.

The problem is that I want to be so much more to her.

But I'll start with being her Dominant. It's what I know.

I walk toward her, still fully clothed, and trail my finger down her cheek, her neck, over the tops of her breasts and lightly over one nipple. She gasps.

"You are beautiful, Frankie. So very beautiful." I softly touch her shoulders and turn her around so her back is to me. I sift my fingers through her hair, and then I slide my hands down her back and cup the globes of her ass.

"This is a beautiful ass. Tell me... Has it ever been spanked?"

Before she replies, I slap my palm against her right cheek.

She gasps again and turns to face me, her mouth forming an *O*. "Hunter!"

"If spanking is a hard limit for you," I say, "we may need to end this now."

"It's... I..."

I rub the cheek of her ass to ease the sting as I move my mouth close to her ear. "I will never do anything you don't want. Not ever. But tell me now if you can't handle this."

"What if I said I couldn't?" Her voice shakes.

"I—"

I stop.

What if she can't? This is the kind of sex I like, but do I want to give her up?

All the more reason why I shouldn't be pursuing any kind of relationship.

"Then I'm afraid we have no future," I force myself to say. "So I'm hoping you won't say that."

She melts against me. As I hold her naked body, I sniff her hair. Fruity and woodsy, like apples and patchouli. An amazing aroma, and for some reason it seems to fit her.

"I *can* handle it, Hunter," she says against my chest. "In fact…I liked it. It just surprised me. That's all."

I push her away from me so I can meet her gaze. "Are you sure, Frankie? You need to tell me the truth. We need to be truthful with each other if this is going to work. You need to tell me if I go too far. I could even give you a safe word."

A smile edges onto her lips. "What if I'm gagged? I wouldn't be able to use the safe word."

I can't help myself. I smile. With that one comment, I know Frankie and I are well matched. And apparently she does, too. "That's not for you to worry about. We'll have an alternative way for you to let me know."

"Hunter," she says, "I'm so tired of vanilla sex. It's all I had with Penn, and it's all I thought I'd ever get. Meeting you was like…getting glasses."

"What do you mean?"

"I used to be horribly nearsighted. I got laser surgery several years ago, but before that, I wore contacts. I first got glasses when I was in middle school. I hated the way I looked in them, but that's another story. Wearing them, though, was"—she chuckles—"eye-opening."

I smile. "Nice pun."

"Couldn't help myself. Anyway, before I ever had them on, I didn't realize what I was missing. I thought squinting my eyes to make the words on the blackboard less blurry was as good as it got. Once I got glasses… Well, you can infer the rest."

"I'm glad to hear all of that. And I'm glad you like what I'm offering." I cup her cheek, press my lips against hers softly. "But you still need to be punished."

"Okay," she says. "How do you want to punish me?"

"Maybe a spanking."

"All right."

I lead her to her small dining table. "Bend over."

She obeys me, bending over the table so her beautiful ass is at my beck and call.

I trail my fingers over one cheek and then the other, and then I dip between the crease, sliding over her asshole and then down to her pussy, where I dip my fingers.

"Wet," I say, my cock getting harder. "You *did* like that spanking."

"I…"

"No more talking," I say. "Unless you want me to stop. In which case your temporary safe word is 'stop.'"

"Why can't that just be my regular safe word?"

"It's not a safe word that's commonly used," I tell her.

"Why not?"

"Because some submissives like to fantasize that they're being overpowered, and they use the word as part of the fantasy."

"I won't ever fantasize that."

"That's fine. It's never been my fantasy to overpower a

woman. At least not in any way where she would tell me to stop. Anyway, no more talking. For today, your safe word is 'stop.'"

She nods.

"Good girl," I say.

I slide my fingers into her pussy once more, loving the sweet suction against my flesh.

Then I bring my hand down on her ass.

"Oh!" she gasps. Then, "I'm sorry. Is that talking?"

"No, but *that* was."

I bring my palm down on her ass again.

She squeals once more but says nothing.

Quick study. I've had professional submissives who don't do as well.

"Such a beautiful ass," I say, my breath accelerating. I adjust my groin. God, I'm hard as a freaking rock. How is it possible I've only had her once?

But my God, I haven't been able to stop thinking about her since that first night I saw her.

And then the next night... The masquerade... When she wore that gorgeous blue mask.

I think that was when I knew for sure that I was feeling something.

"We need to talk about the rules," I say.

Slap.

The sting against my palm makes me harder.

I can tell she wants to respond.

But good girl. She doesn't.

"You will get undressed when I tell you to and only when I tell you to."

Slap.

"You see, Frankie, I like to be in control in the bedroom.

I yearn for your obedience, your submission. Part of that is you waiting until I tell you what to do."

Slap!

"But what if I—"

Slap! Slap! Slap!

"No talking," I say through clenched teeth. "You *will* obey me."

Her body tenses.

Slap!

Slap, slap, slap!

Her ass is delectably rosy, and my palm stings with a force that has traveled straight to my cock.

I turn her to face me. "Are you okay?"

She doesn't speak. Nice.

"You may speak," I say.

She nods. "I'm absolutely fine, Hunter. To be honest? I enjoyed the spanking. I'm probably more turned on than I've ever been right now, and my God, I want you."

A groan comes from my very core. "I want you too. God, I want you." I lead her hand to the bulge in my jeans. "This is me wanting you, Frankie. I want to fuck you right here and right now."

She says nothing, just drops her red lips into a circle.

I turn her back around, caress the globes of her ass. "I'm going to fuck you like this, so I can see this gorgeous ass. So I can see how red I made it. How red you let me make it. Fuck, Frankie. Just…fuck."

I unsnap and unzip my jeans, pull out my hard cock, and cover it with a condom. I slide it between Frankie's ass cheeks, and then against her wet cunt, lubricating myself.

"Are you ready?" I whisper against her neck.

She doesn't answer. Simply nods.

Good girl.

I plunge into her in one smooth thrust.

God, heaven. She's the perfect cast for me, and for a moment all I want to do is stay inside her, joined, completed.

But the urge overtakes me, and I pull out and thrust back in. She moves with me, meeting each of my thrusts. We're in perfect sync as I fuck her hard and fast.

She moans softly but says no words, and I realize I want to hear her talk. I want to know how I'm making her feel. I thrust, thrust, thrust... She's getting tighter, just a few seconds more—

She cries out in climax, and I plunge into her deeply, allowing my own release.

I close my eyes, revel in the nirvana surging through me, and then I open them, dropping my gaze to her perfect pink ass. The ass I spanked for the first time.

The first of many times.

"You may speak now," I whisper in her ear.

"God, Hunter," she says on a soft sigh. "That was phenomenal."

I pull out of her and turn her around to face me. I push some hairs out of her eyes. "It was more than phenomenal, Frankie."

"The spanking. It added so much." She touches my cheek. "I never knew, Hunter. I never knew."

"Is your favorite flavor still vanilla?" I ask.

She giggles softly. "In ice cream? Yeah. In sex? Not so much."

I take her in my arms, my jeans still around my thighs, and we simply embrace. Capture the moment of our afterglow.

A few minutes later, she pulls away. "I'm thirsty."

"Me too."

"Want some water? Or more wine?"

"Just water. Thanks."

I adjust my jeans while she gets us two glasses of water. She gestures for me to follow her to the couch. "Is it okay if I get dressed now?"

"You mean I can't keep you naked?" I waggle my eyebrows. "Like a concubine?"

She gives me a good-natured punch. "That's a hard no."

"You may get dressed. But you may be getting undressed later."

"Fair enough." Instead of donning her dress, she walks behind a door, presumably her bedroom, and then emerges wearing a short, satiny robe.

Damn.

"I don't want to screw up the moment, but something's been bugging me, and I need to bring it up."

She raises her eyebrows. "What?"

"About that article you're writing," I begin.

"I know how you feel about it, Hunter."

"I don't want to be a part of any article. I *won't* be a part of any article."

"You've made that clear."

"Frankie, what people do in the privacy of the bedroom, or club, or even an exhibition room, is no one else's business."

"That's why I'll be changing all the names of my sources. And if someone feels the same way you do—that it's none of anyone's business—then that someone doesn't have to talk to me at all."

"I'm still not happy about it," I admit. "How can you guarantee that anything between us won't turn up in what you write?"

"You'll just have to trust me, Hunter. Trust that I'm a professional and I'd never use anyone as a source who specifically tells me not to. I'm writing the article. Frankly, I'm a little pissed that you'd insinuate otherwise."

"I'm not insinuating anything. I'm just voicing my concerns."

"And I'm telling you there's no reason to be concerned. I'm writing it, whether you like it or not."

"I know you are."

"I won't put you in it. But I'm writing it." She gives me an adorable sneer.

"Did you expect me to physically stop you from writing it? That's not what being a Dominant is all about."

She sighs. "The fact is that I don't know what being a Dominant is about. Or what being a submissive is about. Or how Doms and subs differ from each other. Maybe you should educate me. I was going to go to a class over at Treasure's Chest—"

"A class?"

"Yeah. They have classes, and I can go to their introductory one for free. I thought it would be a great chance to learn something for my article."

"Okay."

I know one of the women who teaches those classes, and she's a good submissive. Her name is Mary, but her submissive name is Blossom. She understands all the nuances, and she's probably good at conveying the lifestyle to others in a classroom setting.

I shouldn't have any problem with this.

But I don't want Frankie attending the class.

I also know I can't prevent her from attending, just like I can't prevent her from writing the article.

"I can teach you all you need to know about being a submissive," I tell her.

"Can you?"

"Of course. I've been a Dominant for most of my adult life."

"So I shouldn't attend the class?"

"You can if you want to, but wouldn't you rather learn from me?"

She smiles then, and I know I've got her. Not that Mary would teach her anything inaccurate, but if she's willing to learn from me, that's better. We can grow together in this relationship.

Yes. Our relationship.

I'm going to have—I *want* to have—a relationship with this woman.

"Okay… But you still don't want me using you at all for the article."

"No, I do not."

"Then I have to take the class, Hunter, if I can't put what you teach me in it."

"Why do you need the class for the article?"

"Because I want to be as educated as I can be. That's what research is. You know this. You're a scholar."

She's right, and I don't have an argument.

My lifestyle is just so private to me.

I feel it should be private to everyone.

In fact, anyone in the lifestyle wouldn't read the article because we understand the need for privacy. Even the exhibitionists need a safe place to display themselves, and they find that at the club, where everyone signs nondisclosures but they can still give the voyeurs something to look at.

"Think about your audience," I say. "People in this lifestyle aren't the ones who'll be reading the work."

"So you're saying I'm writing this for the people *not* in the lifestyle."

"Of course you are."

She doesn't reply. Of course she knows that. No one in the lifestyle needs this information. They all know it.

"You're writing it for the curiosity of the people who would never do this."

"What about the people who might *like* to do it but don't know enough about it?"

"If they're serious, they'll find out about it."

"What's wrong with teaching others about this lifestyle? Showing them that we're not just a bunch of kinky people who get off on getting tied up and being flogged. What's wrong with that?"

My groin tightens at her use of the word "we." She's beginning to identify with my lifestyle. God…

"What, Hunter? Tell me."

"Oh, Frankie. There's nothing wrong with it. I just don't want to be a part of it. I don't like it when…when my privacy is threatened."

Especially now, with my novel being released soon under a pen name, I value my privacy more than ever. My colleagues at Mellville might not take kindly to one of their published professors writing Victorian erotica.

"I won't use you as a subject in the article."

"I believe you. I trust that you won't. But I will still be in the article because you've learned from me, and you can't help but use that in the article."

"I'm a professional. I can limit my sources. I've done it before."

She's getting upset. She thinks I don't trust her, and that's not the case. I need to let this go.

I'm not the kind of Dominant who wants to control my submissive's life. Only during a scene. I like strong and independent women. I always have. It's what attracted me to Allison, and it's what attracted me to Teresa. It's also what attracts me to a submissive to play with. It's a myth that submissives are meek little women. They're not. They're empowered women who aren't afraid to ask for what they want.

"I'm writing it, Hunter. It's an assignment, so I can't just waltz into my boss's office and tell her no."

"I know that." God, do I ever. I've taken on a few bosses in my time, and it never ended pretty. "Will you do me one favor?"

"If it's reasonable."

I can't help a chuckle. Frankie is different from Allison. Different from Teresa. Different from any other submissive I've met. Yet she *is* a submissive. It's quite clear.

A very empowered one. And God, that makes her even more attractive.

"It's only this. I'd like to read it before you submit it."

"Not if you're going to criticize."

"You're a writer, and you can't take criticism?"

"All right. Criticize all you want. But don't force me to change anything."

"Do you really think I could force you to do *anything*?"

She smiles then, and it's a big one. "You got me to want a spanking from you. That's something new."

"Maybe it's new, but it's something you've wanted for a long time."

She smiles again, this time blushing. "How is it that you

know me so well?"

"Frankie," I say, "I've been asking the same thing about you since we met. Now bend back over and keep that sexy little robe on. I'm not done with that ass yet."

CHAPTER THIRTY-FIVE

Frankie

Hunter and I have a date.

A date for dinner tonight.

A date at the club on Friday night.

Before then, however, I have my group chat with the Dominants and submissives who responded to my post.

I'm sitting at my computer, ready to open the chat room. I emailed all of them but got a response only from three. The other two must've chickened out.

I have my questions ready.

I enter the chat room under the name Writerchick.

Writerchick: *I'm here. Welcome! Please introduce yourself as you come in.*

Then I wait.

And wait.

Until finally—

Kinkyboots: *Hi.*

Writerchick: *Thanks for coming, Kinkyboots. May I ask what pronouns you use?*

Kinkyboots: *She/her.*

Writerchick: *I'm hoping we'll get a few more people in here. Do you have any questions while we wait?*

Kinkyboots: *Yeah. What name will you be using for me? In your article, I mean.*

Writerchick: *I can use whatever you wish.*

Kinkyboots: *I don't think I want to be called Kinkyboots in the article. Just call me Jane.*

Writerchick: *Absolutely. Jane it is.*

Godfrey: *Good afternoon.*

Writerchick: *Hi, Godfrey. May I ask what pronouns you use?*

Godfrey: *I'm a male.*

Writerchick: *Welcome. Kinkyboots and I are here so far. I'm hoping we'll get a few more people.*

Godfrey: *I just read through the chat. You can call me Godfrey in the article.*

Writerchick: *Perfect. I will do that. Thank you both for being here.*

Kitten: *Hi there. I'm here. I'm female.*

Writerchick: *Hi, Kitten. Meet Godfrey and Kinkyboots.*

Kitten: *Hi, everyone.*

Writerchick: *We're talking about what names you'd like for me to use in the article. Would you like to be referred to as Kitten?*

Kitten: *No, a regular name would probably be better. How about Jane?*

Writerchick: *Kinkyboots already chose Jane. Do you have another you like?*

Kitten: *Sure. Susan.*

Writerchick: *Susan it is.*

Kitten: *Is anyone else coming?*

Writerchick: *I hope so, but you three are the only ones* *who returned my email today. It's possible you may be the only three, so let's go ahead and get started.*

I pause, gathering my courage to ask these people about their private lives. But that's why they're here.

Writerchick: *I'd like each of you to tell me which types of BDSM activities you engage in.*

Kinkyboots: *I'm submissive.*

Kitten: *Me too.*

Godfrey: *I'm a Dom.*

Well, pretty much what I expected. According to what I could find online, most women are submissive and most men are Dominant. I would've liked to hear from a female Dom or a male sub.

Writerchick: *Are you comfortable sharing your sexual orientations?*

Kinkyboots: *Straight.*

Godfrey: *Straight.*

Kitten: *Bisexual.*

Again, pretty common. It would have been nice to see a different orientation, but I'll work with what I've got.

Writerchick: *Okay, thank you. I'd like you to answer the questions I pose in the order you came into the chatroom, so Kinkyboots first, and then Godfrey, and then Kitten. How did you first find out that you were interested in this kind of lifestyle?*

Kinkyboots: *This is going to sound strange, maybe, but my dad spanked me when I was a kid. It wasn't a sexual thing at all. I hated it then, and he never sexually abused me. But for some reason, I've always wanted my boyfriends to spank me.*

Writerchick: *That's very interesting. It may not be related to your abuse at the hands of your father at all.*

Kinkyboots: *That's what my shrink says. Though she also says it could be.*

Writerchick: *Anything else?*

Kinkyboots: *It took a while to find a boyfriend who was willing to spank me.*

Kitten: *You had trouble finding a boyfriend willing to spank you? Man, most of the ones I find love it.*

Kinkyboots: *Really? It wasn't that way for me. Most of them weren't willing to do it. When I finally found one who was willing, he wanted to do other things as well, like tie me up.*

I wait for her to add more, but when she doesn't, I type again.

Writerchick: *Godfrey?*

Godfrey: *I guess I've known since I was young. At least since puberty. When I started becoming attracted to girls, I imagined them in all these compromising positions. For a long time, I repressed those urges. It wasn't until I was an adult, a couple of years out of college, before I realize that my impulses were normal as long as I had a consenting partner.*

Writerchick: *And you, Kitten?*

Kitten: *Kind of the same as Godfrey. I always had the fantasies, but I never acted on them, not until I was an adult, and then I read some erotic novels that went mainstream, and I realized, hey, this isn't abnormal at all. It's just different.*

Writerchick: *Thank you so much for your answers. Do you have a partner that you play with exclusively?*

Kinkyboots: *I recently got out of a relationship. I'm not comfortable with playing with someone I don't know.*

Writerchick: *How do you deal with that?*

Kinkyboots: *There are online sites where you can find potential partners who share your interests and who are willing to get to know you before you engage in any kind of play. That's where I am now. Looking for potential partners, meeting people for coffee and stuff.*

Godfrey: *I'm married, so my wife is my playmate. We've been together for five years.*

Kitten: *I'm in a relationship as well, though we're not married. And yes, he's my Dominant.*

Writerchick: *Excellent, thank you. Do you play in the privacy of your home? Or at clubs? Or anywhere else?*

Kinkyboots: *I prefer to play at home. I'm not really comfortable going to a club. This part of me is private.*

Godfrey: *My wife and I have been to clubs, and we go on occasion. Usually when there's some kind of theme night. She enjoys that kind of stuff. But we also have a dungeon in our home. That's where we do most of our play.*

Writerchick: *Theme night?*

Godfrey: *Yeah. It can be as simple as a holiday theme, or it can be more involved, like a Star Wars theme or something. One club does foam parties. They actually blow soapy foam onto the dance floor and everyone gets naked.*

Oh my. I wait a minute for Kitten or Kinkyboots to weigh in on foam parties, but neither does.

Writerchick: *Any other thoughts on clubs?*

Kitten: *Clubs for me. I like the club atmosphere. I go clubbing a lot at regular clubs, and I really love leather clubs. They're a feast for the eyes.*

Kitten's not wrong. Black Rose Underground is sensory overload.

Writerchick: *Next question. How do you keep your private life private?*

Kinkyboots: *It's just not something I talk about to people at work. My closest friends know, and I trust them. But I'm not ashamed of what I'm into, so if someone found out, it wouldn't be the end of the world.*

Writerchick: *Are you comfortable telling me what you do for a living?*

Kinkyboots: *I'm a flight attendant.*

Writerchick: *Thank you. I appreciate that.*

Godfrey: *I'm an attorney. So is my wife. We practice law together in a boutique firm with a couple of associates. So we keep it private. It's no one's business. Even when we go to the clubs, we don't worry about being seen because the people who go to those clubs all have an understanding.*

Writerchick: *Confidentiality agreements.*

Godfrey: *Yes, exactly. The best clubs will make you sign one. Sometimes they don't, but it's considered a gentlemen's agreement. No one ever mentions what they see. Kind of like what happens in Vegas stays in Vegas.*

Kitten: *Everybody knows what I'm into. It's no secret. In fact, you want to know why I asked to be called Jane? It's actually my name.*

Kinkyboots: *If you want Jane, I'll take Susan.*

Kitten: *Oh no worries. I probably should be a little more discreet.*

Writerchick: *What do you do for a living, Kitten?*

Kitten: *I'm between jobs at the moment. I was a cocktail waitress at a bar uptown, but I got laid off when the bar changed owners.*

Writerchick: *Thank you all for your candor. I'm going to get a little more personal on you, so if you're not comfortable answering the questions, just let me know. No pressure. What kind of activities do you do with your partners?*

Kinkyboots: *It's probably no surprise that my favorite thing to do is spanking. And by spanking I mean getting spanked. But I also like being handcuffed to a pole, being taken from behind. I like being blindfolded. That's probably my favorite thing next to spanking. It's amazing, not being able to see what he's about to do to me.*

Yes. I warm all over. I remember the night I first went to the club with Hunter. When he blindfolded me to take me. It was hot. Putting my trust and faith in a person I barely knew.

Perhaps not the best idea I ever had, but once we got there and Claude told me my safety was guaranteed…it actually took some of the excitement out of it. Not that being there with Hunter wasn't exciting. It was.

It *so* was.

Godfrey: *My wife and I do animal scenes. She likes to be my dog. I have an anal plug with a tail that I use. That's her favorite thing. My favorite thing is binding her with rope. She likes candle wax, too.*

I shudder in front of my computer screen. This isn't anything new to me, but hearing people talk about enjoying some of these things… It's kind of a turn-on, even though I never want to be led around like a dog.

Kitten: *I like it all. I'm not sure I could say that I have a favorite thing. My favorite thing is submitting and pleasing my Dom. Doing whatever he wants.*

Interesting. Kitten is a true submissive.

Writerchick: *We're about done. I have two more questions. Those of you who go to clubs—which I guess is all of you at some point—do you go to clubs here in the city?*

Three yeses pop onto the screen.

Writerchick: *Have you been to more than one club in the city?*

No. Yes. Yes again.

Writerchick: *Is there anything you can tell me about the clubs? I'm not asking for names or locations, but for example, do these clubs serve alcohol?*

Kinkyboots: *I've only been to one, and only once. And yes, they served alcohol.*

Godfrey: *One that I've been to does. The two others that I've been to don't have liquor licenses. But you can bring your own liquor, and they have bartenders who will serve it to you.*

Kitten: *I've been to two that serve alcohol, three that don't.*

Wow. Five clubs here in the city? Of course, the city is big.

There may be even more than five clubs.

Writerchick: *Thank you, and the last question. How do you practice safe sex?*

Kinkyboots: *I only play with one person at a time, so I make sure he uses a condom until we're both comfortable.*

Godfrey: *Since my partner is my wife, we don't need to worry about safe sex.*

Kitten: *Condoms are a requirement! No one gets near me without a raincoat.*

Writerchick: *Thank you all so much! I'll be in touch, and I hope we can talk again soon.*

Everyone logs off, and I save the chat. Then I copy it onto a document and save that as well. For added safety, I print out a hard copy.

No way am I losing this valuable information.

Very interesting stuff, but not nearly enough for an article.

I need more sources. Hopefully some of the others will respond to my email later.

For now? I need to shower. Hunter will be here to pick me up soon for our dinner date.

A dinner date.

An actual date.

This isn't easy for Hunter.

My God.

He's actually taking me to dinner. As himself. As Hunter.

I smile.

This will be fun.

CHAPTER THIRTY-SIX

Hunter

I'm uneasy as I sit across from Frankie at The Glass House. I chose it because she already knows I was here last weekend.

I was dining with my friend, colleague, and former college roommate, Logan Armstrong—another professor at Mellville—who's been through a tough time. A student falsely accused him of making sexual advances, and he's been through the wringer.

"You were right," I tell her. "I *was* here. And I did order my special martini."

"Why didn't you just level with me?"

"How could I? I stay masked for a reason."

"You're not masked now."

"No. You've unmasked me." I can't help shifting in my chair. "And I'd be lying if I didn't say it's frightening."

"What is there to be frightened about? I'm only a woman—a woman who's intrigued by your lifestyle. Who wants to learn more. And I'm not talking about writing an article for my work. I'll get that information from research. I want to learn more for *me*. And I've been thinking, Hunter. I think I'd rather not take the class at Treasure's Chest. I want to learn from *you*."

"I'm not a teacher."

She laughs then—uproarious laughter—and the absurdity hits me. The truth is I *am* a teacher. It's my chosen profession.

"I'm not a teacher of BDSM," I clarify. "Though I will teach you how to be the perfect submissive for *me*."

"Maybe you *should* teach BDSM. You obviously enjoy teaching. I took the liberty of looking you up on RateMyProfessors.com. Your reviews are great."

"Except for one," I say.

"Who cares? You can't reach everyone. Perhaps your teaching style just isn't quite right for some."

"Perhaps not."

There's no way to know for sure, but I suspect the negative review is from a student whose advances I rejected.

"I have a degree in English literature. That's what I teach. I don't have a degree in BDSM."

"Is there even such a thing?" Frankie's silvery eyes sparkle.

"These days, you can get a degree in just about everything. You can get college credit for all kinds of independent study. Of course, that doesn't guarantee that you're going to find a job."

"Yeah, I suppose not. Who would hire a guy with a PhD in BDSM?"

"Only a college that teaches it."

We laugh again. Our server comes by and takes our drink order—two of my special martinis.

Frankie is easy to talk to. She's warm and smart and funny.

Everything I've always been attracted to in a woman.

Plus, she's beautiful and has a killer body.

Frankie is more beautiful than either Allison or Teresa, who were both warm and smart. Teresa's warmth sometimes came at a cost, though, and that's when she let out her mean streak.

She hid it well…but only for a while.

God, why is Teresa creeping into my head?

I'll never be able to make anything work with Frankie if I can't get Teresa out of my thoughts.

Damn. That's exactly what's going on. It's a defense mechanism. I've built so many walls around my emotions that I'm not sure I'll be able to free them.

But Frankie makes me want to try.

Which is also scary as hell.

We've had sex only twice. Once at the club, and once at her place, and both times I was still clothed. Frankie makes me want more. I want to take her to my place and make love to her in my own bed.

That's a surefire recipe for disaster.

I've kept things distant with my partners for a reason. Part of that reason no longer exists with Frankie. I've already told her my name, shown her my face.

I wanted to do these things.

I could've easily walked out of the coffee shop, told her she was mistaken and to have a good day.

No one would've been the wiser if I got out of there quickly.

But I didn't.

There's only one reason why.

Part of me wanted to let my guard down with Frankie.

This woman—this woman I don't even know but who

knows more about me than anyone I've been intimate with—if you can even call it intimacy when we share the act but nothing else—in the past five years.

Our server comes to take orders.

"I'm so sorry," Frankie says. "I haven't even had a chance to look at the menu."

"That's no problem," he says. "Let me tell you about today's specials, so you have all of the information, and I'll be back in a moment. We have Fish Beaujolais made with Alaskan halibut, and it comes with roasted cauliflower and fresh green beans. We also have a wonderful wagyu ribeye, sixteen ounces, and that comes with a baked potato and also fresh green beans."

"Sixteen ounces." Frankie widens her eyes. "That's a full pound of meat."

"You'd be amazed how many ladies order it," the server says.

"I'll think about it," she says.

"Absolutely. I'll be back in a minute."

She scans her menu, and I realize I haven't looked at the menu either. But I don't need to. I always have the same thing when I come to The Glass House. Prime rib, medium rare, with garlic mashed potatoes and asparagus spears. Is garlic the right way to go tonight? I don't normally worry about that. Sure, I chew a couple of breath mints before a scene anyway, but I don't want anything to go badly tonight. I don't want my breath to have one hint of garlic.

"As good as that ribeye sounds," Frankie says, "there's just no way I can eat that much."

"You don't have to eat it all. You can get the rest in a doggy bag."

"No dog," she says.

"You don't have to have a dog, Frankie."

She smiles. "I know that. My sister has this annoying little dog named Roger who hates me. He's this miniature pinscher and Chihuahua mix that's about three years old, but I swear to God he's like a grumpy old man. He loves her and he loves Jackson, her fiancé. Those are the only two people he tolerates."

"Guess it's a good thing they got together," I say.

"It was a long time coming. I truly am happy for my sister. She's such an introvert, and she never dated much."

"And you?"

"You think I held back on you? I told you. I dated a few times before Penn, but nothing serious. A guy in high school popped my cherry, and I remember his name was Kevin Townley, but I'm not sure I'd be able to pick him out of a lineup today."

"Oh?"

"Does that make me sound bad? He was cute enough, but he wasn't the big man on campus or anything."

I can't help it. I laugh. She's such a delight. And I'm not sure I've ever used the word "delight" before when describing a woman. Not even Allison or Teresa.

Frankie makes me feel like it's okay to be myself.

And it's growing on me, I can't lie.

"I lost my virginity with Allison."

"Really?" Her eyes widen.

"Does that surprise you?"

"Well, yeah, to be honest. Have you looked in the mirror lately? You're gorgeous, Hunter."

"I was kind of a late bloomer. I weighed all of a hundred and forty in high school. I finally had a growth spurt between my junior and senior years, but my weight didn't level out until college. I was kind of gangly, and I wore glasses."

"You're not wearing glasses now."

"I had laser surgery, same as you."

She narrows her eyes as she studies me. "Actually, tortoiseshell glasses would look amazing on you. Give you that professor vibe."

"Since I *am* a professor, don't I already have that vibe?"

She laughs. "I can't see you in one of those blazers with patches on the elbows."

"You'll never see me in anything like that. I hate that look."

She laughs, and again it's such a joyful sound. I'm really beginning to like this woman.

And that's a fucking emotion.

And I wonder… Should I let myself feel more?

I'm not sure I have a choice.

"I think you looked the sexiest the first night I saw you," she says. "You were wearing your mask and your cape, of course, but you were wearing jeans and a white button-down. Very sexy."

"You like that better than the black?"

"On you? For sure. I mean, you look great in black, too, especially with your dark hair and eyes. But something about the jeans and white button-down. The white against the contrast of your tanned skin. It was such a normal outfit, and you looked amazing in it, but then you had this black cape and that white mask. It was kind of contradictory, you know?"

"No, I didn't know."

"Well, yeah. When you think of the Phantom of the Opera, you think of him as this dark creature of the night who wears only black. Which you did, the next time I saw you."

"That's because I was hoping we would go to the club."

"Really? That night at the masquerade?"

"It was my plan. But then... I don't know. I guess I chickened out."

"You don't seem like the kind of man who chickens out much."

"You're right. When it comes to the lifestyle and the sex I enjoy, I never chicken out. But as you know, I'm usually playing with a seasoned submissive who knows what to expect."

"And that's not me."

"Right. That's totally not you."

"What if I *want* it to be me?"

"You can want it all you want, Frankie, but you're not experienced. The only way to get experienced is to—"

"Do it," she finishes for me.

"Yeah. Pretty much. You can study all you want, take all the classes you want, read all the books that are out there—and though some of them are accurate, a lot of them aren't—but none of that is a substitute for real-life experience in the lifestyle."

"Well...I'm ready to get some experience."

"I can help you with that, but as I told you before, I don't want what we do to end up in your article."

"I made that promise, Hunter. None of what *we* do will end up in the article. I'm not even going to take the class at Treasure's Chest. I'm getting my information from some online sources. Some people who agreed to chat with me."

"Yes. Erik with a K."

"Right. And a few others. And I've got some great information so far."

"I can't tell you how to do your job," I say.

"No, you absolutely can't. And I can't tell you how to do yours."

"Right. But thank you. Thank you for agreeing that anything that happens between us won't end up in your article."

"I wouldn't do that anyway, Hunter. I'm as private as you are with regard to my sex life."

"Good. Then we have a genuine understanding between us."

Before she can reply, the server returns. "Have you decided?"

"Yes." Frankie shuts her menu. "I will have that amazing wagyu ribeye, medium rare, and a house salad with balsamic vinaigrette."

"Excellent. And for you, sir?"

"House salad with ranch, and the prime rib, medium rare, with a baked potato and asparagus."

"Very good. Can I refresh your drinks?"

Frankie and I have been talking so much, we've hardly touched our drinks. "Looks like we're good for now," I tell him.

"And would you like to order any wine with dinner?"

I eye the wine list. "I think our red meat orders would pair well with one of your most robust cabs."

"Excellent. May I recommend the Jordan?"

"You may. Two glasses, please."

"Very good. I'll get everything started."

Then I smile across the table at Frankie.

This will be a memorable evening. One way or another.

CHAPTER THIRTY-SEVEN

Frankie

"I'd like to take you home with me," Hunter says.

I try to conceal my surprise, but I fear I'm not very successful.

"Don't look so surprised."

"I just figured. You know. The club."

"I don't go to the club without my cape and mask," he says.

"So you weren't hoping we'd end up there tonight?"

"I'd very much like to take you there, but we have plans for that tomorrow. I'd like to take you home. To my place."

"When's the last time you had a woman at your place?" I can't help asking.

"It's been a long time, Frankie."

"Was it Teresa?"

"Yes." His gaze doesn't waver from mine. "I don't want there to be secrets between us. I've already divulged a huge one to you."

"Then I'd be honored." I wince. "I mean... That didn't come out right at all."

"I understand what you mean. You're saying you'd like to come with me."

"I would."

"I want you to know," he says, "that just because we're not inside the club doesn't mean your safety isn't guaranteed at all times. I would never let anything happen to you, and we don't have to do anything you don't want to do."

"Hunter, I appreciate the sentiment." I reach across the table and squeeze his hand. "I do. But you're taking the romance out of it."

"I'm afraid I don't know how to do romance."

"You keep saying that, but you read all the classics. You know what love is. You know what love is supposed to feel like between two people. In *The Great Gatsby*, Jay Gatsby would do anything to be with his love, even though she wasn't available. I know you understand the concept."

He doesn't reply.

I hope I haven't upset him, and I open my mouth to apologize, but then I shut it.

There was nothing wrong with what I said. I don't want to lose whatever is budding between Hunter and me, but I also can't let everything slide. I'm not Mandy. I'm not an introvert. I wouldn't call myself an extrovert, either, but I'm going to lay my cards on the table. I'm going to say what I want to say.

He's still silent.

"I'd like to go with you, Hunter. If it's what you want."

He clears his throat. "It is what I want. I'd like to show you a little more of myself, Frankie. I'd like to show you my home. Maybe tell you a little bit more about myself. About my work."

"I'd like that very much."

The server comes with the check and sets it down in front of Hunter. This is an expensive place, and I make pretty good money.

"Let me help with that," I say.

He shakes his head. "Absolutely not. When I take a lady out, I pay."

Those words from another man might sound chauvinistic, but I don't get that feeling from Hunter at all. He's simply being a gentleman.

A gentleman and an amazing person. I wish he hadn't held his emotions at bay for so long.

I smile. "Thank you. I appreciate your generosity. I enjoyed the dinner very much."

"I did too." He returns my smile. "But I enjoyed the company even more."

We leave the restaurant and hail a cab.

"I hope you don't mind taking a cab. I don't own a car."

"Are you kidding?" I laugh. "I don't, either. Who could afford to, here in the city?"

Traffic is a mess, but we finally make it to Hunter's brownstone. It's a quaint building, all red brick, and while I'm used to a doorman, the brownstone has an old-fashioned key and no intercom.

He opens the door to the front, and then he leads me up the stairwell to his apartment. "There are two apartments up here," he says. "Mine is the smaller, but it's perfect for me. Two bedrooms, one of which I use as an office. A tiny kitchen, but I'm not the best cook in the world, so I eat sandwiches, mostly, with the occasional takeout." He unlocks the door. "Here it is."

I walk inside, and my jaw drops.

I feel like I've walked into the past.

The house itself is historic, and Hunter has decorated it with what look like antiques, though I honestly don't have an educated eye regarding decor.

"Wow," I can't help saying.

"I take it you like it."

"I love it. It's absolutely beautiful." I walk toward a navy-blue sofa with cherrywood feet upholstered in some kind of brocade with bumblebees embroidered onto it. The coffee table sitting in front of it is the same cherry with a gorgeous silver-and-gold marble top. On top are several books, leather bound, including, of course, *The Great Gatsby.*

Two wingback chairs also flank the coffee table on the other side, upholstered with the same navy blue but no bumblebees.

Between the two chairs is a small cherry table on a pedestal.

The entire apartment floor is dark hardwood, but a blue-and-burgundy Turkish rug sits under the coffee table. A wine rack sits off to the side, made of the same cherrywood with wrought iron accents.

"Let me show you everything else." Hunter leads me to the small kitchen and dining area. Another Turkish rug sits under the dining room table, which is small, to accommodate the size of the apartment, but again it looks like something that came out of the early twentieth century. Cherry again—he must like cherry—and the chairs are upholstered in navy and burgundy stripes.

"Did you decorate this yourself?" I ask.

"I did, actually." He runs his hand over the upholstery of one of the wingbacks. "Believe it or not, I found each of these pieces on the secondhand market and restored them myself."

"Wow. You're an artist, Hunter."

"It's just a hobby. I enjoy it. When you read and teach all day, it's nice to do something with your hands on the weekends."

"It's all gorgeous. I can't wait to see the bedroom." I clamp my hand over my mouth. "I mean… I don't mean…"

He laughs. "I know exactly what you mean, Frankie. I'd love to show you the bedroom, but first I want to show you my working area. My office."

He leads me through one of the bedroom doors, and the first thing my gaze falls upon is an antique rolltop desk, again in cherry.

"Are all these pieces actually made of cherry? Or did you stain them to look that way?"

"They're all cherry, but I did use some stain to freshen up the color."

"They're beautiful. You actually work at the rolltop desk?"

"No." He gestures. "I work mostly in that recliner, with my laptop."

Indeed, the leather recliner—the leather is a dark brown—sits in the corner of the room along with a floor lamp. Two walls are completely lined with bookshelves, and I close my eyes and inhale.

The smoky scent of leather, the crisp and earthy scent of parchment.

I feel like I've walked into an old library.

Hunter has a huge collection of books—a lot of the classics, of course, which he undoubtedly teaches, but a lot of commercial fiction as well, which surprises me. Then of course there's nonfiction, books on teaching, and a few self-help books as well.

Interestingly, no books on the BDSM lifestyle—at least not sitting out in plain view.

"I love this place," I say. "What a perfect place to do your work."

"I've graded many papers in that chair," he says. "Put together many lesson plans. And…it's where I wrote my novel."

A grin splits my face. "Hunter, that's fantastic! Can you tell me about it?"

"It's funny." He shakes his head. "I haven't told anyone about it, other than my friend Logan. But it just kind of popped out of my mouth with you."

"I'm honored. Truly. What did you write about?"

"It's historical erotic fiction," he says.

My cheeks burn when he says the word "erotic." "Really? Romance?"

"There's a love story, but I wouldn't call it a romance. I've done a lot of research into alternate sexual lifestyles in the past."

"I'd love to read it sometime."

"It's actually under contract with Peck and Gold here in New York. It releases in a few months. Under a pen name, of course."

"Erik with a K?" I smile.

He laughs. "No. And not Phantom, either. Damn. Why do I want to tell you?"

"Baby steps, Hunter. But I'd love to read it. I'm absolutely impressed. The thought of writing a book is so daunting."

"But you're a writer, Frankie. You write for the magazine."

I shake my head. "I think my longest article was about five thousand words. You're talking about an eighty- or ninety-thousand-word novel."

"Actually, this one is more like a hundred and twenty thousand words."

"Color me impressed," I say. "You're amazing."

"Don't say that. You haven't read it."

"Just writing that many words is amazing."

He lets out another low laugh. "Like I said, you haven't read it. Early reviews have been promising, though. My agent and the publisher are pleased."

"I know a lot of publishers in the city," I say. "I know Anita from Peck and Gold."

"I've been working with Greta Boss."

"Hmm, I don't know her. But this is something else we have in common, although like I said, I'm not sure I could write a whole book."

"You'd be surprised."

"I don't really write fiction," I say. "The stuff I write for the magazine is usually investigative journalism or fluff pieces."

"What's a fluff piece?" he asks.

"Pop-culture pieces. Things our readers like. Stuff with a lot of information but not much substance. You know. Fluff."

He approaches me, his eyes narrowing. "Do you consider the article you're writing on the BDSM lifestyle to be fluff?"

"That's actually a good question. I've done a lot of research, so I consider it investigative. But I can't deny that while I wouldn't call it fluff, it's definitely got mass appeal."

"Would it upset you to know I've never read your magazine?"

"Of course not. Our readership is mostly women, first of all, and you're a scholar. We don't write scholarly articles."

"Just because I'm a scholar doesn't mean I don't like a little fluff once in a while." He points to his shelves of commercial fiction. "Check me out. John Grisham, Stephen King, and Dean Koontz are some of my favorites."

"You have any books on…BDSM?"

"Of course I do." He opens a small barrister's bookcase, takes out a book, and hands it to me. "This is one of the best ones out there."

I run my fingers over the cover. "*Alternative Sexual Lifestyles.*"

"It gets into a lot of different things," he says, "some of which might make you uncomfortable. I know they made me uncomfortable. The section on BDSM is excellent, though."

"May I borrow this?"

"Absolutely, but I want it back."

I wrinkle my forehead. "Of course I'm going to give it back to you, Hunter."

"Right. I didn't mean to imply that you wouldn't. I'm just kind of weird about my books."

"No need to explain."

"Now…" He grins. "Let me show you my bedroom."

CHAPTER THIRTY-EIGHT

Hunter

I open the door slowly.

While my living area and my office are decorated in mostly antiques that I finished myself, my bedroom is another story.

It's more contemporary, done in stunning black lacquer rather than natural wood.

My king-size bed is covered in a navy-blue down comforter, and my chest of drawers is the same black lacquer as the headboard and footboard of my bed.

Frankie's eyes widen.

"Surprised?" I ask.

"Yeah, a little. I was expecting an antique bedframe and maybe a wardrobe. Definitely a highboy."

"I just redecorated this room," I say. "Now that I've met you, I think I know why."

"I'm not sure I follow."

"I hadn't changed my bedroom at all since Teresa. I haven't had a woman *in* my bedroom since Teresa. I kept my physical pleasures solely at the club. Then, a couple of months ago, for some reason, I had the desire to change my bedroom."

"Did you have antiques in here before?"

"I did. A gorgeous cherry bedframe, and a high- and lowboy. But it always…"

"I get it. It always reminded you of her."

"Yes and no. Yes, because she was the last woman I had here, and it was because of her that I turned off my emotions and decided to indulge purely in the physical. But I also decided not to have a woman here. So I kind of detached from the room. I figured it was a place to sleep. Not a place to have sex."

"The fact that you changed it means you were rethinking that position."

I shrug. "I'm not sure I was rethinking. But…it may have just meant that I was going to meet you."

Her cheeks go pink, and my God she's so beautiful.

"So you believe in premonitions, then?"

"No, of course not. But I can't help but wonder if the universe was sending me a sign. That maybe I would meet someone I wanted to share this bedroom with."

"And do you want to share it with me?"

"I do. I want to make love with you here, Frankie. That's not to say I don't plan to take you back to the club, because I do. But for the first time in a long time, I want to bring a woman home. To my bedroom."

"Do you have any toys here?"

"I have a few. I got rid of most of them after Teresa. They were too much of a reminder."

"That you've never used on her…" she prods.

"No, the ones that I still have I never used on anyone."

"Do you want to use them on me?"

I draw in a deep breath, trying to slow the beating of my heart, the aching in my hard cock. “I do, Frankie. I want to bind you to the headboard of my bed, and I want to spread your legs and suck the delicious cream out of your pussy.”

She sucks in a breath.

“Does that turn you on?”

She nods, chewing on her lower lip.

“This isn’t a feeling I expected to have.” I walk toward her, glide my finger over her cheek. “I’m having feelings for the first time in a long time, Frankie. I’m not sure why or what it is about you. You’re beautiful, of course. You’re smart and engaging. But there’s something else. Something that seems to call to the inside of my heart.”

“I’m feeling something similar,” she says. “And honestly, I didn’t expect to, so soon after ending things with Penn.”

“So I’m not a rebound guy?”

“No, Hunter. I don’t think you are. Because if you were, I wouldn’t be feeling what I’m feeling.”

“You would just want the sex.”

“Right. And you know, we’ve only had sex twice despite the fact that we’ve known each other for several weeks now.”

“I’d like to go for number three. Here. Tonight.”

She sighs softly. The sound goes straight to my throbbing cock.

“Please,” she says. “Please, Hunter. Make love to me.”

Oh, that magic word.

Please.

I walk to my dresser and open the top drawer. I pull out leather bindings. They’re actually safer than handcuffs.

“Undress.”

“Will you undress?” she asks. “I’ve never seen you. I’ve never seen your body.”

"I'll decide whether I undress, Frankie. I'm the Dominant here."

"Okay. Whatever you say, Hunter."

"Good. Good answer."

Normally I'd tell her to call me "sir," but I love hearing my name from Frankie's lips.

I take in her face, her smile, her beautiful hair that flows over her shoulders, that sumptuous body, and her dress that clings to her body. "Undress for me. Now."

She leaves her pumps on. Good—she remembers. She peels the dress from her shoulders, easing it over her chest, and those luscious tits spring free.

Then she pushes it down over her flat belly, her slim hips, her milky thighs. Until it's on the floor and she steps out of it.

She wears only a black thong now, and she turns around and seductively wiggles her ass at me.

My cock grows harder, especially as I remember spanking those creamy cheeks.

"Don't be a tease, Frankie."

She turns back around and faces me, her gorgeous nipples hard and ready to be bitten. "Am I a tease?" she asks innocently.

"I think it might be better if you don't talk."

"Really?"

I yank her toward me, sit down on the bed, and pull her over my knee, bringing my palm down on that beautiful ass.

"Oh!" she cries out.

I slap her again, this time on the other cheek.

Then I watch as the sweet pink bursts forth from her dilated capillaries.

"Absolutely gorgeous," I growl.

She opens her mouth but then closes it abruptly.

Good girl.

I pull her up, kiss her lips, and then set her on the bed. "I believe I will undress for you, Frankie. I'll undress for you, stand before you naked, and shove my cock down that sweet little throat of yours."

She doesn't react, which surprises me.

Is it possible she wants this as much as I do?

Then I remember… The first time we met, I told her I had a fantasy of her kneeling before me, her mouth spread open while I fucked it.

I'm about to make that fantasy come true for both of us.

I don't have a spider gag at home, so she'll have to hold her mouth open herself.

And honestly? Even though I love the look of a woman's mouth being held open by a gag? A mouth feels so much better without it, because she can form her lips around my cock and increase the suction.

My God, I'm pulsating just thinking about it.

I need to calm down, breathe in, breathe out. If I don't, I'll explode way too soon.

Damn. I'm acting like a freaking schoolboy around her.

Does she even know her own sex appeal? She was with that dick for so long, I wonder if she does.

"Has anyone ever told you how beautiful you are?" I ask.

"Occasionally," she says. Then she slaps her hand over her mouth.

"It's okay. You may speak. I asked you a direct question."

"Well, like I said, occasionally. Penn used to say I was pretty. Maybe once or twice he said 'beautiful.'"

"He should've told you every day," I say. "Every day, he should've woken up, looked at you, and wondered how he got so lucky."

She sighs. That soft sound sets my dick on fire. "My God, Hunter. You take my breath away."

And with those words from her mouth, another chunk of cement falls from my heart.

I could fall in love with this woman.

If I let my guard down, I could so easily fall in love with her.

"You're beautiful too," she says. "Did any of those women tell you that? Allison? Teresa?"

My cheeks warm. "Not really."

"They should have." She rakes her gaze over me. "That dark hair that's just a little bit shaggy. Those gorgeous brown eyes that are nearly black. And your eyelashes, Hunter. Women pay good money to have eyelashes like that."

"I assure you I'm nothing compared to you." I unbutton my shirt, watching her gaze at me with desire in her eyes. I tease her a little this time. I go slowly, exposing my skin inch by inch.

Finally I part the two halves of the shirt, slide them over my shoulders, and let it fall to the ground.

It's her turn to suck in a breath. "My God. You truly are beautiful. A work of art."

Her words embarrass me a little. I've never thought of myself as beautiful. It's not really a word I'd use to describe myself, or any other guy, for that matter. I unhook my belt, pull it out of my pants, and toss it onto the floor.

"Kneel before me," I say.

She pauses a moment, but then she drops to her knees.

I should get a pillow for her knees. The small rug by my bed won't give her much cushion, and her knees will begin to ache.

But I don't.

Because I don't want to stop.

I unbutton my pants, unzip them, slide them over my hips, along with my boxer briefs, and my dick springs out, so ready and willing, so throbbing and hot, and so ready.

She gapes at me.

"You know how large I am. I've been inside you, Frankie."

"I know. It's not the size, Hunter. It's the beauty."

Beauty. That word again.

No one's ever said my cock is beautiful. Magnificent, yes. Never beautiful.

Of course, she shouldn't be talking.

But already I know this relationship is different. I've been a demanding Dominant. Normally I don't let my sub speak while we play. A lot of times I don't allow her to touch me.

But here, now, I crave Frankie's touch.

And that fear I've been feeling for so long? Fear at wanting what I shouldn't want?

It's dissipating.

Which of course leads to a new fear.

I don't even know if she shares my proclivities. She's curious, of course, but will she be able to be a full-blown sub? The kind of sub I desire?

I walk toward her, ready to shove my cock into her mouth, but before I do, I cup her cheeks, tilt her head so she's meeting my gaze.

And I realize, as I look into those gorgeous silvery blue eyes, that it doesn't matter what kind of sub she is or whether she turns out to be a sub at all.

All that matters is *her*.

CHAPTER THIRTY-NINE

Frankie

He absolutely mesmerizes me.

Penn was a good-looking guy, but Hunter is a masterpiece. Penn had a good-size cock, but Hunter's is a massive work of art.

Penn was lean and muscular, but Hunter is a freaking Renaissance statue.

There's simply no comparison between the two.

I look up at him as he cups my cheeks, his palms warm against my skin. Is he comparing me to Allison right now? To Teresa? To any of his other partners in play?

I hope he isn't, but how can he not be? I'm doing the same thing.

I've never seen anything like Hunter Stone outside of a magazine, and he puts the best male models in our publication to shame.

"Have you ever considered modeling?" I ask.

He shakes his head slightly. "That's what you're thinking about right now?"

"I'm thinking about how freaking gorgeous you are,

Hunter. You're the most amazing man I've ever laid eyes on, and quite frankly what's even more amazing is that you seem to want *me*."

Then he does something I don't expect.

He drops to his knees so that we're face-to-face—an odd move for someone who's clearly a Dominant.

"How can you say that? You're ravishing. Those eyes—I feel like you're looking right into my soul."

"That's just because they're such a unique color."

"No, Frankie." He cups my cheeks. "That's because they're *yours*."

I suppress a shudder. Then another one flows through me, and this time I can't suppress it.

I'm warm all over. And also cold. And also steaming hot. My pussy is already throbbing.

But I'm feeling more than just the physical reactions.

I'm feeling...something new.

On its face, I want to call it love, but I thought I loved Penn, and already what I'm feeling for Hunter is deeper, more significant.

Which is ridiculous because I barely know him.

I mean, he came to me in a mask with a fake name. He came to me as a character, not as himself.

But honestly, I'm feeling the love so much that I'm afraid if I open my mouth the words may pop out.

So I keep my lips closed. Tightly closed.

The last thing I want to do is scare Hunter away, and me professing my love to him will do exactly that. This is a man who has kept himself out of any relationships with feeling for a long time.

Even now, it's new to him. Bringing me to his bedroom is a huge step.

I don't want to blow it.

He leans into me then, presses his lips against mine. This time I part my lips and allow his wandering tongue inside my mouth.

It's a soft kiss, and for a moment I'm not sure he wants me as desperately as I want him.

Until the kiss turns passionate, raw, and feral. He groans into my mouth, and it vibrates into me, as if I have my hand on a playing piano.

It's like music when we kiss.

At first it's a soft melody, and then a brazen concerto with lots of percussion. That's what the kiss is now.

We kiss for several moments, and then, my hand, seemingly of its own accord, reaches toward him, grasps his cock.

He breaks the kiss.

I widen my eyes. "Is that not okay?"

"No, it's very okay." He smiles. "It's just that normally… my sub waits for permission."

I gasp and release him. "I'm so sorry."

"No." He takes my hand, squeezes it, and leads it back to his cock. "I want you to touch me. I crave it."

"God, so do I."

This is different for him, then.

Different for both of us. I'm certainly not an experienced sub—perhaps not a sub at all—but I'm willing to learn for him. I'm interested enough, curious enough, that I can do it if it's what he wants.

But *is* it what he wants?

We're both changing, growing, blooming.

In ways I never imagined, and probably in ways he never imagined, either.

I grasp him, savor the warmth of him, my fingers barely meeting around his girth.

Then he rises, slowly, and he moves to the bed, grabs a pillow, and brings it back to me. "For your knees."

I smile and place the pillow underneath me.

Then his dick bobs against my lips. "Open. Take me in."

I wrap my lips around his cock head, and I lick the drop of salty liquid that has emerged. Then I move down on his cock, going about half his length, and then edging closer, until he nudges the back of my throat.

I'm able to stifle my gag reflex, and I go farther.

And then I pull back.

He's lubricated now with my saliva, so I use my fist so I can add pressure and go all the way down his length.

I suck him this way, looking upward to see his gaze.

His eyes are closed, his teeth clenched.

Good.

He's enjoying it.

So am I. I'm enjoying it because I want to do this for him.

His large cock makes it uncomfortable at times, but that doesn't matter. This isn't for my comfort. This is for his pleasure. This is for him.

I increase my speed, and I increase my suction, and—

He pulls away quickly. "God, enough."

"Enough?"

"I'm close to coming, Frankie. I don't want to come yet."

"What if I want you to come? What if I want to swallow for you?"

He sucks in a breath. "Fucking God."

"What do you want, Hunter? Tell me what you want, and I'll do it for you. Anything."

He opens his eyes then, stares down at me, burning his

gaze into mine. "I'm not sure you understand what you're asking for."

"No, I do understand." My cheeks are so hot I'm sure they're scarlet. "I mean, if you ask me for anal sex, I'm not going to give you that. At least not tonight. I'm not ready. But anything else, Hunter. Anything."

He groans—one of those low, guttural moans that seems to permeate the whole room.

"I do want to come in your mouth, Frankie. I also want to fuck you. I want to make love to you in my bed."

"So come in my mouth first, and then if you need to wait, you wait. I don't have any plans to be anywhere else. Do you?"

He groans again.

Then he nudges his cock past my lips. This time I'm on a mission. I want to take him as far as I can, give him the pleasure he seeks.

I swirl my tongue around him, probe his tiny slit, and then I take him far in the back of my throat, again using my fist.

I begin slowly, and then I increase the speed and the friction of the suction, and within another moment—

"God." He grabs my head, and he pushes himself all the way inside my mouth.

My gag reflex has become nonexistent because I want this. I want this as much as he does.

I want to give him this gift.

Then later... I'll tell him that I never gave this gift to anyone else. This is the first time I've allowed a man to come in my mouth.

He pumps into me, and as his semen flows against my throat, I know this is something more.

Those words I wanted to say before?

They're true.

The truth of them cracks through me like a thunderbolt.

I'm in love with this man. With Hunter Stone.

I'm his.

And if he wants to mold me into the perfect sub, I will let him.

CHAPTER FORTY

Hunter

I'm floating in a haze—a haze of pleasure and nirvana. I can't put words to the feelings—feelings I've repressed for so long.

Actually, I can... But I'm not quite ready for that yet.

I do know that I want to get to know this woman better. I want to know everything about her. What makes her heart sing. What makes her cry. Makes her laugh.

Every fucking thing.

I withdraw my cock even though I want to stay inside her mouth forever. A tiny drop of my come drizzles down her chin. She wipes it off with her finger and then sucks the finger into her mouth.

And God damn...

Already my cock is tightening again.

I may not have to wait that long to have her in my bed. To fuck her.

No, to make love to her.

This isn't just a fuck to me anymore.

It hasn't been since I brought her here.

Once I let her in—not just into my apartment but into my bedroom—it became something more.

And there's no turning back.

I take her hands, pull her to her feet, and hold her close. "That was amazing," I whisper into her ear.

She melts against me, kisses my chest. "I've never done that before—let a man come in my mouth."

A low groan vibrates out of me, and my dick twitches. Just that admission—the fact that she's never swallowed for anyone—has me ready to go again.

My God, the feel of her lips and of her flesh molded to mine.

Have I ever felt this way? With Allison? With Teresa?

And then it hits me.

I haven't.

And that doesn't mean I loved Allison any less.

"Frankie," I say.

"Hmm?" she mumbles against my skin.

"I want to tell you something."

She pulls away then, her eyes wide. "Of course. What?"

"Sit with me." I bring her to the bed and pull her onto my lap.

Her knees are red. I touch them gently. "Okay?"

"I'm fine. Thank you for the pillow. It helped."

"I'm glad."

She kisses my cheek. "What do you want to tell me?"

"I realize something, and it's probably something I should've realized long ago. When I was with Teresa, I was trying to recreate what I had with Allison."

"Relationships are always different," she says.

"Exactly, but I didn't know that at the time. I was in my twenties, so I should have, but the only significant relationship I'd ever had was with Allison. It was so good in so many ways, and I was lost when she was taken from me. After years of mourning, when I felt I was ready to look for someone new, I was expecting it to be exactly the same."

"But it wasn't."

"No, not at all. Parts of it felt the same, but other parts..."

"She wasn't Allison."

"No, she wasn't. And she kept parts of herself hidden—parts that didn't come out until later—and that's when..."

It's still so painful to think about. To talk about.

"She broke your heart."

"In a way, I suppose she did. She turned on me. Told her friends about our private life—laughed with them about it, even—when she knew how much my privacy meant to me. Once I saw her for who she really was, I realized that our whole relationship was a farce."

"I'm sorry that happened, Hunter. You deserve better than that. So that's why you decided to give up on relationships."

"I did. And I honestly don't regret it. It was the right decision for me at the time."

"And now?" She raises her eyebrows.

"It's different with you. Different from Allison. That doesn't make it any less special."

She smiles, her lips still glistening. "Thank you for saying that."

"You don't have to thank me. It's the truth. The truth I just realized myself. That was what the whole relationship with Teresa was. It was me trying to recreate what I had with Allison. But that was impossible. Quite honestly, it was probably just as much my fault that our relationship ended. I'd convinced myself that Teresa was something that she wasn't."

"Maybe. But don't put that on yourself."

"It doesn't matter. It's ancient history. But I'm hoping..." I clear my throat, gathering my courage. "I'm hoping...that you and I can have something. Something unique. I'm no longer trying to recreate something from the past. I'm interested in the present now."

And in the future.

But I don't say those last words. It's too soon to think about the future, and I don't want to scare her away.

Hell, I don't want to scare *myself* away.

Only months ago, I felt content with scenes that were merely physical. With women for whom I had no feelings other than sexual.

And now?

This beautiful woman with the hypnotizing eyes has changed everything.

Will she accept me for who I truly am?

Will the club still be a big part of our lives?

Already I know that whatever happens, it will be a compromise.

I'm okay with that.

Because this woman means something to me. Something very special.

I can almost put it into words...

But I'm not quite there yet.

I kiss the tops of her breasts, play with her nipples, and then I lie down on my back, pulling her with me.

We lie on the bed for a few moments, and she snuggles into my shoulder.

And for the first time in a long time, I feel completely relaxed.

CHAPTER FORTY-ONE

Frankie

I wake to the sun streaming into the bedroom window. For a moment I don't know where I am, but then I feel Hunter's hard body next to mine.

We're covered, and I don't remember how we got in bed. Perhaps I fell asleep and he covered me.

Sometimes it's difficult to believe that such a gentle soul is a Dominant. But I've learned through my research—and through interacting with Hunter—that being a Dominant doesn't mean you have to be domineering in every part of your life. Hunter is a gentle soul. A student of love and language. Hunter is a Dominant. The two aren't mutually exclusive.

I creep out of bed, trying not to wake him. I have no idea what time it is, only that it's morning and the sun is up. I find my purse sitting on the chair in his bedroom, and I grab my phone out of it. The battery's about to die, but at least I see the time. Seven forty-five a.m.

I'm planning to work from home today, so this is an opportunity for me. I can start some coffee and make

Hunter breakfast.

Start getting him to fall in love with me.

I smile.

I fell in love so quickly. And so quickly after Penn. Perhaps because Hunter's everything Penn wasn't. He's the anti-Penn. I giggle at the thought. But then I stop, still not wanting to wake Hunter.

Does he even eat breakfast? Probably. He's obviously in amazing shape, and I know he works out and runs. Probably a high-protein breakfast for him. Or some kind of smoothie with lots of whey protein and greens.

Blech.

I like to run, but I draw the line at kale protein shakes.

I grab his shirt from the floor and throw it over my shoulders. It covers me like a minidress, and I close my eyes and inhale his musky and masculine scent.

Does anything ever feel better than wearing the shirt of the man you love?

Infusing yourself with the smell and feel of him?

I patter out to the kitchen and look around.

It's a tiny kitchen, smaller even than my own, which surprises me. But when you convert a brownstone, you work with the space you have. He has two bedrooms whereas I have only one.

A drip coffeemaker sits on the counter, so that's my clue that he drinks coffee—that and the fact that he was at the coffee shop. My search yields coffee beans and a grinder. Shoot. As much as I do love freshly ground coffee, I don't want to wake Hunter. But I can't find any ground coffee.

I walk quietly back to the bedroom and shut the door. Maybe that will help keep the coffee grinder noise from waking him.

Once the coffee is brewing, I look in his refrigerator. Sure enough, a dozen eggs sit on the top shelf, along with a package of bacon. I also find some English muffins and strawberry jam.

I have no idea how he likes his eggs, but I like mine scrambled. This is mostly because I never learned the secret to flipping. I always break the yolk. I don't like them sunny-side up because they're kind of gloppy on top.

So scrambled it will be. I make great scrambled eggs. The secret is not to use milk at all and to whisk them until they're really fluffy. Also to fry them in butter. Nothing else will do. Not bacon fat, not coconut oil, not cooking spray.

Only butter.

I start the bacon first in a cast-iron skillet that I find. When it's nearly done, I throw the English muffins in the toaster and begin the scrambled eggs.

I'm lost in my own little fantasy of a life with Hunter when something grazes my neck.

I turn and jump.

He stands there, wearing nothing but his jeans.

I can't help but gawk at him.

"I'm so sorry. I didn't mean to scare you."

"It's okay." I glance down at the frying pan. "I hope you like scrambled eggs."

"Love them." He grabs two mugs out of the cupboard. "Coffee?"

"Absolutely."

"Cream and sugar?"

"Just black, thanks."

He pours a cup and hands it to me, and then he pours his own cup, walks to the refrigerator, and adds a touch of cream.

"No sugar?"

"Nope. I like just a tiny bit of cream to break it up a little bit."

I finish the eggs, and he gets out two plates. The English muffins pop out of the toaster.

"Could you get those?" I ask.

"Sure."

He grabs the English muffins, sets them on each plate, and then I add the bacon and eggs.

He brings the plates to the table while I grab our mugs of coffee.

"Dig in," I say.

He smiles and takes a bite of eggs, swallows, and picks up a slice of bacon. "Frankie, I want you to know that I don't usually let women spend the night with me."

"I figured that, given your history."

"What I'm trying to say is..." He rubs the back of his neck. "I didn't plan on doing it last night."

I stop chewing. Is he sorry? Did he not want this?

"I didn't plan to," he continues, "but I'm really glad you're here."

I resume chewing and swallow. "That's good, I guess. I didn't plan to spend the night, either. I think we fell asleep."

"We did. I woke up about an hour later, and you looked so peaceful I couldn't bear to wake you. So I moved you to the head of the bed and covered you."

"Thank you," I say.

He couldn't bear to wake me. So that means...he kind of wanted to kick me out but then couldn't bear to. I can't quite figure out if that's good or bad.

"I'll be out of your way as soon as we're done with breakfast," I say.

"No. That's not what I mean."

"Look, Hunter." I pick up a piece of bacon. "This is new to both of us, okay? I just got out of a relationship, and you just got out of…the idea that you could never have a relationship. I'm okay going slow. I get it."

"No, Frankie." He reaches toward me and brushes a lock of hair behind my ear. "That's not what I mean. I don't want to go slow."

I stop chewing again. Then I swallow my mouthful of eggs with a gulp. "What *are* you saying?"

"I'm saying that…I have feelings. I don't quite know what to make of them yet. But I'm hoping… That you and I… Together… Maybe we can…"

"You're going to have to finish that sentence at some point." I smile. "I don't want to push you into anything."

"I don't want to push you into anything, either." His gaze doesn't waver from mine. "I want you. I'd do anything to have you. But my whole lifestyle, the things I enjoy in bed—"

"I know what you enjoy, Hunter."

"I wanted to do so much last night," he says, "but after that amazing blow job, I swear to God, Frankie, I don't think I've ever been that relaxed."

I can't help the smile that spreads over my face. "I'm glad you enjoyed yourself."

"Enjoyed myself? That went so far beyond enjoying myself." He reaches across the table, takes my hand, squeezes it. "You're phenomenal. You know that?"

"So are you."

"I'm glad you think so, but what you've experienced is just the beginning of what I have to offer. I'd like to change that, but it's not always pretty, Frankie. I won't make it sound like wine and roses all the time, because it's not. I'm strong-willed, and I get what I want from my sub. Can you handle that?"

My pussy throbs with his words. "Any time."

"After breakfast?"

"Is the club open during the day?"

"No." His gaze turns darker. "But my bedroom is."

I gulp. "I need a shower."

"My shower is also open."

"I have work…"

"I won't keep you too long. I have an afternoon class."

"Hunter…"

He narrows his eyes, and I swear, they're burning right through me.

I bite my lip. "I don't mean I don't want to be here. I totally do. I just… I don't want to push you, Hunter."

"You can't push me. I'm unpushable."

"Okay… Even though I totally should be working on my article today, I have to say spending some more time in your bedroom sounds like heaven."

He squeezes my hand again. "Sounds like heaven to me, too."

"I also want to thank you," I say.

"For what?"

I set down my coffee mug. "For opening up to me last night about Allison and Teresa. I know Allison especially meant a lot to you."

"She did."

"Would you still be with her if she were still alive?"

"I don't know. Does it matter?"

"I suppose it doesn't."

"I understand why you're asking. You're thinking if Allison hadn't died, she and I would still be together, and you and I wouldn't have met."

"Well...yeah."

"But she did die, Frankie, and you and I did meet. And you've already taught me so much."

"I've taught *you* something? You? The scholar? You? The Dominant?"

"Yeah. You taught me how to feel again. You made me *want* to feel. Once I got over being scared of it, once I took my mask off, I remembered what feeling felt like. No pun intended."

"I want to be honest with you, Hunter. I'm feeling something for you that I'm not sure I've ever felt before."

"Not even with the guy you were with for over five years?"

"Not even him. That was a big mistake. But I suppose if I hadn't made that mistake, I wouldn't have been sitting in the bar that night, and I wouldn't have met you."

"See?" He smiles. "Everything that's happened in our lives has led us to this point. And I'd like to make the most of it."

"Then take me to your bedroom," I say, "and bind me. Bind me to the bed like you promised last night."

CHAPTER FORTY-TWO

Hunter

Frankie looks so sexy in my shirt. It's been difficult keeping my hands off of her, but she went to all the trouble to make me breakfast, so I felt I should eat it.

Plus, it was good, and now, with some protein and carbs in my system, I'll be able to really show her what I want to do with her.

As I lead her back to my bedroom, my gaze falls on the Phantom of the Opera mask sitting on top of my dresser. The stark white against the black lacquer of the wood.

I'll still wear it at the club, of course. I'm known there as Phantom, and even though I trust everyone I see there, I still don't want to show my face.

In fact, I think I'll have Frankie wear a mask at the club as well.

But the mask represents so much more than just hiding my identity at the club. It represents a part of me that no longer exists. That part of me that wanted to stay distant from my partners.

The mask was a layer between us.

And with Frankie? I no longer need the mask.

I no longer *want* the mask.

I'm no longer Phantom. I'm Hunter. Professor Hunter Stone.

And I'm…

I think I might be falling in love.

"You look hot in my shirt," I growl at her, "but it's going to have to come off." I grab the collar and rip it off of her, sending buttons flying.

She gasps.

"I hope you know how to sew the buttons back on," I tell her.

Her mouth drops.

I chuckle. "I'm only kidding, Frankie. I don't expect you to be my seamstress."

"Good, because I don't know which end of the needle is up. But I do know a good dry cleaner where I get all my mending done. I'll be happy to take it in for you."

"That's kind of you, but the buttons coming off was my fault, and I'll see that they're fixed."

She smiles.

"Now," I say, "this is normally when I tell my submissive to keep quiet for the rest of the scene, but I'm not going to do that with you. I *want* you to speak. I want to hear what you're thinking, what you're feeling. Okay?"

She nods.

"That's not telling me anything."

"Of course it is. A nod is body language. Telling you yes. That's amazing. And thank you. Because I want to be able to tell you what I'm feeling, Hunter. It's a big part of the experience for me, letting my partner know how I feel."

"Good," I say. "Because I want to hear everything,

Frankie. I want to know how you're feeling, how I'm making *you* feel."

"Absolutely. Will you tell me how *you're* feeling?"

"I'm not sure I'll be able *not* to." I grab the leather bindings from last night. "Now, I'm going to bind your wrists together and then secure them to the headboard. Okay?"

"Okay."

My fingers graze her skin as I secure the leather bindings around each wrist. She shivers slightly, but is she scared? Or is she turned on?

I don't want her to be scared, but I choose not to mention it. I simply say, "If at any time you want to stop, you just need to tell me to stop."

"I will, but Hunter, I'm not going to want you to stop."

God, my cock aches inside these jeans. I'm already so hard, and I'm only getting harder.

But I'll go slowly. I want to show her some of the joys of being bound. When she's secure in place on my bed, I return to my bureau and pull out a few objects. The first is a feather. The second is a flogger.

I return to her, to the delicacy laid out before me, and I fan the feather over her chin, down her neck, between her breasts.

Another shiver.

She's not scared. She's turned on.

Then I hold up the flogger. "Do you know what this is, Frankie?"

"A flogger?"

"Yes." This time I trail the flogger between her breasts, over her mound, and then over one side and then the other.

Then I bring it down upon her with a whip.

She gasps.

The magic… The pure magic of watching her capillaries give rise to the beautiful pink flush. "Your thigh is getting red. Do you have any idea how beautiful you look when you're pink all over? When that beautiful rosiness rises to your cheeks and the tops of your breasts?"

I bring the flogger over her breasts, making sure I hit the nipple with a flick. Pure rosiness…and the nipple. It's hard and straining.

She gasps again, this time arching her back.

Nice.

"You have gorgeous breasts, Frankie. And those nipples? Like a fucking red-hot candy. Amazing. I think I'd taste cinnamon if I sucked on them."

"Would you?"

"Would I what?"

"Would you suck on them? Please?"

"I like that you say please, and I will. I've planned to. But not quite yet."

I bring the flogger down on her breast once more.

Again she arches her back, raises her hips.

I bring the flogger down on her mound, knowing that I'm catching her clit.

"Oh God!" she cries out.

I want to ask her if it feels good, which isn't like me. I never ask a sub. It's up to the sub to let me know how she's feeling through her actions or sounds. If it's not good, if she wants me to stop, she'll use her safe word.

But Frankie isn't my sub. Or she is—I hope—but she's something more.

And I *want* to know how she feels.

"Good?" I ask.

"God, yes." On a soft sigh.

My cock is harder in my jeans. It's already hard as steel, and my God, I ache to be inside her hot little cunt.

But that will wait.

I bring the flogger back down on her breasts.

Then again three times in a row, and with each thrash, what the leather feels seems to creep from the instrument and into my arm, shooting electricity straight to my groin.

She's beautifully red, her lips parted, her eyes closed, her arms bound above her.

"Now spread your legs," I command. "I'm going to suck that delicious pussy."

She doesn't hesitate to obey me.

Still wearing my jeans, I crawl between her legs.

First, I just gaze at her wet and succulent pussy, the beautiful, swollen pink flesh.

And I inhale.

That musky smell that is unique to each female. And I swear Frankie smells sweeter than anyone.

God, even Allison.

And then Allison falls from my mind, just as the rest of the cement falls from my heart.

But these feelings are too much, so I push them aside and clamp my mouth onto her.

I suck at her as she writhes against my mouth, eating the cream that flows freely from her.

When I'm finally sated, I move to her clit, swirl my tongue over it, and then suck it gently between my lips as I thrust two fingers inside her heat.

Her orgasm is instant, and she clamps around my fingers, milking them, as I massage her G-spot and lick her clit.

My promise to suck her nipples falls completely from my mind, and I crawl toward her, shove my cock inside her, and crush my mouth to hers.

She responds to my kiss, and I fuck her almost violently as our tongues tangle.

Thrust, thrust, thrust…

Until–

I rip my mouth from hers and roar my release.

My God…

My God…

I stay embedded inside her for a moment, until I realize I forgot the condom.

I can't bear to leave her, though. She has nothing to fear from me, as I get tested regularly and I always wear a condom.

I doubt I have anything to fear from her, as she's on birth control and she's been in a monogamous relationship for the last five years. Except, of course, her fiancé was cheating on her.

So I withdraw.

"Frankie?"

"Hmm?" she says dreamily.

"I apologize. I forgot the condom."

"Okay," she says. "On the pill."

"I know. I mean…"

Her eyes pop open. "You're not telling me you–"

"Oh no. I'm totally clean."

"And you think I…" She rolls away from me. "For God's sake, Hunter."

"We haven't talked about this."

"For your information, I got tested for everything once I found out Penn had been cheating on me. I'm completely clean."

I resist a sigh of relief. I knew she wouldn't put me in

any danger. Just like I wouldn't put her in any danger.

"I guess we can forget condoms from now on." I smile.

"Yeah, we can, as soon as I get over the fact that you thought I was some kind of danger to you. My God, Hunter. I'm not the one who plays with a new woman every week. Don't you think I would've stopped you if I knew you were at risk?"

"Of course I do. Frankie, this isn't a reason to get upset."

"You know? It kind of is." She pulls at her bindings.

"Don't. I don't want you to chafe."

"Unbind me, Hunter. I want to go home."

"I thought you said you needed a shower."

"I do. I'll get it at my own place."

"Frankie..."

"This isn't over, okay? That's not what I'm saying. I'm just a little pissed right now, Hunter. And I need to get over it. I need to go home, take a shower, and maybe do some work. I'll call you later."

Ten minutes later, she's out the door, summoning an Uber on her phone.

I told her I'd take her home, but she said no.

I sigh and head to the kitchen for another cup of coffee.

Something good came into my life and dissolved the concrete around my heart.

And now I've managed to fuck it up.

CHAPTER FORTY-THREE

Frankie

I slam my door when I get back to my apartment.

This is my own damned fault. I went and fell in love with the rebound guy. Who does that?

I've read all the magazine articles. Hell, I've *written* the articles. I know better.

I'm not even angry with Hunter. Why *shouldn't* he be concerned? He knew I just ended a relationship because my fiancé was cheating on me. Of course he'd wonder if said fiancé may have infected me with something.

On the other hand, though, he routinely has sex with many women. One at a time, sure, but still. If one of us had reason to be concerned, it certainly wasn't him.

And I *wasn't* concerned.

I trust him. He's a college professor, a scholar. He knows all about sexually transmitted diseases, so of course he wears condoms and tests himself regularly.

Who wouldn't?

Just as I got myself tested as soon as I found out fucking Penn was cheating on me.

It was a month ago, and everything came out clean.

But I will get tested again in five months, just to make sure.

Still, I'm pretty confident I'm clean. Penn did say I had nothing to worry about, that he was always safe during his cheating sessions.

Now that I know said sessions took place at the club? I'm pretty damned sure no partner would let him near her without a condom.

I've just pulled out my laptop to work on my article when someone knocks on the door.

I hope—yet I don't hope—it's Hunter. I'm so not in the mood right now. Except I want to see him anyway.

I walk to the door and check through the peephole.

It's Mandy.

I open the door. "What do you want?"

"Hello to you too." Mandy brushes past me as she walks in.

"I'm working today, Mand. How'd you know I'd even be here?"

"I took a chance. Maybe I was hoping you wouldn't be." She rubs at her forehead. "There's something that's been bugging me that I really want to tell you. I had a long heart-to-heart with Jack last night, and we agreed that we wouldn't violate any agreements and that I should tell you."

"Violate any agreements? What are you talking about?"

Mandy bites her lower lip. "Can we sit?"

"Sure. Are you and Jackson all right?"

"Yes, of course. We're fine."

"Mom and Dad?"

"Of course."

"Jackson's mom and dad?"

"Frank, for God's sake. Everyone's fine and healthy."

"What is it? And why are you mentioning some kind of—"

Oh my God. Violation of an agreement. Like an NDA, maybe?

I don't even want to think about where this is going, but I already have an idea. Mandy's strangeness at dinner when I mentioned the subject of my article...

"The thing is," Mandy says, "the reason Penn came to you and told you he was cheating is because Jack and I made him."

"Oh… Okay." I narrow my gaze. "And why would you do that? How would you even know he was cheating?"

Mandy pauses, and her cheeks turn bright red.

"You see… Jack and I saw him."

"Saw him where?"

"We saw him…cheating on you."

God…

Probably the same place *I* saw him having sex.

At freaking Black Rose Underground.

"How exactly did you see him cheating?" *Except, oh my God, I don't want to know.*

"I can't tell you where, but it was at a…"

"It was at a leather club," I finish for her.

Mandy jerks backward against the wall. "Yes! How did you know?"

"How did *you* know, Mandy?"

"I…"

"Please, don't. This is already too much information about my sister."

My God. I could run into my sister at the club. Not just Penn but Mandy. And Jack.

"I only told you because I felt you had the right to know

that Jack and I started this. It's between you and me, Frankie. We all have to sign a nondisclosure agreement to get into the club. I can't tell you where it is or who I see there."

"Right, I understand." More than she knows. "So you like to get tied up. What's the harm in that?"

Easy for me to say, since I was bound this morning.

What is this going to mean for Hunter and me? I'm not going to feel comfortable going back to Black Rose knowing I may run into my sister. It's bad enough I might run into Penn.

Granted, Hunter and I don't do anything out in the open, but still.

What if Mandy and Jack *do*?

Ugh. I just got an image in my mind that I'll never be able to unsee.

"It's…a very private part of my life."

"How private can it be, if you do things in the club?"

"We…have a private room."

Thank God. I never have to worry about seeing my sister tied up and getting fucked in the bondage room.

Still…it's just too weird.

The whole thing is too weird.

This stuff I'm feeling for Hunter? It can't be love. It's rebound sex. That's it.

And now I know I have to end things with him.

I can't go back to Black Rose Underground. Not ever. And I can't ask him to give it up. It's a big part of his life as Phantom. He'll go back to his life, back to playing with different partners and having no feelings.

It won't be too difficult for him.

It'll rip *my* heart out, but he'll be fine.

"I'm taking a risk telling you all of this," Mandy

continues, "but Jack and I decided you really should know. That he and I are the reason…"

"That Penn told me?"

"Well…yeah."

"Are you kidding me? I'd still be with the jerk if you hadn't. I should thank you."

"No. I don't want your thanks, Frankie. I want your forgiveness. For so many things."

"About forgetting what date it was when you and Jack announced your engagement? I'm over it, Mandy."

"Yeah, for that, and also for being the catalyst that ended your relationship."

"I don't want to be with a man who cheats on me," I say. "If you hadn't seen him and made him tell me, we'd probably still be together—God, we'd be *married*—and I would be completely in the dark."

"I know that. And I know you're better off without him. You've always been better off without him. But still…I feel badly. I feel badly because you were planning this lovely wedding, and now you're alone."

I open my mouth to tell her that I'm not alone, but then I close it abruptly.

I have to end things with Hunter.

Crap. I told him when I left that it wasn't over. I just needed to get away, and at the time, that was true.

But now? Knowing my sister and her fiancé, as well as my ex, go to that club?

I can't ask Hunter to choose between me and the club. I can't. I don't believe in giving a partner an ultimatum.

But I can't go back to the club, knowing I may run into my ex or my sister. It's just too…*icky*.

I was looking forward to exploring more of the club and

everything it had to offer Hunter and me.

But I can give it up. It hasn't been a part of my life up until now.

The problem? Giving up Hunter.

I can almost hear my heart cracking in two.

"You okay?" Mandy asks.

"Yeah, I'm fine."

"You don't look fine. You look…kind of tired, actually."

"I had a busy night."

"Frankie, are you seeing someone?"

"No."

Not anymore, anyway.

"You know, Jack works with a lot of single guys. I bet we could—"

I hold up my hand to stop her. "No. No blind dates. No fixups. I am perfectly capable of finding dates on my own."

"I know that, Frank. You never had any problem in that area. That was all me."

"Only because you made yourself a wallflower, Mandy. You were always pretty. Beautiful, even. You had eyes only for one man."

That gets a smile out of her. "I did. I know I missed out on other guys, but Jackson was the only guy for me. I'm just thankful he finally returned my feelings."

"I'm happy for you, Mandy. Truly."

The words are true. My big sister deserves happiness. She deserves the best.

I just wish she hadn't found it at Black Rose Underground.

But I don't want to take that away from her. And I *can't* take it away from Hunter.

"Can I take you to lunch?" Mandy asks.

I check my watch. "It's after one."

"I haven't eaten yet. You want to get some sushi or something?"

"You and Jackson and your sushi. But I don't think—" Then I change my mind. I have to deal with this whole Hunter-club thing, but I still have to eat. "You know what? That sounds pretty good. Let me grab my purse."

I head into the bedroom, grab my purse and my phone. "Let's go."

"Great. Jack and I found a new place that's not too expensive and serves amazing portions. I can't wait to treat you."

"You got it, sis." I force a smile as we head out.

CHAPTER FORTY-FOUR

Hunter

"I'd call Heathcliff the classic Byronic hero," Laura Snyder says in my second-period Romantic Literature class.

"So would everyone else who's familiar with the term," I say. "You're going to need to dig a little deeper."

Laura's cheeks blush. "I mean, he's dark, you know? A loner."

"So you're saying all loners are dark?" I decide to cut Laura a break by calling on someone else whose hand is raised. "Dina?"

"I agree that he's a Byronic hero, of course, but there's more of an edge to Heathcliff than, say, even the phantom in Leroux's masterpiece."

"Darker than being physically scarred?" I ask.

"For sure. Erik in *Phantom* had physical and emotional scars. Heathcliff's are all emotional."

"So you're saying emotional scars can be worse than physical?" I ask.

"Yes, that's exactly what I'm saying."

"I'd agree, though unless one is as physically scarred as the phantom was, I'm not sure the question can be answered accurately. But let's get back to the Byronic hero. The dark-and-brooding type with mysterious origins. Usually a troubled past. We may be able to understand Heathcliff better if we compare him to other Byronic heroes. Can anyone give me an example of a Byronic hero in contemporary literature?"

"Bruce Wayne?" a guy from the back row says with a chuckle.

I smile. "He definitely fits the type, though I'd be hard-pressed to call comic books literature."

"Anakin Skywalker." Another guy from the back.

"You know the type for sure," I say. "Now...contemporary literature?" I nod to a young man in the second row whose name escapes me. "Yes?"

"Severus Snape," he says. "From *Harry Potter.* Is that considered literature?"

"Of course. Young adult literature is still literature, and Snape definitely fits the bill. Any others?"

Laura raises her hand again.

"Laura?"

"Jaime Lannister, maybe? From *A Game of Thrones*?"

"Jaime is definitely an antihero, but I wouldn't classify him as Byronic."

"Why not?"

"He's intelligent and cunning, and clearly he doesn't care about social norms, since he's doing his sister—"

Chuckles permeate the room.

"—but he's not a loner, and he doesn't have a mysterious or troubled past."

"I see." Laura blushes again.

"But you got close." I smile at her. "Any others?" Then I glance at the clock. The period is over. "Maybe next time. See you all next time."

The students gather their books, rise, and leave the room, murmuring together.

I shuffle through some notes on my desk, and I've just pulled up a lesson plan on my iPad when a figure appears in my doorway.

"Could I speak to you for a moment, Dr. Stone?"

I look up from my iPad.

My classes are over for the day, and I don't recognize the attractive young woman standing at my desk.

"Sure. What can I help you with?"

"I was wondering…if you'd like to have a cup of coffee sometime."

"I'm sorry," I say, "but it's against the rules of the university for a professor to date a student."

"But I'm no longer *your* student."

No, she's not, and I wish I remembered her name so I could address her. But I don't.

"But you're still a student at the university," I say.

"It's a ridiculous rule," she says. "I could understand it if I were in your class, but I'm not."

"It's still the rule."

She smiles. "I know a professor who bends that rule."

I know several, but it's never led to anything good. "I don't," I say succinctly.

Crestfallen, she—God, I wish I remembered her name—leaves the classroom.

This happens to me a lot, but this is the first time it's happened since I met Frankie.

Frankie, who I'm falling for.

Frankie, who didn't call me last night as she said she would.

I'm giving her some space. The last thing I want to do is smother her. I've been smothered before, and it's not pretty.

Then another knock on my open door.

I look up. "Oh, hey, Linda. Come on in."

Linda Burnett, the chair of the English Lit department, enters. Linda's about ten years older than I am, and she's a great person. We've had many chats over the years about *The Great Gatsby.*

"Hey, Hunter. Who was that just leaving your classroom?"

"A former student." I shake my head. "She wanted to have coffee with me."

"You turned her down, I hope."

"Of course I did. You know me better than that."

Her forehead is wrinkled, and she wasn't smiling when she entered.

"You look glum." I frown. "What's going on?"

She clears her throat and sits down across from my desk. "There's no easy way to say this, so I'm going to just blurt it out. Are you publishing an erotic novel under the pen name of Sterling Parker?"

I drop my jaw. No. Just no. "I'm not sure what business that is of yours."

"Normally, it wouldn't be, Hunter, but you're one of our most published professors in academic journals. I would have appreciated a heads-up about this."

"I haven't admitted to anything."

She sighs. "I suppose you haven't been on social media lately."

"I'm never on social media, Linda."

"I'm afraid you've been outed," she says. "Did you ever

have a copy of this manuscript in your office?"

"I haven't admitted to writing anything other than my publications in academic journals and my nonfiction book on F. Scott Fitzgerald's works."

"I'm not your enemy here, Hunter. I'm trying to help you."

"Help me with what?"

"Did you write the novel?"

"For Christ's sake, Linda. Yes, I wrote the novel. I'm Sterling Parker. I'm not ashamed of my work, but I chose to use a pseudonym for exactly this reason. I didn't want any blowback here at work."

"I'm afraid it's a little late for that."

"I'm still not ashamed. The book is damned good, and though it's fictional, it's based on years of research into alternative sexual lifestyles during the Regency and Victorian eras. My agent says she's never read anything like it, and—"

Linda holds up her hand. "I'm not questioning the validity of the work, Hunter. You're an excellent researcher, an original thinker, and a talented writer. We all know that. The issue is the potential scandal that's brewing on social media."

I roll my eyes. "It'll blow over. Things like this always do."

"I hope so," Linda says. "The university can't afford another scandal—not after what happened with Logan Armstrong."

"That was a witch hunt. Logan never touched that young man."

"I know that, and so do you. And so does he. And so does that kid. But Title IX requires the school to investigate everything."

"Logan told me all about it," I say. "He rejected the guy's advances, and the guy got pissed, so he started everything. It's over now."

"Yes," Linda agrees. "That's over, but it was enough for Logan to leave Mellville. I don't want to lose you, too."

"Because someone thinks I wrote an erotic novel? So what? I did. I'm a human being, Linda. I'm allowed to have a life and interests outside the university. But this is a private matter. I do not like when my privacy is threatened."

"Of course. I understand." She twists her lips. "But I'm not going to lie, Hunter. I have a bad feeling about this." She rises, leaves, and closes the door.

I gather my stuff, head to the subway, and get on the first train. I'm pissed. I never wanted my pen name to become known because my private life is private. It's not the end of the world, but who outed me?

I'm always careful, so it couldn't have been anyone at the college. I never had my manuscript on the university system, and I certainly didn't keep a hard copy anywhere on campus.

The only people who know are my agent and my publisher, and they wouldn't...

Shit...

I ride along, watching the subway doors open at each stop. I have no idea where I'm going until I get off the train and somehow end up in front of Frankie's building.

It's six o'clock, so she may still be at work.

I walk into her building, nodding to the doorman.

"Can I help you, sir?"

"I need to see Francesca Thomas. She's expecting me."

"Sure, I remember you. Go on up."

I head to Frankie's apartment and knock on the door.

A few seconds later, she opens it. "Hello, Hunter."

I walk briskly in. "You said you'd call me last night, Frankie. What's going on?"

"I..."

"Damn it!" I grab her and crush my mouth to hers.

Her lips are already parted, and I dive my tongue between them.

She kisses me back, her need apparently as great as mine.

Until she breaks the kiss.

She gasps as she wipes her mouth. "What are you doing here?"

"I needed to see you. Why didn't you call me last night?"

"I had to think," she says.

"You told me when you left that it wasn't over."

"I..."

"I've had a shit day, Francesca, and I cannot take any lies tonight. What the fuck is going on?"

"I just..." She buries her face in her hands. "I don't think it's going to work, Hunter."

"You're feeling what I'm feeling." I rake my gaze over her as emotion—anger, passion, rage—boils through me. "I already know this. The way you react to me. The way you're looking at me now. The way your cheeks are red, the way you're squirming. I know your pussy is wet for me, Frankie. So why do you want to end this?"

"It's not that I want to, Hunter. It's..."

I advance on her, grab her, and pull her to me. I slide my lips over her neck up to her earlobe and tug on it harshly. "Tell me I'm not making you hot right now," I whisper. "Tell me you don't want me the way I want you. Tell me my cock can't possibly be this hard for a woman who doesn't want me."

"I... I..."

I sweep her into my arms, walk into her bedroom. Her bed is unmade, which is endearing to me.

"Have you forgotten you were spanked in this apartment, Frankie? Because I'm going to spank your ass until it's so red and burning and your pussy is so wet that you beg me to fuck you."

"Hunter... Please..."

"Please what, Frankie?" My tone is harsh, the way I speak to a disobedient sub who isn't disobedient for long. "Please stop? All you have to do is tell me to stop, and I will."

"Please..." she breathes.

"Please... What...?" I say through clenched teeth.

"Please... Please fuck me. Spank me. Then fuck me. Make me hurt, Hunter. Please."

I say no more.

Normally, at the club, I have them undress for me. It's part of the fantasy, part of the turn-on.

Tonight, I want Frankie to be naked, and I want to get her that way as quickly as possible.

She's still in her work clothes—a short black skirt, a white blouse, and a gray blazer.

And those pumps she always wears. Those freaking black patent leather platform pumps, with the bright red soles that make her legs look even longer, and damn, they're sexy as hell.

I like it when she leaves them on while we fuck, but not tonight. Tonight, they're coming off. I lay her down on the bed and pluck them off of her feet.

She's wearing pantyhose. First time I've seen her wear them. Her legs are usually bare. But Frankie's a professional woman, and when she goes to work, she looks the part.

I ease my hands under her skirt, ready to rip the hose off when—

"God..." I groan.

They're not pantyhose after all, but nude-colored nylon stockings held in place by a garter belt.

My cock hardens further.

"Fuck it all," I say through clenched teeth. "My God, you're sexy."

"It's a brand-new pair of stockings, Hunter."

"So what?" I rip the first one from the garter belt, and then the second, until her legs are bare.

If I ruin them, I'll buy her a new pair. I don't give a fuck right now.

I rip the garter belt off her next, and then her skirt, pulling it over her thighs and throwing it on the floor. Lace panties. Fucking nude-colored lace panties. I take the waistband between my teeth and rip as hard as I can.

The waistband disintegrates under my attack, and I throw the panties on the floor.

Frankie's eyes are closed, her cheeks flushed.

She's enjoying this.

And so am I.

Only her jacket, blouse, and bra separate me from her nude body.

I'd tear them off her, but part of me doesn't want to ruin her work clothes. I already trashed her stockings, garter belt, and panties.

"Get up," I command. "Sit up and take the rest of them off. Right now. As quickly as you can."

She pops up and obeys me. Within seconds, the blazer, blouse, and bra have joined the rest of her clothes on the floor.

Her gorgeous tits fall gently against her chest, and her nipples are ripe and hard.

I smash my mouth to one, sucking hard as I twist the other with my fingers.

"Oh my God!" she cries.

I bite harder, twist harder. She tangles her hands in my hair, pulling at it and then caressing my scalp.

I work her tits until they're close to raw, and then I let them go, flip her over, bring her up onto her knees.

Then I shed my own clothes quickly, and I thrust my cock into her from behind.

She's so wet that I slide right in.

I stay there a moment, allow myself to simply enjoy the completion, allow myself to forget the horribleness of this day—Linda's visit and the imminent social media scandal surrounding my novel, yes, but even more so, the memory of Frankie telling me it's not going to work out.

Right then, I realize what's important.

I'll fight against any social media scandal.

But even more? I'll fight for Frankie.

And I'll win. I will win both fights.

I fuck her hard and fast, and once my rage subsides, I slide in and out of her slowly, savoring every second of it.

Beneath me, she sobs into her pillow. "Hunter, Hunter… So good."

So good? I'll give her so good.

I pull out of her, flip her over onto her back, and then thrust back inside. I roll us onto our sides so we're facing each other, and I look down, watching our bodies come together.

The beauty and the simplicity of two bodies coming together.

But there's more beauty in our souls coming together.

Surely she must feel it too.

"You're not ending this," I say through gritted teeth. "I will not let you."

"There, there are… There are… My God!" She cries out as she comes, clenching around me.

That's all it takes to send me over the edge.

I thrust into her once more, hard and quickly, and I release. Release into her.

In that moment, I give her not only my body but my heart and soul.

She cannot end this.

I won't allow it.

We lie there, still facing each other, for what seems like an eternity but is only seconds. Finally, I pull out of her, my cock still semi-hard.

"My God," she says. "That was phenomenal, Hunter. I've never experienced anything like that in my life."

"Then you've changed your mind? You're not ending this?"

She doesn't reply.

"Spit it out, Francesca. I've had a shit day, and I need you to lay it on the line."

She opens her eyes. "You know we saw Penn at the club."

"I know."

"I just found out…today…that my sister and her fiancé go there as well."

"So what?"

"It's just too weird, Hunter. What if we saw them there? It was bad enough seeing Penn there."

I drop my jaw and keep myself from rolling my eyes. "You're kidding me, right? *That's* why you're ending this?

Because you don't want to go to the club anymore?"

"It just feels too strange to me. And I can't ask you to give up the club, Hunter. It's a huge part of your life. You love it."

She's not wrong. I do love the club.

But I love her more.

My God. I'm in love, and it's different from Allison. Different from Teresa.

It's unique, just as love should be. With Teresa, I was trying to duplicate what I had with Allison. Now? I realize love can never be duplicated. Love can't be reproduced because it's always unique between two individuals.

I love Frankie. I love her so much.

Am I willing to give up the club for her?

Damn. I never thought it would come to this.

For a moment, I consider it. I consider giving up the club and all it's meant to me over these years.

Granted, if I pursue a relationship with Frankie, I will need the club less. But still…it can be a place where she blooms. Where we bloom together. Where we find her fantasies.

I love Frankie more than the club, and yesterday, I might have agreed to give it up.

But not today.

Today, I will fight.

I will fight whatever scandal comes my way. I will fight for the club.

Most of all, I'll fight for Frankie.

I'll fight for what I deserve.

CHAPTER FORTY-FIVE

Frankie

Silence.

Hunter is silent for so long that I wonder if he's lost the use of his voice.

Finally, he says, "I can't give up the club."

"Which is why I won't ask you to."

Sadness rips a hole in my heart. It really is over.

He's just the rebound guy, I tell myself.

Though I desperately want to believe those words, I know them to be false. Hunter is *not* a rebound guy for me. Hunter is the real thing.

Love.

Love that I never felt for Penn or anyone else.

That's how I know it's the real thing.

"So if I don't agree to give up the club, we're over."

His words are a statement, not a question.

"What about a different club?" I ask. "I know, from my research, that there are at least four more in the city."

"I've been to all of them. They're not for me."

"Compromise, Hunter. It's part of every relationship."

He shakes his head. "I chose Black Rose Underground for a reason. It fits me. So I paid for a lifetime membership, Frankie. Lifetime. No refunds. It's not just a club. It's *my* club."

"But..."

"You're sticking to this? Even after I told you I shelled out mid five figures for a lifetime membership? Really?"

I bite my lip. I don't want to say it. I don't want to—

"Say it. I need to hear you say it."

"I..."

Why won't the words come? I've already said them. But now...they're lodged in my throat like a dry crust of bread that refuses to go down. I love the club. I love how it's opened up a whole new world for me, but...

He sighs. "This has been the shittiest day of my life."

I lift my eyebrows. "Has it? Think back, Hunter. Really think back. Is this truly the worst day of your life?"

He wrinkles his forehead.

He's thinking about Allison. About the day he lost her. Then about the year of mourning.

This is *not* the shittiest day of his life. Not by a long shot.

He finally meets my gaze. "Yes, Frankie. Yes, it is."

My heart cracks in two. I can almost hear the symbolic break. "Please, Hunter. Have you forgotten that I know what you went through with Allison? How you lost the love of your life?"

"It hurt," he says. "It hurt like I never thought I was capable of hurting. At least at that time. I remember it like it was yesterday, how I felt like my heart had been torn from my body. Like I would never feel again. But you know what? Allison *wasn't* the love of my life."

"She wasn't?" I swallow.

"No, she wasn't." He takes my hands. "You are, Francesca Thomas. You, with all your quirks. You crashed into me and melted the ice around my heart. And now you're going to leave me. So clearly you don't feel the way that I do."

"But I *do*."

"Save it. You already told me it's over."

"Hunter, I had no idea."

"Of course you didn't." He drops my hands. "To you, I'm simply expendable. You want to toss me aside because you're afraid we might run into your sister at the club. That makes me feel pretty insignificant, which I clearly am to you."

"But you're not." Tears well in my eyes. "Can't you see that this is destroying me? I love you too!"

He freezes, as if he's made of stone. Seconds pass, seconds that seem like hours, until he finally speaks.

"What?"

"Is there something wrong with your hearing? I said I love you."

"Then how can you do this?" He shakes his head and pulls at his hair. "What am I missing here?"

"It's just too weird for me, Hunter. I might run into my sister and brother-in-law there. We've already run into my ex. How *can't* you see that it's weird for me?"

"So your discomfort is more important to you than I am."

I drop my jaw.

I don't know how to answer him, because though I wasn't thinking of it in that way, he's absolutely right.

"You know what?" He clenches his hands into fists. "I'm sick of worrying about other people's discomfort. I'm going to fight. I'm going to fight for you. And if the prude asses at the university aren't comfortable with the kind of literature

I write, they can all suck my dick. I'll fight them, too. I'll fight for my job."

"Wait..." I shake my head to clear it. "What? What about your job?"

"Yeah, I told you it was a shit day. Someone found out about my upcoming novel and is spreading my pen name all over social media."

"You didn't tell me your pen name."

"It's Sterling Parker."

"So you're only telling me because I can find out on social, right?"

He balls his hands into fists. "Jesus, Frankie, I would have told you. You didn't fucking ask me!"

"Because you're so private, Hunter. You didn't want me using anything from you in the article, and you—"

"God, yes! I'm private. My privacy means a lot to me. That's another reason why I chose Black Rose. It has the best NDA and the best security. This is *my* business, Frankie. Mine and no one else's."

"I... I understand. But is your job in jeopardy?"

"Not yet," he says.

"That's good. I mean, shouldn't you be allowed to do what you please during your free time? I think it's in the Constitution."

He simply shakes his head.

"You have to fight it," I say.

"Absolutely, Frankie. I will fight it. And I will fight for you, too."

"You already have me. I love you."

"You love your comfort more." He shakes his head. "I asked you to stop writing the article. You refused. If you ask me to give up the club, I will also refuse."

"I know that, which is why I'm not asking you to leave the club."

"I think we can have everything." He paces around the room and then back until he comes face-to-face with me. "I think I can keep you *and* the club."

"I suppose I could ask Mandy and Jack to stop going to the club." Then: "Shit!" I clasp my hand over my mouth.

"Jackson Paris?"

"My God. What a mess I've made of things. I've violated my NDA in so many ways already."

"Actually, you haven't. I know Jackson, and I know his fiancée, Mandy. I've met her a few times. I'm not sure I ever knew her last name, but now that you mention it, your eyes are similar to hers."

"I've done it now."

"You've done nothing. We're all members of the club and all bound by the same confidentiality agreement. I already know they go there. You haven't done anything."

"They…know who you are?"

"No. Only Claude and Braden Black—and his brother, Ben—know my real identity. But they know me. They know Phantom."

"Oh." I look down.

"So back to this. Your discomfort."

The look on his face guts me. The full-lipped frown. The tight jaw. But his eyes are what get me. They're shadowed, sad, distraught.

What a fool I'm being. I enjoy the club. I'm finding so much of myself there. Hunter enjoys the club. Hunter and I love each other. Nothing else is relevant.

"You know what? I'll get over it. We'll use the club. Jackson already knows who you are, and Mandy's my sister, so the two of you will meet."

"Would it be different if Jackson and I didn't know each other?"

"You know what? No, it wouldn't." I reach toward him, cup one of his stubbly cheeks. "I've been an idiot, Hunter. I love you. And honestly, I had no idea you felt the same way about me. I didn't think there was any possibility of that."

"After I brought you to my home and everything?"

"Honestly, no. The stories you told about Allison. How much she meant to you and how gutted you were when you lost her. And then Teresa and how you got burned by her, trying to recreate what you had with Allison. I wasn't sure you would ever let yourself feel again. That's what I told myself, anyway."

"I'm sorry, Frankie."

"Are you kidding me? You have nothing to be sorry for. I'm the one who's sorry. I'm the one who put my personal comfort ahead of what we have together. It won't happen again, Hunter. I promise you that. In fact, if you want me to put the kibosh on the article, I'll do it. I'll do it for *your* comfort."

"Absolutely not," he says. "You don't give up the article, and I don't give up the club. We can both be happy with both of those decisions. We have to make allowances for each other. Compromise. I'm not thrilled about the article, but it's important to you. If you can get past your discomfort of possibly running into your sister at the club, I can certainly get over my discomfort with your article."

He kisses me then—a long, slow, passionate kiss, different from our normal raw and savage kisses.

This is a kiss that says everything's okay between us.

This is a kiss that says *I love you.*

CHAPTER FORTY-SIX

Hunter

Snickers from my students greet me when I enter the classroom the next morning.

Then silence.

And stares.

I suppose this is what I get for ignoring social media. Who knows what kind of shitstorm is taking place online?

"All right," I say, setting down my messenger bag, pulling out my iPad, and finding today's lesson plan. "We ended last time talking about Heathcliff and how he's a classic Byronic hero. Today, I want to focus more on Catherine and her role in the story in preparation for your next paper."

The expected groans don't come.

I raise my eyebrows. "Great! I see you're excited about the next paper. That's good news. It will be a compare and contrast of either Heathcliff or Catherine with a similar contemporary hero of your choice. And yes, it can be Anakin Skywalker or any other movie or comic book hero. I won't limit it to literature only."

They're still eerily silent.

I breathe in, hold it, and exhale. Best to be proactive in situations like these.

"You've no doubt seen what's happening on social media. Yes, I wrote a novel of erotic fiction under a pen name. It will be releasing in a few months. That's all I'm going to say on the matter. Now, let's talk Catherine Earnshaw. Dina, could you tell us some of the characteristics of our heroine?"

Dina Strauss always sits in the front row, always participates, and always has something insightful to say.

"Uh...yeah. Sure, Dr. Stone." She grabs her paperback of *Wuthering Heights* and flips through it.

Unusual for her.

"Anyone else?" I ask.

"Do you teach erotica?" someone asks from the back.

Here it comes...

"No. Anyone have anything to say about Catherine? You should have all finished the novel by now." I glance at the student next to Dina who's trying hard to focus on whatever is in front of her. "SueAnn? Anything?"

She looks up, her cheeks red. "I'm afraid I haven't had time to finish reading yet."

"I see. David, how about you?"

"Catherine is clearly torn between her ambition and her aching desire for Heathcliff."

"Aching desire," I say. "An accurate way to put it."

And an odd way, coming from David Larson, a science geek who's taking this class for general ed credit.

David looks back down at his iPad, his eyes moving back and forth as if reading.

"Do you have something more interesting, Dave?" I ask. "Or are you rereading *Wuthering Heights*?"

David meets my gaze, pushing his glasses up. His cheeks

are red now. I've embarrassed him.

"Yeah." He clears his throat. "Just rereading."

"Tell me. How did you come up with the description of 'aching desire?'"

"You said it was accurate."

"It is. Just wondering how you came up with it?"

"It just…came to me."

Snickers and murmurs float through the room.

"Does anyone have anything they'd like to tell me?" I ask.

Radio silence.

I walk to the first row of desks and face David. I pick up his iPad. "You don't mind, do you?"

I begin reading, and I keep my jaw from dropping.

This is my work. My fucking novel. My novel that hasn't been released yet.

I throw his iPad back down in front of him. "Where did you get this?"

"It's… It's circulating online."

"For God's sake." I breathe in. "Class is over until next time, when I expect every one of you to be prepared to discuss Catherine Earnshaw. Get out of here."

The students gather their belongings and shuffle out the door. Dina stays behind.

"Dr. Stone?"

"Yes?"

"I just want you to know, I think it's brilliant."

"That's kind of you, Dina, but you also may want to know that you have a pirated copy. The book doesn't release for several more months. May I ask where you got it?"

"Online. And I'm sorry."

"Ebook piracy is a serious offense. It's copyright infringement and can result in a fine up to thirty thousand dollars."

Her blue eyes go wide. "I didn't put it out there."

"But you have it in your possession."

"I'll delete it. I'm so sorry."

"Dina, I'm not going to make a case out of this, but I need you to tell me where you got it."

"I…don't know. It was uploaded to one of the Mellville message boards over the weekend. Everyone was talking about it, so… You know."

"I'm afraid I don't know, Dina. This is a huge invasion of my privacy, not to mention a violation of the law. I have a contract with my publisher to sell the work. Someone is giving it away for free and has attached my real name to it. Tell me. What would you do in my shoes?"

"I… I don't know, Dr. Stone. Please. I'll delete it. I won't say anything more about it."

"You do that. Have a good day, Dina."

She slinks out of the room.

I sigh.

Time to talk to Linda before this gets out of hand. I gather my stuff, head to my office, dump it all on my desk, and then walk down the hallway to Linda's office. Our secretary, Lonnie, blushes as I pass.

Oh God…

I knock harshly. "Linda, it's Hunter."

"Come in," she says.

I open the door and take a seat across from her desk. "Apparently I'm a household name around the student body now. I just wanted to give you a heads-up, since you demanded one."

"Hunter…"

"Let me say my piece, please. My students somehow have a pirated copy of my novel, which hasn't yet been released.

Someone released my pen name and my work on social media, and they're not only violating my privacy, they're breaking copyright law. This is serious, Linda."

"Yes, Hunter, but—"

"I won't have it," I say, interrupting her. "My private life is private, damn it."

"Hunter, please. This is the least of our worries."

I lift my brow. "Oh?"

She sighs. "The dean of students contacted me a half hour ago. There have been some allegations."

"What kind of allegations?"

"That you're a member of some secret club and that's how you did all your research."

"Christ... That's no one's business."

"It is," she says, "if you're engaging in illegal activities."

I stand up, knocking over the chair. "What?" I say through clenched teeth.

"It's all over social, I'm afraid."

"Linda, you and I both know that rumor and innuendo travel faster than the speed of light. I assure you that I don't engage in anything illegal. Ever." I look down at my white knuckles. "What I do in my private life is my own fucking business."

"I know that, Hunter. But this may get ugly."

"Fuck," I say. "Why does everything have to be a fight?"

"It doesn't have to be. You could...come clean. If you *are* a member of a club, Hunter—and I'm not saying you are—you could tell the dean and make sure she knows nothing illegal is going on there."

Right. Not happening, and not just because of the NDA I signed. Because it's none of the dean's fucking business.

"Bullshit. It's none of her business what I do in my free

time. What I do in my private life. Who the hell started these rumors?"

"I'd tell you if I knew." She sighs.

"I don't care. I'm fighting." I rise and look out the window at the red brick buildings where I once roamed the halls as a student, at the cobblestone pathways and the granite statue of Clark Mellville, the college's founder. "Mellville is my alma mater. I got all three of my degrees here, and I've been a professor here for the last five years. I'm not going quietly. This place means a lot to me, and I should mean a lot to *it* as well."

"You do mean a lot to me and to the rest of our department."

"If you say so." I turn. "I need a fucking drink."

• • •

I text Logan.

Hunter: *You up for a drink at Smitty's?*

Logan: *Sure. Be there in fifteen.*

I'm already halfway through my martini when Logan saunters into the bar, his muscular build, shaved head, and blue eyes drawing attention as they always do.

"Bourbon," he tells the barkeep as he sits down next to me and eyes my drink. "I see you started without me."

"Remember when we sat here last year, drinking and commiserating about your situation?" I ask.

"How could I forget?"

"You didn't deserve any of it, Logan." I take a drink, letting the alcohol float over my tongue. "And now…" I shake my head.

"What's going on, Hunt?"

I pour out the story, finishing my martini in the process.

"Man." Logan takes a sip of his bourbon. "Social media sucks, for sure. How could they have gotten your manuscript?"

"Hell if I know." I signal the bartender for another. "But they're not going to get away with it."

"I don't know." Logan shakes his head. "You saw what I went through. It may not be worth the headache."

"How is it so easy for you to walk away, Logan?" I ask. "Mellville has been a huge part of our lives."

"For sure," Logan agrees. "But it now has some shitty memories for me, too. Sometimes it's not a bad thing to move on to greener pastures. Sometimes we don't know how much further we have to go—or grow—until we change scenery."

I've known Logan since freshman year of college. We roomed together for two years, until Allison and I moved off campus into an apartment together. Logan and I shared drinks together at Smitty's every week while we were in school. Now our visits to the bar are few and far between, but we're always here for each other. Still, Logan doesn't know about my private life. He doesn't know about the club.

"Here's the thing," I say. "I *am* a member of a club, Logan."

Logan's eyes widen, but then he tries to look nonchalant. "Oh?"

"Yeah. And that's all I can say about it, other than that nothing illegal goes on there."

"I know that, Hunt. For God's sake."

"The point is… How did someone find out? I mean, the rumor had to start somewhere."

"You may never know," Logan says. "But everything

you say to me is safe."

"I know."

The bartender hands me my second martini. "Ready for another?" he asks Logan.

"I'm good." He turns to me. "The rumors will eventually die down, but even if they don't, this doesn't have to be a fight, Hunt. It can be a message. A message that it's time to move forward. Away from Mellville."

I inhale and let it out slowly. "I'll think about it. I do see your point. But fighting for what's right is in my nature."

"Mine too," he says, "but sometimes, when you look through the trees, you can find a path you didn't see before. You can find a way to leave something behind and have even more."

CHAPTER FORTY-SEVEN

Frankie

Embrace Your Dark Side in the City

At first glance, it's a club like any other. The wooden bar in the back that stocks top-shelf liquor. A large dance floor with strobe lights and a disco ball. Tables line the dancing area, and couples talk intimately. Jazz plays across the sound system, and a few people take to the dance floor.

Only then do you notice their garments.

Some don gorgeous clubwear, but others?

Leather, lace, lingerie...and some wear nothing at all.

No shame or stigma here at a private BDSM club in the city. In this dimly lit fantasyland, individuals, couples, and more enjoy safe, healthy, and consensual sex without judgment. Large rooms provide a safe space for exhibitionists to enjoy their play and give voyeurs a chance to watch. Smaller suites can be reserved for private play.

Research shows that more and more people are enjoying steamier times between the sheets. A recent survey conducted by Lovely *confirms this. Of 4,389 adults surveyed, 67 percent said they had experimented with some type of BDSM, and*

11 percent had done so in one of the exclusive clubs located in the city.

The clubs routinely are membership only. Guests are sometimes allowed, but they must be accompanied by a member and they must sign a confidentiality agreement. The clubs take the privacy of their members very seriously.

Jasmine (names changed to protect privacy), twenty-eight, is new to the scene. "I wouldn't say I'm a submissive exactly," she says. "This isn't really a lifestyle for me. It's just something I engage in sometimes. When the mood strikes me and when there's someone that I trust to dominate me."

Reputable clubs make security a priority. Plus, a responsible Dominant will offer their submissive a safe word. "I haven't had to use my safe word," Jasmine says, "but I know it's there in case I need it. A good Dominant will always respect your safe word. But a good Dominant will also talk to you about the scene beforehand, make sure you're comfortable with everything they're about to do, and make sure they know your hard limits. That's something you won't ever do, no matter what."

Candy, forty-seven, has visited a few BDSM clubs in the city. "They all offer different things," she says. "For example, one of the clubs I like gives you a lot of privacy for your scenes. I'm not an exhibitionist by nature, so that's what I prefer."

Candy is a submissive, meaning she takes the submissive role in BDSM activities. She has played with both male and female Dominants. "I'm a late bloomer," Candy says. "I've only been doing this for a few years. I got a divorce five years ago, and I wanted something different. I wanted to try something I'd never tried before, so I got online and looked around. When I found a BDSM chat room, I was intrigued."

Candy dived right in. She's not looking for a relationship, so she plays with people—both men and women—she meets at her clubs.

According to BDSM Today *by Cleric Foster, being a submissive means yielding to the Dominant; however, a submissive is far from passive or unintelligent. In fact, submissives and Dominants have equal control in a BDSM relationship. Submissives are often confident and competent and work in high-powered jobs. Their submission is limited to the bedroom. Others choose to be submissive full-time at home but maintain an outside career, sometimes in a demanding role.*

Jane, another submissive, says she had difficulty finding a boyfriend who was willing to do what she craved—spank her. "My dad spanked me when I was a kid," she says. "It wasn't a sexual thing at all. I hated it then... But for some reason, I've always wanted my boyfriends to spank me."

Jane, unlike Candy, isn't comfortable playing with someone with whom she's not in a relationship. "There are online sites where you can find potential partners who are interested in what you're interested in," she says, "and who are willing to get to know you before you engage in any kind of play. That's where I am now. Looking for potential partners, meeting people for coffee and stuff."

"Being the submissive partner," says Ryan Coats, PhD, a sex therapist in Manhattan, "doesn't necessarily come from anything that happened in your life. It can, but sometimes it's just a kink that a person enjoys. There's no right way to be a submissive, or to be a Dominant partner, for that matter. What is crucial is consent. It's basically a contract between or among all parties that the Dominant will keep the submissive safe and protected at all times, and the submissive

will communicate effectively to aid the Dominant in that task."

Erik, a Dominant, has been in the lifestyle for ten years. "I like regular sex as much as the next person," he says. "But I always felt like something was missing. I crave danger. I crave the forbidden. I crave taboo." Erik plays with one partner at a time, but he's not in an outside relationship with any of them. "My sub is my equal in every way, more so than in a conventional relationship in some ways. My submissive consents to everything I do. We talk beforehand about what her limits are and what my limits are. About what I expect out of the scene, about what she expects out of the scene."

Godfrey, another Dominant, plays only with his wife of five years, who is his submissive. He's been a Dominant most of his life. "I've known since I was young," he says. "At least since puberty. When I started becoming attracted to girls, I imagined them in all these compromising positions. For a long time, I repressed those urges. It wasn't until I was an adult, a couple of years out of college, before I realized my impulses were normal as long as I had a consenting partner."

While Godfrey, Erik, and Candy enjoy frequenting the lifestyle clubs in the area, Jane prefers to play at home. "I'm not really comfortable going to a club," she says. "This part of me is private."

Susan, another submissive, has a different perspective. "I like the club atmosphere. I go clubbing a lot at regular clubs, and I really love leather clubs. They're a feast for the eyes."

"Those who go to the lifestyle clubs usually have voyeuristic or exhibitionist tendencies, even if they're very subtle," Dr. Coats says. "It's a chance to see and be seen. Be around others who share your fetishes. To see and hear

things you won't see and hear in your own home. It's all very normal, as long as there is mutual consent all around.

"Participating in BDSM—whether you're Dominant, submissive, or a little of each—puts you in a vulnerable position," Coats continues. "Consent is essential, and you must choose your location wisely. Wherever you choose to play, you must feel safe. For some, that's at home. For others, it's at a club."

But ask about the name or location of the club, and everyone becomes close-lipped. They take their confidentiality agreements seriously. But one informant told me, "Don't be surprised if you see someone you know. Someone in the public eye. More people than you would think enjoy this naughtier side of sex."

"Whether you choose to find a club or not, it's important to remember that sex is good and it's healthy for you," Dr. Coats says. "However and with whomever you choose to engage, be free to acquiesce to your desires as long as there is mutual consent. And always remember to be safe."

—Francesca Thomas for Lovely *Magazine*

CHAPTER FORTY-EIGHT

Hunter

"So what do you think?" Frankie asks me that evening. "I know it's short, but my boss wants to have a lot of insets and photos. Thank goodness I'm not the photographer on this assignment. I've told them all that no cameras are allowed in any of the clubs, so I imagine it's going to be stock-photo city."

"You didn't use the book I gave you. You used a different one."

"Of course I did. You asked me not to use anything I learned from you."

She's right. I'm angry, and I'm being short with her because of what happened at work today. I haven't yet told Frankie of the most recent development. Not only do they have a bootleg copy of my novel, but now someone has decided to accuse me of frequenting a club where illegal activities occur.

This is Frankie's time to shine, and she doesn't need me being a downer.

"It's brilliant," I say. "Absolutely brilliant."

A smile splits her face, and it is so beautiful. I need to remember beauty in this moment.

"Really? You think so?"

"Frankie, I never say anything except what I think. You should know that by now."

"Thank you." She kisses my lips lightly. "It means so much to me that you like it. I know you were against this article from the get-go, and I appreciate you not forcing me to choose between it and you."

"I appreciate you not forcing me to choose between the club and you. I know that was difficult for you."

"Not really. Not when I sucked it up and saw my discomfort for what it was. Me being a cranky whiner." She laughs. "Mandy will tell you I was the spoiled brat of our family, and she's not wrong in a lot of ways. I was the baby, and I was also the one who was popular at school while she was such a wallflower. When you live a life like that—a life of privilege—you start to feel entitled. I thought I had gotten over that a long time ago. I mean, I worked my way up to this job that I love, and I did it without any handouts or nepotism along the way. But I suppose old habits creep back in every once in a while."

"You're hardly a whiner, Frankie."

"Not anymore. I'm determined. I don't like ultimatums, which is why I wasn't going to give you one."

"No, you were going to break up with me instead."

"Yes. Until I realized that just wasn't possible. We're in love, Hunter, and that means accepting each other for who we are. It also means putting someone else and their needs first."

"That's true. And we'll notice that even more when we have kids—"

I stop abruptly.

"Kids?"

"In the future, Frankie. I'm not saying now."

Indeed, I may not even have a job when all of this is over. As much as I hate touching the trust fund, I'll do it if I must.

"You know what I'd like to do to celebrate my article?"

"What's that, baby?"

That beautiful smile splits her face once more. "I think that's the first time you've ever called me 'baby.'"

It is, because it's what I used to call Allison. I won't say that to Frankie, but I never used it again with another woman, and I dislike endearments like "sweetheart" and "honey." But now I know Allison was never the love of my life. We would've been happy together had she lived. I've no doubt about that. But she wasn't my true soulmate.

That moniker belongs to the woman in front of me now.

Francesca Thomas.

"I'd like to go to the club. To Black Rose Underground. And I don't care who we see there, Hunter. Whether it's my sister, my ex, my future brother-in-law. I don't care."

"You won't. She and Jack always use a private suite, like you and I do. There's no chance of any of us seeing the others in intimate acts."

"Right." She swipes her forehead. "She told me that, and it does make me feel a little more at ease. It's not that I have a problem seeing people doing that. But you know, she's my sister."

"I get it. She probably feels the same way."

"Here's the thing, Hunter. I never imagined that my sister would engage in such stuff. She was a wallflower if there ever was one. And now…"

"You'd be surprised what some of the people at the club

do on a daily basis. There's a senator who goes there."

"A senator?" she gasps. "I know one of my informants said I'd be surprised, but…a *senator*?"

"Yes. And look all you want. He usually disguises himself like I do, but sometimes he doesn't. He's under the same confidentiality agreement as the rest of us are. That's the beauty of the people who go to the club. You can trust them, Frankie. There's only been one time when someone blew the whistle on some of the members. They sold the story to some tabloid, but the owner paid off the tabloid not to print it. Then he bought the tabloid and fired everybody."

She drops her jaw. "Really?"

"Yes. He takes the club very seriously, and he takes the nondisclosure agreement very seriously. No one has violated it since."

And I won't be the one to violate it. Not even to prove some stupid social media allegations are false.

• • •

"Are you ready?" I ask Frankie.

She's bound, laid out on a table, her legs spread, a feast for my eyes, nose, and everything else.

She's naked. I walk toward her, cup her breasts, pinch each nipple. "I'm going to clamp your nipples now, Frankie. Are you ready?"

"I am."

Again, I haven't told Frankie not to speak. I want her to speak. I still consider her my submissive here in the club, and of course I collar her for her own protection, but she's different from all the others. She's not *just* my submissive. She's my lover. Hopefully my life mate.

And I never want her to be silenced.

I got some ice from the bar, and it sits in an ice bucket on one of the tables.

First, the nipple clamps.

They look like tiny clothespins, but I can determine the tightness. This is Frankie's first time, so I only give her a slight pinch.

"Okay?" I ask.

She smiles. "More."

I tighten the clamp and then apply the other to her other nipple.

"More," she says again.

My God, I'm hard as a rock.

"All you have to do is tell me to stop if you ever want to stop," I say.

"I know. More."

I tighten the clamps until she gasps a bit.

But she doesn't tell me to stop.

I tighten them slightly more, and then I stop. This is as tight as I go. Her nipples are flattened out and protruding like a mouth blowing a bubble with gum.

She's so fucking hot.

Time for the ice.

I walk to the table, grab an ice cube, and bring it back. I trail it over Frankie's clit.

She gasps once more.

"Ice, Frankie. The heat of your body will melt it quickly."

I insert the ice cube into her pussy.

She lifts her hips, sighing.

"You like that, baby?"

"Yes. The sensation is…cold…except hot."

"Exactly. Feels good, doesn't it?"

"You have no idea."

I kneel and swipe my tongue across her pussy, which is cold from the ice yet hot from her flesh. "Actually, I do." I suck at her then, and I suck out the ice cube, or what's left of it.

Then I suck her pussy. I eat her. Shove my tongue deep inside her. She lifts her hips. Her arms and legs are bound, and she struggles against the binding.

And I know it's making it better for her.

She can't move. She can't grind against me. And that's what she desires.

Soon, I will let her.

But not yet.

Not until I have my feast.

I eat her and I eat her and I eat her, and when I'm ready for her to come, I nibble her clit and force two fingers inside her.

She comes instantly, and I undo my pants, free my cock, and thrust inside.

As she comes around me, I fuck her hard. I pump and pump and pump, and within a few moments I'm coming as well, shooting inside her, filling her, taking her, branding her with my come.

She's mine, and that collar she wears?

She will never take it off.

CHAPTER FORTY-NINE

Frankie

"I have a meeting with my department chair and some of the administrators this morning," Hunter tells me a few days later.

"What about?"

"Remember how I told you that someone outed my pen name?"

"Yeah."

"Well…now social media is all agog about the contents of the book. They think I must have gotten my information at some underground club or something."

Though I've been curious, I've resisted the temptation to search for Hunter and his pen name on social media. He'd hate that, and I don't want to upset him.

"I see. The NDA."

"Right. Not just the NDA, but rumors are flying that I engage in illegal and immoral activities."

I drop my jaw. "Hunter, why didn't you tell me?"

"I was hoping it would go away on its own."

"I'm sorry."

"I'll take care of it."

"May I go to the meeting with you?" I ask.

"God, no."

"But I want to be there. I'm part of your support system."

"You're sweet to want to go. It would be different if we were married, or—"

I widen my eyes.

He went too far.

He fingers the 14-karat gold chain around my throat. It's a simple style, sixteen inches long, with a crystal heart dangling from it.

It's my collar.

I never take it off.

"I've never collared a woman outside the club before," he says.

"I know."

"But I collared you, and I want you to know I'm in this for the long haul."

"I am too, Hunter."

"This is a commitment from me," he says. "And Frankie, I'd put a ring on your finger right now if I had one. But this collar, to me, means the same thing."

I warm all over. "Hunter, I didn't mean to—"

He quiets me with two fingers against my lips. "You're not pushing me into anything. I love you, Frankie Thomas. I'd love for you to be my wife if you'll have me."

I jump into his arms. "Of course I'll have you. You're everything I've ever wanted. You're everything I never knew I wanted."

"I feel exactly the same." He draws in a breath. "If you come with me today, you'll come as my fiancée."

"Thank you. Thank you for letting me come and

support you."

"They may say some terrible things about me. None of which are true."

"I understand that."

"All right. Let's go."

• • •

"Dr. Stone," a gray-haired man with a rumbling voice says when we enter the conference room. "And who is this with you?"

"This is my fiancée, Francesca Thomas. She's here to support me."

"Very well. Ms. Thomas, you may take a seat next to Dr. Stone right there." He indicates two seats on the opposite side of the table.

"Have you brought counsel?" the man asks.

"Counsel. Are you kidding me?" Hunter shakes his head. "I haven't done anything wrong. I wrote a book that was illegally distributed before publication, and whatever allegations are spreading like wildfire over social, I assure you they are without merit."

"Very well. This meeting will come to order." The man pounds a gavel on the conference room table as if he's some kind of judge. "My name is Forrest Tucker, and I am legal counsel for Mellville University. To my right is the dean of students, Leslie Nelson, and to my left is Linda Burnett, chairperson of the Department of English and Literature.

"Dr. Stone," Mr. Tucker says, "you'll be happy to know that we've uncovered the source of all of this unpleasantness."

"Oh?" Hunter raises his eyebrows. "Who is responsible, then?"

"A senior by the name of Lukas Moore. He's a student intern at your publishing house, Beck and Gold. He admitted to illegally distributing your manuscript."

"Good. I'll be suing him."

"You are certainly free to do so, but we've already dealt with the situation. He's been dismissed from Beck and Gold, and he's been put on probation here at the university."

"Probation? He should be expelled."

"He's a senior, Dr. Stone," the dean of students says. "He's almost ready to graduate."

"And you think I care? He violated my privacy, and he broke the law."

"You are certainly free to pursue your own remedies against Mr. Moore," the dean says. "This is what the university is doing."

"And you agree with this, Linda?" Hunter glares at the department chair.

"No, I don't agree," she says, "but I was outvoted."

"Let me guess," Hunter says. "This kid's some kind of legacy, and his family gives Mellville a lot of money. Am I right?"

Silence.

Yeah, he's right.

The attorney clears his throat. "What's more important at the moment, Dr. Stone, is the social media scandal concerning your illegal and immoral activities."

"All allegations are completely false."

"We all know that," he says. "The issue is that our phone lines and email have been blowing up with communications from angry parents who want you fired."

"Then fire me."

I grab his arm. "Hunter, no!"

"Frankie..."

"He's the best professor you've got. Just look at his reviews on RateMyProfessors.com. He's brilliant, and you'd let him go because of some gossip on the internet?"

"Ms...Thomas, is it?" the attorney asks.

I nod.

"We don't want to lose Dr. Stone. But we need to figure out a way to put out this fire."

"All because some snot-nosed, privileged jerk decided to out my pen name." Hunter shakes his head. "Damn all of you. I've given this university the better part of my adult life. I studied here. Got all my degrees here. I taught here. I published here, giving you the status you wanted with my award-winning articles in academic journals. And this is how you treat me? My private life is private, damn it."

"Of course it is," Linda says.

"The issue," the dean begins, "is how to deal with the fallout."

"Just tell the truth," I say to Hunter, keeping my voice low.

The dean lifts her brow. "What truth is that?"

Fuck. She heard me? I look around. Every eye is trained on me. Why isn't Hunter standing up for himself? Pressure settles in my gut. Pressure to answer, and if I don't...Hunter will lose his job.

I gulp, knowing I may well be shooting myself in the foot. "It's a club. A BDSM club in the city, and I can assure you that nothing illegal or immoral goes on there because I've been there. I've been there with Hunter."

CHAPTER FIFTY

Hunter

"How could you?" I demand once we're back at Frankie's place.

I stayed silent all the way back to her apartment, because first, I needed to think clearly. Second, enough of my laundry has been aired to the public, and I didn't want to include our cabbie in that ever-increasing number. Third, I'm so damned angry that if I said anything I may have blown up.

"I'm sorry, Hunter. I didn't think they heard me, and I couldn't lie. I'm so sorry. But you're not fired."

"So what? You violated your NDA *and* mine. You know how I value my privacy."

"They won't say anything. They promised."

"That's not the fucking *point*." I rake my fingers through my hair as my pulse pounds.

Frankie looks so beautiful in her work clothes. Those fucking platform pumps. Those luscious red lips.

But no.

It's over.

She and I are over.

"The club isn't anything to be ashamed of. Nothing illegal happens there, and what the hell is immoral, anyway? To each his own, as long as there's consent."

"I'm *not* ashamed, Frankie. But it's private. It's private to me, to you, to the other members."

"Hunter, I—"

"Shut up!" I roar. "Just shut the fuck up. You betrayed me. You knew I wouldn't want you to mention the club. You knew, Frankie, and you did it anyway. What did I have to do? Order you not to mention the club? Consider yourself ordered."

She nods, parts her lips, her blue eyes on fire. "I only follow your orders in bed, Hunter. Can't you see I did this for you? For us? For our future?"

"We no longer have a future." I turn, stomp out, and slam her door behind me.

CHAPTER FIFTY-ONE

Frankie

I don't bother going after him. Nothing will help until he calms down. I call him, knowing he won't pick up. He doesn't, and I leave a voicemail.

"Hunter, I love you. Everything I did was out of love for you. To protect you. I hated what those people were saying about you, and I hated that the asshole who started it all is only getting a slap on the wrist. I did betray your trust. I admit that. I made a grave mistake. I thought I was helping you. That's what you do for people you love. You help them. You protect them. Even if it means hurting them sometimes. And"—I gulp back a sob—"even if it means losing them. But I hope I haven't lost you, Hunter, because I love you. I love you so much. Please call me."

But I don't expect him to call me.

And he doesn't.

• • •

A month later…

"Congratulations, Frankie!"

I look up from my computer. Lisa is standing there with a huge smile on her face.

"For what?"

"Your article was nominated for a Best Buzz award!"

My eyes pop open. "How? It just came out two days ago."

"I secretly submitted it a week ago," she says. "I have an in with the committee, and they let me submit it early. I was so impressed by it, and I knew they would be, too. I was right! In my opinion, you're a shoo-in."

The Best Buzz award… It's a coveted honor, but they usually look at serious investigative reporting from publications like ours. Not something frivolous like sex clubs. Then again, it's all about the "buzz," as they say.

"Wow." I stand up and give her a quick hug. "Thank you for submitting it, Lisa."

"You're welcome. It's so good. I think I may have you do more articles that go into more detail. One that focuses on submissives, and then one on Dominants. If only you could get into one of those clubs…"

"I'm afraid that's impossible," I say.

"I know, and I understand why. But the article is outstanding and so informative."

"Thanks," I say.

"The award will be given out at a gala in a couple of months. As soon as I have the date, I'll let you know. You'll definitely want it on your calendar."

"Absolutely. Thanks again, Lisa."

She whisks away, and I smile…for a moment.

Because my next thought is Hunter.

I've left several messages over the last few weeks, and

he hasn't answered any of them.

So I call Mandy instead, and then Izzy. Gigi doesn't answer.

I finish the workday, go home, and once I'm alone, I cry.

CHAPTER FIFTY-TWO

Hunter

"Hey," I say into the phone to Logan.

"Hey. You doing okay?"

No.

"Yeah. I suppose. Things are finally dying down on social, but the fucking university had to send out a letter to all the students and parents attesting to my upstanding moral character. The whole thing makes me sick, Logan."

"You going to sue that kid?"

"I'd like nothing better, but he comes from old money, and he'd get an attorney to stick it to me."

"You come from money, too, Hunt. So you get an attorney and you stick it to him. What about your publisher?"

"I decided I'd rather not waste my money on a lawsuit where the kid'll get off scot-free. And my publisher feels the same way."

"Is the book release still on?"

"Yup. End of next month."

"That's awesome, man." He pauses a moment. "I've got some news."

"Yeah? Good news, I hope. I'd love some good news."

"I got a new position at NYU."

"That's great, Logan."

"And...they have another opening in their English Lit department, and they want you."

I nearly drop the phone. Logan's words from our visit to Smitty's sail into my mind.

Sometimes it's not a bad thing to move on to greener pastures. Sometimes we don't know how much further we have to go—or grow—until we change scenery. Sometimes, when you look through the trees, you can find a path you didn't see before. You can find a way to leave something behind and have even more.

Logan has moved on. Maybe it's time I move on as well. Move forward. Grow. Bloom.

"NYU wants me?"

"They do. After I talked you up, of course. I even told them about your novel, and they think it's great. It's more money than Mellville, Hunter—and let's face it, Mellville has left a bad taste in both our mouths."

"True enough. I used to love this stupid place."

"I know. Me too. Talk it over with your other half and let me know. They want to talk to you and get an answer as soon as possible."

My other half...

Has it been that long since Logan and I have talked? Not since Smitty's? I haven't reached out to anyone since Frankie and I fought.

I've been pretty miserable.

"Frankie and I... We split up."

The words crush my soul.

"I'm sorry, man."

"I'm okay."

"You don't sound okay."

I sigh. "I'm not."

"Then work it out."

"It's not that simple."

"Hunter, my friend, if you love her, it's always that simple."

"It's not. She…told Forrest Tucker, Leslie, and Linda something that I asked her not to."

"Was it a lie?"

I swallow. "No. It was the truth. But it was personal. I asked her not to say anything, and she did anyway. She betrayed me."

"*That's* what this is about?"

"You don't understand, Logan. You have no idea what it was that she told them."

"You want to tell me what it was?"

"No."

"Okay. Then you want to tell me why she said it?"

"She thought she was helping me. She wasn't."

He lets out a soft huff. "That's not betrayal, Hunter. That's love."

"You don't understand."

"Maybe I don't," he says, "but don't throw love away. I've watched you all these years. I've seen how lonely you've become. And that's all I'll say."

"I appreciate the sentiment, Logan. Thanks for the in about the job. I'll get in touch with NYU right away."

After I end the call, I replay Frankie's voicemails. I do it several times a day anyway, just to hear her sweet voice. Just to make myself feel all the emptiness I deserve. After the first one, she left another the very next day.

Hunter, hi. It's me again. It's been a day. Surely you can't still be angry. Please let me make it up to you. Please. I'll do anything.

Then again a week later.

I promised myself I wouldn't call you again, but here I am, doing it anyway. Because I love you, Hunter. You made me see we're worth fighting for. Remember when I tried to end our relationship because I didn't think I could go to the club anymore? And you helped me see that I was putting my own comfort over you? Aren't you doing the same thing now? Putting your own comfort over me? I mean, I know you didn't want anyone to know about your personal life, but now some of them do, and that makes you uncomfortable. I'm sorry for that discomfort, but please don't put your discomfort over our love.

Two weeks after that. Her last call.

This will be my last call, Hunter. I still love you more than anything, and I miss you so much. Do you even miss me a little bit? Did I truly mean so little to you that you can just give us up? Please call me. Please, Hunter. I won't call again.

And she hasn't called again. That was a week ago. Every time the phone rings, my heart jumps. I want it to be her, even if I have no intention of answering.

Is Logan right?

Is it really that simple?

Frankie did betray me. She did something I specifically asked her not to do. But she didn't do it out of meanness or spite.

She did it out of love.

She was trying to protect me.

Funny. I don't ever think of myself as needing protection.

I'm the Dominant. I'm the one who *does* the protecting.

I punished myself for not being able to protect Allison.

I punished myself by trying to convince myself that Teresa was as kindhearted as Allison.

And now, am I punishing myself again, under the guise of punishing Frankie for her betrayal? She made a mistake, for sure, but Linda and the others are trustworthy. They'll never reveal that I go to a club. And Frankie didn't mention the club's name.

My phone buzzes…and my heart jumps.

Frankie.

Out of habit, I let it go to voicemail. I tremble as I play back her message.

I know I promised that I wouldn't call you again, but Hunter, my article—it came out a couple days ago—has been nominated for a Best Buzz award! I can hardly believe it. You were the first person I wanted to tell, but I couldn't, so I called Mandy, Isabella, Gigi, my mom. They were all ecstatic for me, but I didn't care. I wanted to tell you, Hunter, so here I am, telling you, even though it's clear you no longer care. I miss you, though. I miss the club. I miss our talks. I miss our intimacy. But mostly I just miss you. Goodbye. And this time I mean it. Goodbye.

Sweet Frankie.

How I love her.

Love isn't about recreating the past or about trying to make something work that just isn't workable. Love isn't about finding someone who's perfect, either. Someone who will always do what you want her to do.

Love is about cherishing someone, protecting someone, even when you know they'll be angry at you for it.

That's what Frankie did. She cherished me. Tried to

help me. All while knowing how I'd react.

And boy, did I prove her right.

I miss her so much, and I love her even more. So I call her.

And it goes to voicemail.

I chuckle to myself. I can't blame her.

"Hello, my beautiful angel," I say. "This is Phantom. I'm so sorry for being such a fool. I love you so much. Meet me at the bar tonight, and together I hope we can make some beautiful music."

CHAPTER FIFTY-THREE

Hunter

My breath catches when she walks into the bar wearing the black dress from masquerade night with her black pumps and a gold lace wrap.

I sit at the bar, dressed in my Phantom garb and holding a bouquet of red roses.

I know the moment she sees me. Her gaze meets mine, and a fire ignites in my groin.

"My angel…" I say when she approaches.

"Hunter."

I hold out my hand, and she takes it. Then I fold her into my arms.

"I'm so sorry, Frankie," I whisper. "I'm so fucking sorry."

She pulls back a little. I knew it would take more than a simple "I'm sorry" to fix what happened between us. More than twenty-four long-stemmed roses. Even more than the ring I have hidden beneath my cape.

I look into her silvery blue eyes—the eyes that first mesmerized me only months ago but are seared permanently into my soul.

"Listen to me." I cup her silky cheek. "I understand now. In a way, I think I always did, but it took a good friend to help me see the truth. We're in this together, Frankie. We're growing together. We'll both make mistakes along the way. It's normal."

"I did what I did for—"

"Shh." I place two fingers over her beautiful lips. "It's okay. You were protecting me, and I would have done the same for you."

"But I—"

"Wait. Please. Let me finish." I trail my fingers over her lower lip. "You mean more to me than anything, Frankie. More than my job. More than the club. More than my book. More than anything."

"More than your privacy?" She gives a nervous smile.

"Yes. More than my privacy. More than anything, Frankie."

"I—"

"Frankie—"

This time she places her fingers over my lips, making them tingle.

"Please, just let me talk now, Hunter."

"All right."

"I'm sorry too. So sorry. It was a terrible mistake, and I promise it will never happen again."

I gaze into her eyes. "I know. I should have called you before today. I don't deserve your forgiveness, but"—I rise from my stool and drop to my knees in front of her with the roses—"but I humbly ask for it anyway, baby. I ask for it because I love you and I can't imagine my life without you in it."

She takes the flowers and then my hands.

"I'll forgive you if you forgive me."

"It's already done." I rise as she places the flowers on the bar.

"I hope that little maggot intern gets what's coming to him," she says.

"Yeah. He'll get a free ride through life on Daddy's money. But I'm letting it go, Frankie. It doesn't matter anymore. You're everything to me. I've been miserable without you."

"Me too." She sniffles.

"I'm so happy about your article, baby."

"It hasn't won yet."

"It will." I gesture to the two martinis sitting on the bar. "Have a drink. I have a few things to tell you."

"What?" She grabs the stem of her glass and takes a sip.

"I'm leaving Mellville."

"But Hunter—"

"It's my choice. Logan got a position at NYU, and they want me to fill another one."

"That's great! I think. I mean, you love Mellville."

I roll my eyes. "Not anymore."

"Yeah." She sighs. "I feel the same way."

"There's something else I should have told you."

She bites her lip.

"It's nothing bad. It's just…" I chuckle. "You always made such a big deal about your ex being a trust-fund baby, so I didn't want to… Oh, hell. I have a trust fund, Frankie."

Her eyes nearly pop out of her head. "You do?"

"Yeah. It's from my great-grandfather. I only use it occasionally. To buy my lifetime membership at the club, for example. And when I want to impress a lady by ordering an excellent wine."

"The Jordan cab," she says. "From The Glass House."

"Right."

"It was delicious."

"It was. And you are worth every penny. Anyway, the money's there if I need it, but I like working. I like teaching. But I'm thinking you and I can use it to build a house. Maybe on Long Island."

Her cheeks redden as she fingers the collar around her neck. "I never took it off," she says.

"And you never will." I lean over, kiss her cheek, and then nip at her earlobe, whispering, "Now, my angel, I'd like to take you underground. There's a spider gag calling your name."

CHAPTER FIFTY-FOUR

Frankie

Once we're inside a private suite at Black Rose Underground, Hunter removes his mask, but he keeps the cape on. He brought a small leather case with him, and when he opens it, the stainless steel and black leather instrument draws my gaze.

The spider gag.

I shudder as excitement rolls through me.

I did my research. I know what this is. It's a variation on the common ring gag, except it has stainless steel hooks around it that look like spider legs. The ring goes in my mouth, and the metal pieces hold the lips out of the way. Dominants like them because their sub is unable to speak, and also because they make the sub salivate, which increases lubrication for blow jobs.

I wasn't sure how I felt about the whole thing until I see the gag in Hunter's large hands.

I want him to use it on me.

I want to please him.

"This is one of my favorite toys, baby," he says. "Though

I'm not sure it will be with you."

I raise my eyebrows. "Oh?"

"Yes, but I'd like to try it anyway. Just this once."

"Whatever you like."

He narrows his gaze, and those dark eyes smolder. "Undress for me. Slowly."

I peel off my cream-colored camisole, unhook my bra, and let it fall to the floor. He sucks in a breath as my breasts fall against my flesh. Then I urge my skirt down my hips until I'm wearing nothing but my panties and my pumps.

I need to get some club gear.

"Take off the panties," he growls, "but leave the shoes on."

I obey, and he grabs a pillow from the bed and sets it on the floor.

"Kneel."

I drop to my knees on the cool silk of the pillowcase.

"You won't be able to speak, and that will seem odd. It may be scary, even."

"I'll be all right."

"Yes, you will be, but you won't be able to tell me to stop. I'm going to bind your wrists behind you, but your hands will be free. Snap your fingers once if you want to stop at any time. Can you do that, Frankie?"

I swallow as anticipation whirls through me like a tornado. "Yes, Hunter. Yes, sir."

A groan comes out of him. "Good. Good little sub." He fits the gag into my mouth, and already a rush of anxiety ripples across my body.

I'm at his mercy. I can't speak. Can't even move my mouth. And yes, there's a lot of saliva, but I knew there would be.

"God, you look so hot, Frankie. I can't wait to shove my cock into your sweet mouth."

A current skitters over my flesh, and my nipples are hard, my pussy tingling, aching for his fingers, his cock.

But I have to wait..

I have to be a good sub and obey my Dom.

God, the thought…

Such a turn-on.

Hunter walks behind me and takes my wrists, caressing them gently. "Such beautiful hands, Frankie. I'm going to use simple nylon rope that's easy to loosen if necessary."

I breathe in as the rope slides against my skin.

"Too tight?" he asks.

I shake my head.

"Good. Now snap the fingers of your right hand for me."

I comply.

"Excellent. That's what you do if you want me to stop and remove the gag at any time. Understand?"

I nod.

He moves back to the front, and then he slips a cool silk blindfold over me.

I gasp, causing drool to drip from my lips. I wasn't expecting that.

But I don't snap my fingers.

He groans. "Do you have any idea how beautiful you look to me at this moment? Completely at my mercy, under my control. My God."

I can't see, but I can hear, and the sound of his zipper rings in my ears as if it's a freaking concerto. I know what's coming, but still I gasp as he slowly pushes his cock inside my mouth.

The sensation is so odd. The urge to clasp my lips around

him overwhelms me, but I can't.

Is this truly pleasurable for him?

Wouldn't it be more pleasurable for me to close my mouth around him, suck him, create friction with my teeth and tongue? He sure enjoyed that the last time I gave him head.

But his groans, his heavy sighs, the movement of his cock in and out all indicate that he's enjoying himself.

Enjoying himself immensely.

"Yeah, Frankie. God, you're so hot, my sweet little sub. Fuck. Fuck, your hot mouth."

He moves in and out, and I'm aware of the drool, but it doesn't seem to matter.

So I let go.

I let go and concentrate on his pleasure, because his pleasure is my pleasure.

He slides in and out of my mouth, grabs my head, and moves me with him. Discomfort morphs into arousal, just because this makes him happy. And that makes me happy.

Until–

He pulls out and unclasps the spider gag.

"That's enough for your first time." He removes my blindfold and then massages my jaw and my lips. "You did great, baby. God, you're so fucking hot. Thank you. Thank you for this. I know the gag is uncomfortable, especially at first, but you did it for me."

His words are like a warm glove around my heart. He understands, and he appreciates that I put him over my discomfort. We've come a long way. We've bloomed together.

He undresses then, letting me watch, and I savor each inch of new flesh that's exposed as I continue to kneel before him, my hands still bound behind me.

His cock is glistening from my saliva, and the rest of his body is shimmering with perspiration. He's magnificent.

"Rise," he says.

I obey, and strangely, it's difficult with my wrists bound behind me. I make it to my feet, and he removes the rope and massages my wrists.

"Any chafing?"

"No. I'm fine."

"I think you know how much I love you, Frankie," he says, "but in case you don't, let me tell you. You are the love of my life. The other side of my soul."

"Oh, Hunter," I say.

"I love you." This time he drops to his knees, brandishing a velvet box that seems to have come from nowhere. "And I want you to be my wife, the mother of our children, my partner in life, and my submissive here in the club and in our bedroom. Will you have me, Frankie? For the rest of our lives?"

I kneel and meet his gaze, and he takes my left hand and slips a gorgeous sparkler on my ring finger.

"Yes, Hunter. I'll marry you, I'll have your children, and I'll submit to you. Most of all, I'll love you for the rest of my life."

Continue the excitement of
Black Rose Underground with* Blossom*, coming soon!

ACKNOWLEDGMENTS

Bloom was particularly fun to write, as I got to keep a secret from my readers for almost half of the book! I hope you enjoy it as much as I loved writing it.

Huge thanks to my brilliant editorial team, Liz Pelletier, Lydia Sharp, Rae Swain, and Hannah Lindsey. You all helped *Bloom* shine. Thanks also to my proofreaders, Claire Andress and Aimee Lim, for your excellent catches. And of course Bree Archer, who designs the most beautiful covers. *Bloom* is so gorgeous! Thanks to everyone else at Entangled whose tireless efforts always amaze me—Jessica, Riki, Meredith, Curtis, Heather, Katie, and so many more—and Toni Kerr, for your marvelous formatting.

Thanks also to the women and men of my reader group, Hardt and Soul. Your endless and unwavering support keeps me going.

To my family and friends, thank you for your encouragement. Special shout out to Dean—aka Mr. Hardt—and to our amazing sons, Eric and Grant.

Thank you most of all to my readers. Without you, none of this would be possible. I am grateful every day that I'm able to do what I love—write stories for you!

Don't miss the thrilling series that started it all!

The first in the Deviant Kings series, set in a modern world but with a dark, erotic fantasy twist.

I thought a weekend away would be the perfect escape. Until I woke up married and trapped...by the king of the Dark Fae.

For Bryn Meara, a free trip to the exclusive and ultra-luxe Nightfall hotel and casino in Vegas should've been the perfect way to escape the debris of her crumbling career. But waking up from a martini-and-lust-fueled night to find herself married to Caiden Verran, the reclusive billionaire who owns the hotel and most of the city, isn't the jackpot one would think. It seems her dark and sexy new husband is actual royalty—the fae king of the Night Court—and there's an entire world beneath the veil of Vegas.

Whether light or shadow, the fae are a far cry from fairy tales, and now they've made Bryn a pawn in their dark games for power. And Caiden is the most dangerous of all—an intoxicating cocktail of sin and raw, insatiable hunger. She should run. But every night of passion pulls Bryn deeper into his strange and sinister world, until she's no longer certain she wants to leave...even if she could.

From achingly tender to utterly taboo, these ten historical stories will stir, and entice, every desire…

fetish

anonymous

Step into a world of secret appetites, carnal longing, and dark cravings with this erotic collection set in the Victorian era. From achingly tender to utterly taboo, these ten historical stories will stir, and entice, every desire…

A young wife lures men into erotic trysts—and spills all the tea to her husband at night.

An heiress rekindles her friendship with a school mate who coaches her husband in the fine art of fisting.

A burly builder can't get enough of the feathery touch delivered by his level-headed bricklayer.

You're invited to a feast of these and seven more tantalizing tales. Fetish will shatter expectations, defy every convention…and awaken the lust inside you.

Don't miss the exciting new books Entangled has to offer.

Follow us!

@EntangledPublishing

@Entangled_Publishing

@EntangledPub

@EntangledPub

AMARA
an imprint of Entangled Publishing LLC